THE GOOD DAUGHTER

SARAH EDGHILL

BLOODHOUND
BOOKS

www.bloodhoundbooks.com

Print ISBN: 978-1-917214-74-2

For all the good daughters out there...

ONE

'If you loved me, you wouldn't leave me here.'

'That's not fair.'

'It's true though.'

Eve closed her eyes and took a deep breath. 'You know I love you,' she said. 'But we can't carry on like this, Mum. It's not safe for you to be in the flat anymore.'

Someone pushed a trolley past the open door, china plates rattling against each other on metal shelves.

'But it's my home,' said Flora. She looked up at Eve, her eyes brimming. 'Don't make me stay here, I'd rather kill myself.'

'Mum!' Eve couldn't keep the shock out of her voice. She glared at her mother, who glared back, sticking out her chin and folding her arms.

'I mean it.' Flora was shaking her head now. 'If you make me stay in this bloody awful place, I don't know what I'll do. There will be no point in me carrying on, and it will be all your fault.'

Eve stood up so suddenly that the chair tipped backwards and her coat slid off, landing in a heap on the carpet. She really didn't need this; her head was thumping and she hadn't eaten since breakfast. It had been one of those days when she'd been planning to achieve so much, but from the moment she woke up, she'd known some of it wouldn't get done.

It was also a day when she needed to be at her most calm; 'Be kind, Eve,' she'd told her reflection in the bathroom mirror, earlier this morning. 'Be patient and understanding. Don't lose your rag.' Several hours ago, that had seemed achievable. Now, not so much.

'Stop talking like this,' she snapped. 'It's ridiculous.'

Her mother was still glaring at her. Bending down, Eve picked up her coat and took her time shaking out the sleeves, before draping it over the arm of the chair. She breathed in deeply and made a conscious effort to drop her shoulders. 'Isn't this a lovely room they've given you, overlooking the garden? Such big windows as well! Those trees outside are beautiful – are they apple? Hard to tell with no leaves on the branches. I bet you'll get the sun first thing in the morning, on this side of the building...'

She was gabbling. She had no idea which side they were on: they'd followed the young girl down several corridors, through fire doors that slammed behind them as Eve struggled with Flora's old leather suitcase. This room was no better or worse than any of the others she'd glanced into on their way past. Some had been empty: beds neatly made, a handful of personal possessions on bookcases and chests of drawers. In others, she had caught glimpses of elderly people folded into armchairs, the volume turned up overly loud on televisions, cups of tea going cold on bedside tables. One woman had been standing in the middle of her room, swaying gently in time to music no one else could hear.

Further along the corridor Eve had glanced through a door on the left and seen a man propped up in bed: his mouth and eyes were open, and his cheeks so pallid and hollow, he'd clearly taken his last breath.

'Shit!' she'd whispered, stopping in her tracks. Had any of the staff realised? She ought to tell someone. 'Excuse me!' she'd called out to the girl who was leading them down the corridor. 'I think this gentleman–'

At that moment, the man had given out such a thunderous fart that his legs jerked under the bed covers. He'd then opened his eyes and smiled cheerfully at Eve.

Flora had now stopped glaring and slumped back into her chair, her chin resting on her chest. 'I hate this room,' she muttered.

'This is just for now,' said Eve. 'When one of the rooms upstairs becomes free, you can have one of those. Apparently, they're bigger, with better views.'

Flora began to sob, her shoulders shaking, her fingers clawed over the ends of the wooden arms of the chair. 'Please,' she whispered. 'I'd rather die.'

Tears were prickling at the edges of Eve's eyes too, a lump in her throat making it hard to swallow. She was used to her mother's mood swings, the way she oscillated between angry defiance and terrified vulnerability. But she'd never come out with anything like this before. 'Mum, I promise you it's going to be fine,' she said, her voice catching. 'It's one of the nicest homes in the area – you know that, we read all the reports. Do you remember? We were lucky they had a room available...'

There was a knock, and Eve turned to see a man in the doorway. He had a name badge pinned to his red polo shirt, but through the tears everything was blurry and she couldn't make out what it said.

'Hello,' he said. 'Sorry to disturb you. I just wondered if you needed some help with anything. Unpacking? Putting your clothes away?'

Eve dashed the tips of her fingers underneath her eyes,

forcing a smile. 'No, we're fine. Thank you. I've put my mother's things into the drawers.'

'Well, just call if you do. I'm Nathan, I work on this floor with Helen, who you saw earlier. It's lovely to have you here, Mrs Glover. I'm sure you'll get to know us all very quickly.'

He was young, possibly just out of his teens. There was a smattering of acne across his forehead and his chest didn't quite fill the shirt, which had the care home's insignia embroidered on one side. He shifted from one foot to the other, not meeting Eve's eye, staring at a point slightly to the right of her head.

Flora looked up at him, sniffing. 'You're a good boy,' she said. 'But I won't be here long, so there's no point in all this unpacking. I'll be going home soon.'

He smiled, but was already on his way out of the door, his feet shuffling backwards. Before Flora finished speaking, he had disappeared down the corridor.

Eve knelt beside the armchair, putting one hand onto her mother's forearm, the papery skin crinkling beneath her fingers. 'Let's give it a go, shall we, Mum?' she said, reaching out her other hand and gently pushing a strand of white hair away from Flora's face. 'I know it's different to your flat, not as homely...'

'Tiny,' said Flora.

'Yes, this room is smaller than your bedroom. But there was that communal room we saw when we came in, the one with a television and...'

'It stank.'

'No, it didn't! There was the library as well, remember? It looked like they had the most amazing collection of books...'

'Books are boring,' muttered Flora.

'You love books! Anyway, the girl said they have talks there in the evening?'

'I won't be going to any of those stupid things. Bloody, bloody stupid.'

4

'Mum, there's no need to swear.' Eve sat back on her heels, glad the young lad had left the room. 'Anyway, you may find you're interested.'

'I don't want to carry on living if it means being here...'

'Listen...'

'This isn't where I'm meant to be. What about my flat? I want to go back there now. You have no right to keep me here.'

Eve sighed: she was dog tired. She'd been hoping to get Flora settled in quickly, so she'd have time to pop to Tesco on the way home. There was no bread at home and she was pretty sure they were running out of loo roll as well – and teabags; oh yes, and washing-up liquid. She was invariably running out of quite a lot of things, including stuff you couldn't grab off the shelves in Tesco, like patience, energy and resilience.

She pushed herself up from the floor and walked across to the bed, fastening the buckles on the empty suitcase that was lying on it. Her mother had owned this old case for as long as she could remember; it had gone with them on summer holidays to Cornwall, when Eve was growing up. They had hauled it on and off trains, dragged it down steep streets and up narrow staircases in B&Bs. At the end of each holiday, they'd filled it with sand-encrusted swimming costumes and towels, Eve shovelling handfuls of shells into the zip pockets, thinking her mother wouldn't notice. Flora had always refused to replace this old case, even when Eve recently offered to buy her a new hardshell one with wheels.

'Nothing wrong with it,' she'd insisted. 'They don't make them like this anymore.'

Now, they had used this battered old case to bring some of her mother's most treasured possessions to this soulless, depressing room, where Flora was likely to end her days. The guilt weighed almost as heavily on Eve's shoulders as the case, as she heaved it up on top of the cupboard in the corner.

'I want to go back to my flat!' Flora was muttering. 'It's mine. I want to be there. I hate it here.'

'We can't go back to the flat because it's not safe,' Eve said. She heard the irritation in her voice, and forced herself to smile again as she turned and sat down on the bed. 'You know what happened – you know why we've had to make this decision. This is your home now, and we're both going to have to get used to it.'

Flora's brow was knitted angrily, but there was confusion there too. Eve's chest felt tight, and she ran her fingers through her own hair, pushing it away from her face. *Be kind*, she told herself, yet again. *Be patient; think of the big glass of wine you can have when you get home tonight.* But bloody hell, being kind and patient was sometimes so hard. Right now, Flora looked lost: more like a child than a seventy-seven-year-old woman. It was heart-breaking and Eve was crushed by the responsibility of having single-handedly made the decision to bring her here. There were many wonderful things about being an only child, but having to be a parent to your elderly mother, without help or support from anyone else, wasn't one of them.

'Let's go to the lounge and get a cup of tea.' Eve hoped she sounded more positive than she felt. 'Maybe we can meet some of the other residents. Ask them about the afternoon activities?'

'They're sad old bastards who just sit in chairs all day,' said Flora.

Eve had to stifle a laugh; Flora had a point. 'Mum, behave!' she said.

As she helped Flora up from the chair, she ran through the things they'd put into the suitcase earlier. Had there been some paracetamol in the washbag? Any scissors? What about her mother's sharp metal nail file that used to sit on the bedside table in the flat; had she thrown that into the case, at the last minute?

But she was worrying unnecessarily: of course Flora wouldn't really try to kill herself. She wouldn't know where to start. Just recently her memory had been getting so bad, she'd had to ask Eve how to do everything from using the washing machine, to changing the TV channel: when Eve told her about iPlayer – and explained she could rewatch dozens of old episodes of *Antiques Roadshow* – her mother had been appalled. 'But I can't do that unless it's a Sunday!' she'd gasped. '*Antiques Roadshow* is only ever on Sunday night!'

Eve put her arm through Flora's and guided her out into the corridor. It was all fine: in an hour's time, it was unlikely Flora would even remember she'd been threatening to kill herself, let alone be able to work out a way of doing it.

A wailing noise started suddenly from the room next door, building up to a keening monotone that sounded like an animal in pain; impossible to tell if it belonged to a man or a woman. As they went past the open door, Eve couldn't help looking in, the cries drawing her eyes like a magnet. The old man who'd taken such delight in his monumental fart earlier, was now curled into a foetal position, his head cradled in his arms.

Eve wanted to walk more quickly, to get away from the sound that followed them down the corridor and reached right to the back of her skull. But she had to slow her steps to match those of her mother, who was putting her hand on the wall to help her balance. Flora didn't seem to notice the noise. She was concentrating on not tripping over. 'Slippers indoors,' she mumbled to herself.

'I wonder what you'll have for tea tonight?' said Eve. 'Whatever it is, it smells nice.' It didn't. The air in the corridor was thick and stuffy: the stench of burnt meat mixing with the sulphurous cloy of overcooked vegetables.

They pushed through the last of the fire doors and turned into a large room filled with sofas and mismatched armchairs.

Some people were reading newspapers and a couple of elderly ladies were watching a wildlife programme on the television, both of them having separate one sided conversations with the presenter. 'You're quite wrong,' one was saying to the screen. 'Cheetahs are much faster.'

Eve found Flora a chair.

'How about a cuppa?' called another care assistant, her chest mountainous beneath the red polo shirt. She was pushing a tea trolley towards them. 'We've got some chocolate digestives.' She grinned at them, silver fillings glinting somewhere in the back of her mouth.

They sat in silence and watched the woman clatter cups onto saucers and lift an outsized metal teapot. The liquid she poured from it was stewed to the colour of treacle. There was a strange hollowness in Eve's chest; she wanted to grab her bag and race for the door. At least she had that option; her mother was stuck here.

'I'll be in to see you as often as I can.' She reached across and took Flora's hand. 'Maybe not every day; it depends how busy I am at work, and on what Daniel's doing, of course. But I'll be here regularly, I promise. And you'll start to feel at home in no time.' She was aware she was trying to reassure herself, as much as her mother.

Flora had started crying again. 'I won't,' she whispered, so softly that Eve had to put her head right next to hers to hear what she was saying. 'I will never feel at home in this place.'

Eve sighed and twined her fingers through Flora's, noticing as she did that the varnish had smudged along the tip of her own thumbnail. She wasn't surprised: she'd painted her nails in a rush yesterday afternoon, balancing the bottle on the dashboard of the car when she found she had three minutes to spare before an appointment. She'd got out of the car, blowing frantically on the still-wet varnish, but thinking she'd got away with it. Clearly not. She must touch it up before she went back into work tomorrow.

The care assistant brought across two cups, together with a plate of biscuits. 'Enjoy!' she said.

Flora turned to Eve, her blue eyes steely. 'If your father was here, he wouldn't have let you get away with this.'

'Mum, stop it, you're being ridiculous!'

'He would have done something about it. He wouldn't have allowed you to put me into such a horrible place.'

Eve took a deep breath; she mustn't rise to this. Flora didn't mean it; she wasn't herself. It had been a difficult few days, and she was probably in shock; she'd not had much warning that they were going to pack up her entire life and come here. With hindsight, the speed of this move might have been a mistake.

She glanced surreptitiously at her watch: she really did need to get to Tesco. There wouldn't be time to cook, she'd have to pick up some ready meals as well.

'Your father would have looked after me in my own home,' Flora was saying, her voice brittle. 'He would never have allowed you to bring me somewhere like this.'

Eve shook her head and swallowed; her mouth dry. 'That's not fair, Mum.'

'It's true though.'

TWO

Eve was awake before the alarm went off. Rain was pattering against the window and she could hear the rhythmic swoosh of passing cars displacing puddles on the street outside.

Forty-five: she rolled the words around on her tongue. It sounded so old! Forty-five was an age by which you should know where you were going, have a definite game plan. An age by which you should be settled and content. But Eve felt like she was now in the wrong bit of her forties – hurtling towards fifty for God's sake – out of control in a rusty car without a handbrake, and she *still* hadn't got her life sorted.

She rolled over in bed, and her knee clicked, making her wince with pain. She kept meaning to get that checked out. Bloody forty-five. She was sure the bags under her eyes were bigger than they'd ever been, and it was getting to the stage where she might need some professional help covering up the wiry patches of grey in her hair. For the last few years, she'd kept it at bay by spending a fiver on the occasional box of hair dye from Boots. But she was rubbish at home root control. Last time she'd picked the wrong shade by mistake and the – rapidly growing out – roots were currently less her natural auburn, more a soft ginger. 'Mummy,' Daniel had said. 'Why has your hair gone rusty at the parting?'

The door flew open, crashing against the frame, and her boy leapt onto the bed, winding her as his elbow landed on her chest. 'Happy birthday!' His breath was slightly sour, his lips dry as he planted kisses on her cheek, the corners of his eyes full of crusty sleep. He was far and away the most gorgeous thing she'd ever seen.

'Thank you, sweetheart. Wow, what's this?'

He was pushing something against her chest, its cardboard edges scraping her skin. 'I made it myself.'

'Well, I can see that. It's amazing!'

Turning over the piece of card, she saw glitter around a red felt tip border, with *hap burday* written across the top in uneven letters. She'd guessed there might be a card: last night there had been prickles of glitter all over the bathroom floor, together with a Pritt Stick, the end of which had been so badly mangled it looked like a melted candle.

'Look at it!' he shouted, bouncing up and down on her stomach.

She gasped as the breath was pummelled out of her and pulled him down onto the bed beside her as she opened the card, glitter tumbling onto her T-shirt. Daniel had cut out a picture of *Doctor Who's* Tardis, and glued a photo of an overweight woman in a bikini onto the front of it. Next to her was a picture of Lassie and, further along, a very young George Clooney.

'That's you, Mummy, and that's Daddy. And that's the dog I want now – with that long hair.'

She laughed and pulled him towards her, kissing his cheek and burying her face in his hair, smelling the honey shampoo she'd massaged through it the previous evening. He'd been badgering her to get a dog for months now, ever since his friend Robbie had been given a kitten. At first, Daniel had demanded a spaniel, then he'd changed his mind and gone for a black Labrador. Most recently, it had been a Dalmatian, but he'd clearly moved on yet again. She dealt with the ongoing demands as she did with so many other things, by trying to ignore them.

'Thank you, my lovely boy. What a brilliant card. I can't believe you did this all by yourself. You are so clever.'

He grinned and pulled himself away from her arms. 'I'm hungry,' he said, jumping off the bed. 'Going for breakfast.'

'Okay, be careful when you get the cereal out of the cupboard. Don't spill it.'

As she listened to his feet pound down the stairs, she looked at the card again, noticing that the overweight woman was carrying a bottle of beer in one hand and a cigarette in the other. She peered more closely; it didn't look anything like her. But it was even more irritating that Ben got to be George bloody Clooney.

She got out of bed and wandered into the bathroom, leaning across the basin to pull up the blind. She put her fingers to her face and patted the puffy skin underneath her eyes. Cucumber slices were meant to help. When was the last time she'd bought a cucumber?

'Mummy!' yelled Daniel from the kitchen. 'The milk just dropped and went all over the floor, but it wasn't my fault!'

'Oh, for God's sake!' She reached for her toothbrush. 'Don't step in it, I'll be down in a minute.'

They were late leaving the house, as always, and the traffic was heavier than usual on the run into the city centre. It was well after 9am by the time she parked.

As she pushed open the door to the office, Caroline squealed from behind the reception desk and ran around to give her a hug. 'Happy birthday! How are you feeling? Another year older!'

'Ah, yes. Indeed,' said Eve, disentangling herself and moving towards her desk. 'That's what tends to happen with birthdays.'

'Oh Eve, you are funny!' said Caroline. 'Wait, we've got a surprise for you.'

As Eve shrugged off her coat and leant forward to turn on her computer, she saw Gav coming out from the kitchen at the back, holding something in front of him.

'Happy birthday!' he shouted. 'Come on everyone…'

They clustered around her and launched into song, as Gav placed the cake on her desk. She smiled and waited patiently until the last 'to yoooo' had faded away.

'Come on then, blow it out!' Gav was still shouting, even though he was standing two feet away from her. He shouted at everyone. Caroline had a theory he used his voice excessively to make up for the fact that he was so short, but over the years Eve had decided he was probably just a bit deaf.

'Not much to blow out,' she said. There was actually only a single candle: a spindly gold one, planted right in the middle of the frosting.

'You're too old. We couldn't fit that many on the bloody cake!' yelled Gav, laughing uproariously at his own joke. 'Come on, get on with it.'

Eve obediently blew out the candle, and smiled at the others while Gav cut slices, which were handed around on pieces of kitchen roll.

'Mmm, delicious,' she said. It actually wasn't bad. It was a Tesco Finest Carrot Cake; she recognised it because she'd bought one exactly the same herself, a couple of weeks ago, to donate to a cake sale at Daniel's school. She'd never got round to contributing to one of those before and didn't know the form; she only realised she'd dramatically failed the Mummy test when she put the cake onto the table alongside the trays of home-baked delicacies. There were fruit muffins and chocolate brownies, cupcakes with coloured icing, slices of lemon drizzle with a crunchy sugar topping, flapjacks with raisins and chocolate chips.

And then there was one Tesco Finest Carrot Cake. Still in its box. How embarrassing. She'd ripped open the packaging and pulled out the cake, hastily combining two plates of biscuits so she could slide the empty plate under her cake. For good measure she used her finger to mess up the perfect buttercream frosting on top. It didn't exactly look *homemade* but would have to do. Then she'd tugged up the hood of her coat and slipped back out of the school hall, hoping no one had seen her.

'Right, that's enough of all this partying!' shouted Gav. 'Back to work you lot, we've got maisonettes to market, semis to shift.'

He walked back to his desk at the far end of the office, chuckling to himself. He said this regularly, but was the only one who ever laughed.

Eve licked the remaining cake crumbs from her fingers and began to go through her emails. There was the usual mixed bag: conveyancing information from solicitors, new contact sheets of colour prints from the guy who took all the agency's photographs, requests for updates from impatient clients.

'There are some messages from Mr Timpson,' called Caroline. 'He phoned twice yesterday after you left and wants you to call him.'

'I know,' said Eve. 'I'm reading his emails now. I've already had four from him this morning.'

Sometimes she hated this job. Mr Timpson was the owner of a particularly unattractive Victorian house on the outskirts of the city. He had insisted they market his property at £50,000 above Eve's valuation, and was now incandescent because there'd been no viewings in the first fortnight. She would have to speak to him, but needed coffee first. Just as she sat down again, her phone rang.

'Eve?'

'Hi Mum, how are you?'

'Not good. I'm not sleeping at all. I've been awake for seventy-four hours.'

'Seventy-four, eh? It was eighty-three yesterday. I'm sure things will get better. You've only been there for a week. It's bound to take time to settle in. What did you have for breakfast this morning?'

Flora sighed on the other end of the phone. 'Cold toast. You've got your happy voice on – the one you use to jolly me along. But I don't want to be bloody well jollied. I want to go home.'

Eve put her elbow on the desk and rested her head in the palm of her hand. 'Mum, please don't swear. Three Elms is your home now. You know this. Listen, I'm going to pop in to see you after work today – is that okay? Juliet is having Daniel for tea then dropping him home, so I've got a bit of extra time.'

'Who's Juliet?' asked Flora.

'Robbie's mother! You know who Juliet is. Anyway, I'd like to see you later – it's my birthday, did you remember? We talked about it yesterday. I've been given a lovely carrot cake here, at work, I'll bring you a piece.' There was silence on the other end of the phone. 'So, if you haven't got anything else on, I'll pop in about half past four.'

'What else would I have on?' snapped Flora. 'I'm always here. I'm stuck in this horrible place.'

'Okay, I'll see you later. I've got to go now, lots of work to do.' She put the phone on her desk and brought up her on-screen appointment diary. This wouldn't be the last of Flora's calls she'd have to field over the next few hours. Yesterday, there had been five, the day before, seven.

There was a whoop from the other side of the office and Gav leapt to his feet, sending a box of paperclips flying onto the floor, the contents spilling out onto the carpet in a long silver arc, like a mermaid's tail.

'Get in!' yelled Gav. 'Four hundred grand asking price offer on Mountview Road!'

Everyone cheered and Caroline stood up behind her desk and did an awkward little dance, before sinking down into her seat again when she realised they were all looking at her.

'Cash buyers, no onward chain,' shouted Gav. 'This, my friends, is how to work the property market.'

Eve smiled and gave him a thumbs-up. How did such an irritating little man manage to sell so many houses?

Gav was still on his feet, shuffling on the spot and looking like he was trying to do a robot dance. He saw her staring across at him and grinned, before putting his head on one side and looking at her quizzically.

'You done something to your hair, Eve?' he yelled. 'You've gone all ginger on the top.'

THREE

The house was a tip. There were shoes lying abandoned just inside the front door, a pile of newspapers and a dirty mug at the bottom of the stairs.

Looking through to the kitchen, she could see the sink stacked with unwashed saucepans and plates, and the laundry basket full of dirty clothes had been sitting on the table since yesterday. The leg of Daniel's school trousers dangled over the side of the basket, a reminder that he'd had no clean uniform to wear this morning so Eve had sent him into school wearing his PE shirt and yesterday's crumpled, mud-splattered trousers, hastily sprayed with Febreze.

She'd been intending to write a note for his teacher, but had forgotten to do that as well in the rush to leave the house.

She was on her way to Three Elms to see Flora, but had popped in at home on the off-chance that some birthday cards might have come in the post. One friend had called earlier and sung *Happy Birthday* and a few others had texted, but it hadn't been the most exciting of birthdays. Disappointingly, there were only two cards on the mat: one was from an elderly friend of her mother's – Eve recognised the writing – and, ripping open the other, she saw it was from her old university friend Cath. Sweet of her to remember.

There was an unpleasant, sour smell that got stronger as she walked down the hall: as soon as she saw the screwed-up J-cloth on the worktop, she remembered the spilt milk that had been nothing whatsoever to do with Daniel.

'Bugger.' She threw the stinking cloth into the sink on top of the pans. She'd love to be able to blame someone else for this, but sadly it was all down to her.

The landline answerphone was giving out an insistent bleep, so she pressed play. Her heart gave a little jolt when she saw there were five messages: this was more like it.

The first message was from British Gas about an overdue boiler service. The second was from another friend of Flora's, asking for her new address. The third, fourth and fifth were automated recordings from the same company, informing Eve that she'd recently been involved in a car accident, and could win substantial damages if she put in a claim through their no win, no fee system.

She pressed the delete button and stared at the display for a moment as it reset itself. She wasn't sure who she'd been expecting to hear from anyway – most of her friends didn't use the landline anymore: they sent texts or WhatsApp messages, or wrote emails from abroad, passing on six months' worth of news in a dozen tightly packed lines. She was no good at remembering other people's birthdays, so it was unfair to expect them to think about hers.

It was only four o'clock, but she fancied a beer. What the hell, it was her birthday. She pulled a bottle from the fridge, opened the back door and stepped out onto the patio.

Daniel had left his new red truck on the grass a couple of days ago, and she could see a white splodge of bird poo trailing down the side. The truck had a flashing light and siren, but there had been so much rain last night that the battery compartment would probably be full of water; if it worked again, it would be a miracle.

She ought to bring the truck inside and clean it. Ben had only bought it a couple of weeks ago, and he'd be furious if he saw Daniel had left it out here.

But that could wait. She slumped down onto the bench outside the kitchen door, feeling the wooden struts creak ominously beneath her.

'Cheers, me!' she said out loud, lifting up the bottle towards the garden in a toast, before raising it to her lips.

'Cheers, you!' said a voice.

Eve jumped, then spluttered and choked as her mouthful of beer went down the wrong way.

'Oops, sorry.'

She turned and saw a face staring at her over the fence.

'Jake! You gave me a shock.'

'It's just an automatic thing, isn't it,' he said. 'When someone says cheers, you say cheers back?'

Eve grinned, wiping a dribble of beer from her chin. 'Maybe when you're sitting in a pub. But not when they're in the garden next door!'

He laughed and wandered up to the fence, resting his arms on it. 'Sorry. Did I disturb you having a private alcoholic moment? How have you been?'

'No! Of course not. Fine, thanks,' she said. 'And you?'

This was the sort of conversation they always had. They'd lived next door for years, but the relationship had never progressed any further than a neighbourly chat over the shared boundary.

Jake and Ben had been out for a couple of drinks, years ago when they first moved in, but it had felt like the sort of blokey thing they ought to do, rather than something either of them really wanted. Ben worked in insurance; Jake was a housing officer with the local council. Ben liked cars and rugby, Jake cycled to work and had been taking an evening course in life drawing. She wondered if he'd ever completed it.

'He's nice enough, but a bit dull,' she remembered Ben saying. 'We've got nothing in common.'

Eve didn't think he was dull; she just didn't know him very well. Their over-the-fence chats revealed very little, other than that he took better care of his garden than she did of hers, and he had pretty awful dress sense: today he was wearing a blue checked shirt under a brown and beige tank top. The collar of the shirt was tucked underneath the tank top on one side and her hand itched to reach out and pull it straight. He had a mop of dirty blond hair, which looked as if it hadn't been brushed for days, and his fringe was slightly too long, so he had to keep swiping it out of his eyes.

'How's Katie?' she asked, for lack of anything else to say. Eve had asked his teenage daughter to babysit a few times recently, but after handing over a couple of hard-earned tenners at the end of an evening, she'd been relieved to shut the front door on Katie's scowls and teenage shrugs.

When she was that age, Eve had been a prolific babysitter, keeping a wall chart in her bedroom crammed with future bookings. At the age of sixteen, she'd already started to save most of the money given to her by grateful, exhausted parents. But looking after small children clearly wasn't Katie's idea of fun, and Eve suspected the money she earned would be blown on make-up and the vapes she smelt drifting out through her open bedroom window.

'Oh, she's fine,' Jake said, nodding. 'Don't see much of her at the moment, to be honest. She's got a new boyfriend and they spend most of their time at the park, doing God knows what.'

Eve snorted. 'Do you mind that?'

'I don't have much choice,' he said with a shrug. 'My daughter is a law unto herself. If I tell her to stop doing something, you can guarantee she'll make a huge effort to do it twice as much.'

Eve had no idea where Katie's mother was – or whether she even had a mother anymore. Ben had never asked about anything personal during their boys' nights out – much to Eve's frustration – and, after living next door to Jake for all this time, it now felt as if it was far too late to bring up the subject.

'All good with Daniel?' he asked. He had a nice voice, she realised: deep and measured. He could be a television announcer.

'Yes, fine.' She nodded. She stared down at the bottle of beer in her hand, imagining Jake reading out the football results on a Saturday afternoon: *Sheffield Wednesday 3... West Bromwich Albion 1*. Or maybe he could present the BBC's six o'clock news: *And now, live from Westminster, our reporter...*

She looked back to the fence: Jake was staring at her. She blushed and took a swig of the beer, turning her eyes towards her garden, which was hideously overgrown. Weeding and pruning were way down her list of priorities; not even on the list, if she was honest. She got up and stepped onto what had once been a lawn, picking up the red truck and holding it at an angle while the water flooded out of it.

'Jake, do you have a lawnmower I could borrow?' she asked. 'I don't mean right now, just at some stage. Ours is rubbish. In fact, I don't think it even works anymore. But this garden is in such a state I need to do something about it.'

'Of course,' he said, nodding. 'I'll pop it round at the weekend. I can give you a hand if you like. It might be tough getting through that long stuff at the edges – you'll be better off strimming it.'

'Good idea,' she said, wondering if it would be cheeky to ask if he could lend her a strimmer at the same time.

'I'll lend you a strimmer too,' he said, grinning.

She felt herself blushing again – was she that easy to read? He did have a very nice smile.

She suddenly remembered she was supposed to be on her way to Three Elms. 'Shit, got to go!' she said. 'I promised to see my mother. That's great about the weekend, thank you. Are you sure you can spare the time?'

'Yup, not a problem. Good to see you.'

'You too,' she called, as she turned back towards the house. Should she have mentioned that the collar of his shirt was tucked in?

Hey, guess what? she wanted to add. *It's my birthday today, Jake with the lovely voice! That's why I'm having a beer – I don't normally drink alcohol this early in the day, you're not living next door to a sad old soak.*

But the words stayed in her head and it was probably just as well; he might have felt awkward if she'd mentioned her birthday. Although it would have been nice to have just one more card to put on the shelf above the fireplace. She shook off the self-pity, putting the half-empty beer bottle on the worktop. There was no point feeling low; by the time you got to this age – horrible, going-nowhere forty-five – a birthday was just another day.

As she walked past the answerphone, she saw the red light was flashing again: she'd missed another call while she was outside. Things were definitely looking up. She pressed the *play* button, trying to second-guess who else might be about to sing *Happy Birthday*.

It was another message from the company that was offering help after her recent car accident.

FOUR

Eve was starting to dread walking through the front door of Three Elms. She'd only been coming here for a week, but already her nostrils were growing accustomed to the harsh smell of disinfectant that didn't quite mask the combination of urine and stewed cabbage that seeped around corners and along corridors.

The care home smelt of something else as well: old age. Eve had never thought about it before, but now realised that many old people had their own smell – slightly grassy, musty like an unaired bathroom. She could sometimes smell it on Flora, beneath the Chanel No 5 her mother dabbed behind her ears every morning. She made a mental note to buy a reed diffuser to put on the windowsill in her room.

'Good afternoon!' called a man, standing behind the reception desk. Eve had seen him before, and felt she ought to know his name, but there were so many members of staff here and the shift patterns seemed to change all the time. She smiled and waved, immediately feeling foolish and turning the wave into a strange little flick, where she grabbed her own hair and threw it back over her shoulders. God, why did she *do* that? She was going to be the ultimate embarrassing mother when Daniel was old enough to be aware of these things. Poor kid.

The overhead light was broken in the corridor leading to the bedrooms, and a man was wobbling on a ladder, replacing the tube. It made a nice change not to be able to see the stains on the taupe carpet or have the white walls thrown into sharp relief by the harsh glare of the fluorescent bulb. On sunny days, the air along here was often full of dust motes, millions of flakes of ancient skin dancing in the rays of light.

Nathan suddenly appeared from a doorway, clutching a clipboard and frowning. Eve had bumped into him a couple of times now and had realised he was painfully shy. The abrupt exit he'd made on the day Flora moved in hadn't been intentionally rude; he just didn't know how to bring conversations to a conclusion – so he walked out before they ended.

'Hi Nathan,' she said. 'How are you?'

'We've lost six chairs!' he said. 'They're on the spreadsheet but they're not in the dining room.'

'Oh dear,' Eve said. 'At least you haven't lost six residents.' But he was already scuttling away down the corridor.

Flora was sitting in her room, glaring at the door. 'You're very, very late.'

'No, I'm not, Mum. It's 4.32 – I'm precisely two minutes late.'

'Don't speak to me like that! You were meant to be here hours ago.'

Sometimes Flora had good days, sometimes bad. Today she was foul-tempered: refusing to answer questions, turning away to stare out of the window. It was impossible to know what had upset her, but this was happening all the time now.

On Saturday, Eve had arrived with arms full of flowers, which she spent ten minutes arranging in vases, putting a purple and white display on the chest of drawers, with a colourful bunch of red and yellow carnations beside the bed. When she came in the following day, there was no sign of any of them.

'Where are your flowers?' she asked.

'They smelt of wee,' said Flora. 'I threw them out of the window.'

'What about the vases?'

'Them too.'

When Eve went across and looked out of the window, she'd seen the stems of the flowers lying on the grass outside, amongst shards of broken glass.

'It's a lovely day out there,' she said now. 'We can go and have a wander around the garden. I picked you up some magazines when I left the office – there's the latest *Good Housekeeping* and I've got you next week's *Radio Times*.'

'Don't want them,' said Flora.

'Fine.' Eve put the magazines on the bed. 'Maybe you'll feel like looking at them later.'

'I won't!' Her mother crossed her arms in front of her chest and shook her head angrily from side to side.

Eve was itching to answer back, but there was no point both of them behaving like children. 'Oh, is that for me?' She noticed a card on the bed, her mother's handwriting skewed across the envelope.

Flora nodded, so Eve picked it up and opened it.

'Mum, thank you, it's... lovely!'

The picture on the front was an overly twee drawing of a little girl, dressed in pink, holding a balloon and a bunch of flowers. Not the sort of thing her mother would have chosen in a million years: clearly one of the care assistants had bought it on her behalf. Inside, Flora had written, *To my dearest darling Eve, happy birthday xxx,* the words wobbling and shaking across the card at an angle.

Eve suddenly wanted to cry.

The signs of Flora's dementia had been there for more than a year. A series of little things at first: forgetting the names of friends, going out without her handbag, buying herself a new dress in completely the wrong size. Once Flora had got on a train to go and visit a friend, then forgotten where she was going and why, phoning Eve in tears from the ticket inspector's office at Taunton Station.

A few weeks later, the staff at Marks & Spencer in the city centre had called the police when Flora shut herself in a changing room and refused to come out. When Eve finally got her back home, Flora had no idea where she'd been or what had happened.

'I was frightened,' she whispered. 'I thought you'd left me. They were banging on the door so hard, it hurt my head.'

Eve had been frightened too. This was such strange behaviour, so erratic and unpredictable from a woman who had worked in social services for forty years, and had always been so organised. Flora had been a list-maker and a planner, keen that her efficiency would rub off onto her daughter. 'Take control of life, before life takes control of you,' she used to say. Even as a flaky teenager, Eve had recognised the sense in what she was being told and had grown up relying on the fact that her mother invariably knew what to do, and the best way to do it.

But now that confident woman was losing herself. Flora's friends began to phone Eve to voice their concerns and one in particular, Deirdre, insisted they cancel a planned trip to Cornwall. 'I don't think I can cope,' she'd confided to Eve. 'Your mother seems confused most of the time now. She forgets everything I tell her. I'm too old to be any use to her in a crisis.'

Finally, there had been the incident with the gas fire. Eve

had found it left on before – even on baking summer days – but one Sunday morning she opened the front door of Flora's flat to be met by a searing wall of heat. The fire must have been on all night and the air was so stifling it was hard to breathe.

As Eve threw open the windows, she saw a towel hanging over the back of a chair, inches from the naked flame. The cream material was turning brown, the fibres starting to crisp and curl up. She dreaded to think what would have happened if she'd arrived an hour later.

'I thought I'd dry some washing,' Flora said.

Eve had sat down on the sofa beside her mother and picked up both her hands. Flora wouldn't meet her eye and kept trying to pull her fingers out of her grasp.

'Mum, we can't carry on like this,' Eve had said, hearing her voice tremble. 'It's not safe for you to be living here on your own anymore.'

As Flora finally looked at her, there was resignation in her eyes. Somewhere deep inside, what remained of the old Flora knew that none of this was right, none of it made sense. 'I'm sorry,' she'd whispered.

Eve had begun to visit care homes the following week, booking appointments for whenever they could fit her in, sometimes dragging Daniel along after school. The cost of care shocked her, but she'd have to find a way of funding it until they could sell Flora's flat.

She'd briefly wondered whether her mother could move in with them. But there were only three bedrooms in the house; if Granny came to live with them, Daniel would have to move into the tiny back room which was barely large enough for a single bed.

Eve also realised it would mean her giving up work: Flora couldn't be left on her own for long periods. No sooner had that possibility entered her head, than she immediately discounted it. However much she might occasionally moan about her job, she loved everything that came with it. She'd grown up revelling in the fact that she could have a career, earn a living and be independent. Some sainted middle-aged daughters might be prepared to give up everything to care for their elderly parents – and Eve was full of admiration for them – but she was too selfish to count herself among them.

She'd visited five different care homes and Three Elms hadn't been her first choice. But it wasn't bottom of the list either, and there had been a room available immediately. Eve had done the right thing. She had to tell herself, constantly, that she really had done the right thing.

Now, she walked across the room and balanced the birthday card on the windowsill. 'Let's pop it up here for the moment,' she said. 'I've brought some cake – they gave it to me in the office this morning. Shall we go for a walk outside and find a bench somewhere? I'm starving, I didn't have time for lunch.'

Flora slammed her hands down on the arms of her chair. 'I don't want to go out,' she shouted. 'There are boring old people everywhere in this place – I hate it.'

Her mother's face was pink and she was breathing heavily and Eve felt her own heart rate increasing. She sat down on the bed and reached across to put her hand on Flora's arm. 'Okay, no problem. We won't go out,' she said. 'It's fine, we can stay here and have the cake.'

She'd read that this was a common symptom of dementia: a refusal to accept the onslaught of old age. On the surface it seemed ridiculous that white-haired Flora, with her shaking hands and unsteady gait, couldn't understand that she herself was old. But Eve knew that, inside her mother's head, there was a younger version of herself, struggling to understand why her mind and body were failing her, fighting desperately to prove she was in full charge of her faculties.

'I know it's hard meeting new people,' she said gently. 'But if you chat to some of them, you'll find they're very friendly and you may have things in common.'

'Don't tell me who I will or won't like,' said Flora. 'You don't know anything about me.' Now she'd started weeping again, her face crumpled, tears glistening on her cheeks. 'I want to die,' she whispered. 'I can't go on being in this place. Please help me, Eve. Please do something. You can stop all this.'

Eve stroked her mother's arm. There was a lump in her throat, but she mustn't cry as well.

'Do something!' Flora pushed away Eve's hand and started wailing. 'Make it go away!'

Eve stood up suddenly. 'I can't! I bloody well can't do that.'

'This is all your fault!' screamed Flora.

Eve clamped her hands over her ears and closed her eyes. 'Jesus, Mum!' she shouted back. 'Stop it please! Just stop. Stop talking! Stop moaning!' She opened her eyes again to see Flora staring at her wide-eyed and shocked. 'Sorry,' she whispered. 'God, Mum, I'm so sorry. I know this isn't your fault.'

And then, as suddenly as it had roared into life, Flora's fury died away again. She looked up at Eve, frowning. 'Why have you got your hands over your ears like that? What are you shouting about? I'd quite like some of that cake now.'

Eve sank onto the edge of the bed, her pulse racing. She felt drained, as if she'd run miles to get here.

'Your father would have been so proud of you,' said Flora, suddenly. 'He always said you'd go far.'

Eve couldn't help smiling. 'Mum, I'm just a part-time estate agent. I don't even sell many properties!'

'Darling, you are so much more than that!' Flora said. 'We always knew you'd do well in life. I remember him bobbing you up and down on his knee, when you were a baby. There was that rhyme – do you know it? This is the way the gentlemen ride, clip clop, clip clop...' She clapped her hands in front of her. 'This is the way the farmers ride,' she sang, her voice quavering. She laughed, even while the tears still glistened in her eyelashes, holding her hands out in front of her, grasping imaginary reins.

Eve smiled, as her heart ached. This was still her wonderful mother. But, at the same time, it was someone else entirely.

'You used to love that song so much,' Flora was saying. 'You'd scream with excitement and he'd be jiggling you up and down on his knee.'

Eve's father had died when she was very young and she had no memory of him; the image she carried around in her head was of the handsome, smiling face that stared out at her from the photograph that sat on her mother's bedside table.

There was nothing else: no sense of how broad his shoulders had been, how warm his hand had felt when it had held hers, how deep and reassuring his voice had sounded. She had spent her entire life wishing for more, but nothing could fill the gaping hole in her memory where those reminiscences should have been; all she had were moments like this, when her mother shared her own memories.

'Then he'd throw you into the air,' she was saying now. 'Toss you up so high it seemed like you were flying. It terrified me, but you screamed with laughter.'

Eve knew she had some of her mother's traits – the same colour eyes, a shared sense of humour, a similar tone of voice. But she often wondered which bits of her had been donated by this mystery man.

'Am I like him, Mum?' she asked now, as she'd asked many times before. 'Can you see anything of him in me?'

But Flora had closed herself off again. She stared at Eve, confused. 'Are you like who?'

Eve sighed. 'Never mind. Come on, let's have some of that cake.'

She reached for her bag, pulling out the slices of carrot cake that Caroline had carefully wrapped in silver foil. As she started to unwrap the package, her mother turned towards the windowsill.

'Who's that birthday card for?' she asked.

FIVE

'Out here, we have the utility area,' said Eve, pushing open a door. 'As you'll see, it's fully equipped: washing machine, tumble dryer, a second dishwasher and, of course, no modern home would be complete without a drinks fridge!'

She swept forward and opened the glass door, revealing rows of horizontally stacked wine bottles. 'Ta-dah!' she sang, stepping back and opening her arms wide. 'Isn't that wonderful? This really is the perfect party house!'

There was a stony silence. The woman was sending a text, her husband took a cursory glance around the utility area before wandering back into the kitchen again. Eve shut the fridge door. Had she misjudged these two? They were probably the sort of people who paid someone else to put their plates into the dishwasher. And maybe they didn't drink wine? His belly was more likely to have come from beer, and her clackety heels and tight skirt didn't exactly scream Chablis.

'As you'll see, the views are spectacular,' said Eve, following them into the kitchen and moving ahead to open the floor-to-ceiling glass doors that led to the balcony. 'A wonderful outlook onto the Suspension Bridge – I haven't seen another property along this road which has as much space, and the finish is of an exceptionally high standard. I'm sure you'll agree that the renovation work has been carried out extremely well.'

She had done several viewings at this flat now, and loved everything about it. Each time she came here, she mentally moved herself in: imagining cooking tea for Daniel at the marble-topped island in the middle of the kitchen, while carelessly tossing her recycling into the specially designed wall unit in the utility room. She would wander along the galleried mezzanine library, chatting to friends on her phone, watching the sunlight stream through the self-operating Velux windows in the sloping ceiling. In the evening, while Daniel watched the seventy-two-inch television in the sitting room, she would pour herself a gin and tonic and take it out onto the wooden decking, collapsing into one of the Adirondack chairs, carefully placed to combine a view of the Avon Gorge with the last rays of the setting sun.

'Phone signal's a bit crap,' said the woman, holding up her mobile and waving it around over her head. 'Can't pick up anything. Do they even have 5G round here?'

'Oh, absolutely,' said Eve, who had no idea.

'Not convinced by the décor,' said the man. 'Bit old-fashioned for my taste.'

Eve smiled tightly. Irritating shit: he clearly had enough money to gut the place and start again if he wanted. 'I'm sure it wouldn't take much to put your own mark on things, Mr Sewell,' she said with a smile. 'What sort of effect are you after?'

'I like black and white,' said the woman. 'With gold touches – mirrors, sculptures, like Michelle who won *Love Island* has in her penthouse. You know, classy.'

She was at least twenty years his junior and, although there wasn't a wrinkle on her face, Eve could see the swollen flesh around the outside of her mouth where the Botox had spread, leaving the skin puffy and the lips bee-stung and inflamed. When Mr Sewell kissed Mrs Sewell, was it like putting his lips against a rubber ring? It made Eve think about blowing up Daniel's armbands when she took him swimming, her mouth clamped around the squeaky plastic.

'Thing is, Steph babe, you've got excellent taste,' said Mr Sewell. 'So, I'm willing to go with your judgement on this one. What do you think of the place?'

'It's not bad,' said the woman, tipping her head onto one side and bringing her forefinger to her lips.

Eve guessed she was trying to look thoughtful, but it wasn't working. A colossal diamond glinted on the third finger of her hand; the more Eve tried to look away, the more her eyes were pulled towards it.

'This sitting room's a bit poky though,' she was saying. 'Where would we put the L-shaped sofa?'

'Maybe up against that long wall, over there?' asked Eve. They both turned and stared at her, as if they'd only just noticed she was there.

'Is there a separate bog?' asked the man.

'Yes, of course, just through here.' As she was showing them back through to the entrance hall, her phone began to ring. 'Sorry, I have to take this call, it's the office. Do wander round and have a look at the bedrooms and I'll join you again in a minute.' She walked out onto the balcony and slid the glass door shut behind her.

'Mum?'

'Eve, it's me – your mother!'

'Yes, I know. What is it? I'm right in the middle of a viewing.'

'I can't find my glasses!' wailed Flora. 'I had them this morning because I was writing a letter, but now they've gone. I think someone has stolen them.'

'Of course they haven't. Who would steal an old pair of prescription glasses?' snapped Eve. This was the third call in the last two hours. She had spoken to the care home manager, Mrs Donaldson, the other night, asking if it was normal for residents to take this long to settle in.

'Oh yes, it can take months,' the woman had said. 'Some of our guests never stop missing home. It just depends on the individual situation.'

It wasn't the answer Eve had been hoping for. Over the last couple of weeks, she had fielded calls from Flora while she was in the bath, on the loo and getting Daniel ready for school. The familiar number had come up on her phone while she was shopping, cooking, cleaning and doing the ironing.

She had once spent ten minutes trying to placate Flora over the phone as she stood outside the library, having left Daniel reading on a beanbag in the children's section. Each call followed a pattern. Flora would initially be angry: needing an important question answered or desperate for Eve's help to find something that was lost – the glasses disappeared on a regular basis. But the anger would soon turn to misery and she would end up sobbing, begging to be taken home.

Eve could never bring herself to ignore the calls, but had come to dread the vibration of the phone in her pocket. It was exhausting and mentally wearing, but the hardest part was that these calls left her feeling unbearably cruel.

She knew Flora's request to help her die wasn't coming from a rational part of her mother's mind, but it was breaking Eve's heart that the one thing she was asking her to help with, was something she could never consider doing in a million years.

'Listen Mum, I'm working so I can't talk now. But I'll come over later.'

How on earth was she going to manage that? She would have to take Daniel again, even though he'd started to hate the regular trips to the home, which Eve could totally understand. It had been hard for him to see his granny change over the last few months: the warm, smiley woman who used to open her arms wide and crush him against her, saying, 'You lovely boy, I'm going to eat you all up!' had shrunk in on herself and now rarely smiled. She always knew who he was and patted his back when he gave her a hug, but the light had gone out in her eyes, and six-year-old Daniel had no idea why. 'Is it my fault Granny's so unhappy?' he'd asked Eve a few months ago.

Now his granny was living at Three Elms, he wasn't just seeing her upset, he was seeing other miseries too. A few days ago, they had been walking past the lounge when an old man toppled over, landing feet away from them, face down on the carpet. As a care assistant rushed to help, Daniel had buried his head in Eve's coat, clasping his little hands across his ears to block out the low moans of distress and pain.

No, she couldn't take him with her again tonight; maybe Katie would babysit for a couple of hours?

'I'll be in later, I promise,' she said, and ended the call.

Looking back through the expansive glass window, Eve could see the couple gesticulating in the corner of the sitting room. The woman was pointing her manicured nail at one of the walls, the man had dug his hands into his pockets and was shaking his head. Something had clearly gone wrong with negotiations over the position of the L-shaped sofa.

Eve took a deep breath. She really needed this sale: there were fewer buyers around than this time last year, and her commission – which was paying for Flora's stay at Three Elms until they could sell her flat – was dismal. She was damned if she was going to let this couple get away.

Yesterday she had shown them around another – more expensive – apartment down by the harbour, but they'd been disappointed by the size of the third bedroom and when they stood out on the balcony Steph had been traumatised by the swooping seagulls, convinced they were deliberately dive-bombing her hair. Eve had had higher hopes for this flat, sure that the two of them would fall in love with it immediately: they could afford it and it was in a perfect location.

The argument inside was now turning ugly. Steph was prodding one long nail into her husband's chest, adding painfully sharp emphasis to whatever she was saying. Turning on her high heels, she stomped out of the sitting room and disappeared into one of the bedrooms.

'Shit,' said Eve. 'Fuck, bollocks.' The last thing she needed was a marital tiff, she must get back in there and sweet-talk them.

But when she pushed against the door, it didn't budge. She tried again: nothing. It had locked behind her. She knocked on the glass but the man didn't turn around, and she could only stand helplessly, watching as he stormed after his furious wife – the triple glazing silencing whatever profanities he was shouting at her. After repeatedly tugging on the handle, Eve moved to the far end of the balcony, where a window to the utility room was slightly ajar. She kicked off her shoes, pulled the window fully open and threw the shoes through it, before starting to crawl in herself, onto a section of marble worktop. Wriggling through the gap, she wondered how many of those currently driving their cars across the Clifton Suspension Bridge would notice the slightly wobbly bottom of a middle-aged woman sticking out of a window of one of the most exclusive apartments in the area.

It was, she decided as she collapsed onto the shiny black floor tiles, ripping a hole in her tights in the process, a new low.

SIX

'Have you got teddy?'
  'Yes, he's in my backpack.'
'Good. What about your reading book?'
'I don't need to do reading, it's the weekend.'
'Actually, you still need to do it, I'll get the book.' When Eve came back downstairs, Daniel was perched on the edge of the armchair, leaning towards the sitting-room window, straining to look up and down the street outside. The car always came from the same direction, but it didn't stop him checking the other way, just in case.

'We're going to do soft play,' he said, bouncing up and down. 'It'll be brilliant. I can't wait.'

Eve unzipped his backpack and slid the book inside. She hated this bit: the few minutes while they both waited for him to be picked up. Daniel was always full of excitement, while she fought a sense of impending doom.

'He's here!' Daniel leapt off the armchair and ran towards the door. As Ben's car pulled up outside, the boy was already running down the path and tugging at the gate.

'Daniel, watch the road!' she called, walking out after him.

'Hey, Danny boy!' Ben was out of the car, bending over, arms thrown wide. 'How've you been, mate?'

Eve crossed her arms and smiled, even though neither of them were looking at her. Was this another new car? It seemed like Ben had only had the previous one for a few months.

'Daddy, are we going to soft play today?'

'Yup, we'll definitely do that. And maybe a pizza too afterwards – would you like that?'

'Yes! Mummy, we're going for pizza!'

The joy on his face as he turned back towards her, sent tiny daggers of hurt stabbing at her heart. 'That will be good,' she said.

Ben hadn't acknowledged her; he put Daniel back on the ground and pulled his phone out of his pocket. It looked like he was sending a text.

'Hi Ben, everything okay?'

'Yup, fine.' He'd had a haircut, shorter at the sides than usual. It suited him.

'Where's Keira?' Daniel was running towards the car. 'Keira! We're going for a pizza!'

As he opened the door and started to climb into the back seat, Eve saw the little girl strapped into a car seat; her arms waved in the air and she chuckled as Daniel covered her in kisses. The sight of her always made the muscles contract, deep in Eve's belly. She was a pretty little thing, with chubby cheeks that would disappear as she got older, her golden curls a contrast to Daniel's thick brown hair.

'Come on, matey, let's get going.' Ben leant in and reached for the seatbelt.

As he stepped back and pushed the door shut, Eve bent forward and waved. 'Bye darling. Have a good weekend. I love you.'

But Daniel was concentrating on Keira, tickling her to make

her scream with delight, holding her little fingers as he blew raspberries into her palm.

'Right, see you tomorrow,' said Ben.

He was wearing sunglasses so she couldn't see his eyes. She wanted to snatch them off his face: since when had he turned into the sort of person who wore sunglasses in winter?

'Okay. Please make him do some reading. If he gets through this book, he can move on to a new level on Monday.'

'God, Eve, give it a rest, will you?' Ben was shaking his head. 'It's the weekend. The poor little sod needs to have some time off.'

'Yes, of course he does, but he's so tired during the week that we sometimes don't get to read every night so...'

'Well, that's not my fault. If you can't keep up with all his schoolwork, why should I have to make up for it at the weekend? I hardly get to see him as it is.'

Her face was burning and there was a stab of hurt in her chest. 'I can keep up! It's not that at all, he just needs routine. His time with you is always so busy...'

'Oh, I get it, so you're saying that when he comes to us, his routine goes out the window, is that it?'

'No! That's not what I meant.' She hated it when they argued in front of Daniel, but he was still screaming with laughter and tickling Keira, so he wasn't hearing any of this.

'Whatever,' sighed Ben, managing to fill the word with the weary exasperation of a man much put-upon. He opened the car door, jiggling his keys up and down in his hand, and slammed the door behind him without saying goodbye.

She stood on the pavement as the car disappeared down the street, waving, even though she knew Daniel would be too intent on Keira to look back.

'Thanks for remembering it was my birthday this week,

Ben,' she muttered, as the car turned onto the main road and disappeared.

Bloody Ben. Was it unreasonable to ask him to spend five minutes reading with his son? He ought to be able to squeeze it in, between the soft play and the pizzas and the cinema and whatever other wonderful stuff they'd be doing.

She was happy for Daniel that his weekends were always jam-packed with excitement, but couldn't quell her own irritation. She would love to make their son's life equally as thrilling, but as much as anything, she couldn't afford it.

There seemed to be no shortage of cash for Ben and, if he had yet another new car, it meant work was going well. But he and Lou had never been short of a penny: she ran her own florist's, which by all accounts was thriving. She'd won a Businesswoman of the Year award in the summer; Eve had seen an article in the paper, and read it despite herself, glad that nowhere in the copy did this super successful local entrepreneur mention her loving family, and that the photo was just of Lou on her own, surrounded by extravagant green foliage.

Eve had only met Ben's new wife on a handful of occasions. Lou had blonde hair worn in the sort of sharp pixie cut that few women could carry off; she was ten years younger than Eve, and possibly a stone lighter. On the rare occasions when she was with Ben when he came to collect Daniel, she always stayed in the car, smiling and waving but never getting out – clearly no more enthusiastic than Eve to progress the relationship.

She and Ben had been together for nearly four years now, married for three of them: Daniel had been their pageboy at a big glitzy wedding with a reception at The Watershed. Afterwards, Ben gave Eve a photo of their son dressed up in his smart little suit, beaming at the camera, his unruly hair neatly slicked across to one side. He looked adorable, but Eve had never put that particular picture on display.

She turned around and stared up at the house; it was a narrow brick box, with hardly room inside to swing the proverbial cat. But it felt cavernous and empty at weekends, with signs of her little boy everywhere, from a dropped jumper on the sitting-room floor to a discarded toy on the stairs.

Ben had him to stay overnight every other Wednesday as well, but that was all right: having a night to herself during the week felt quite indulgent, and she invariably arranged a trip to the cinema or a drink with Juliet or Caroline.

But the weekends dragged.

What she kept having to remind herself was that it was great Daniel had such a close relationship with his dad. It was the last thing she'd expected. Ben had always seemed so distant when Daniel was a baby, so angry to have been forced into something he didn't feel ready for.

'I just don't know if I'm parent material,' he'd said, one night towards the end. By then, Daniel was nine months old and rarely slept for more than two hours at a stretch; she and Ben were shattered and fractious with each other. Despite the demands this tiny person made on her time and her body, Eve had been overwhelmed with love for the baby, amazed at her capacity to adore everything about him – but increasingly angry that Ben didn't seem to feel the same way.

When she suggested they take a break from each other, the words which came out of her mouth were almost as much of a surprise to her as to Ben. But what was even more shocking was the immediacy with which he agreed, and the speed with which he packed an overnight bag.

'I want you to still see him,' she'd said, as she stood at the front door, jiggling the baby against her shoulder while he wailed plaintively in her ear. 'This isn't a get-out clause for you, Ben.'

For a few hormonally charged weeks, she panicked that she'd chased away her son's father. But Ben did stay in touch – and not just to sort out the painful logistics of extricating himself from a long-term relationship. He came over to the house regularly to help feed his son, give him a bath and put him to bed. He strapped him into the buggy and took him out to the park while Eve caught up on sleep.

By the time Daniel was eighteen months old and staggering around drunkenly on chubby little legs, they had a good routine in place. Ben was more relaxed and so much happier than he'd seemed in such a long time, that Eve thought the split had benefited their relationship; she had begun to plan for the time when he would move back in and they'd be a family again, convinced everything would be so much better than before.

Then, one rainy Sunday afternoon, he'd told her about Lou.

'She's great, you'd really like her. Fantastic sense of humour. We met through Alex at work, and hit it off straight away. We've started talking about moving in together.'

Eve didn't ask him many questions about his new life over the next few months but, even while they were signing legal papers and agreeing access and maintenance details, a part of her still hoped the relationship wasn't truly over. How could it be? She was the mother of Ben's child; they had five years of shared history. Sometimes she even managed to persuade herself that this thing with Lou was just one last fling before he came back to her and they settled down and became a proper family once more.

But a year later, Ben and Lou were married, and Daniel was a perfectly behaved little pageboy. Three months after that, they'd announced Lou was pregnant, and the man who hadn't known if he was parent material, was on his way to having a new family of his own.

Eve went back inside, kicking the front door shut behind her. In the kitchen she stood at the sink filling the kettle, staring through the window at the chaos in the garden. It was kind of Jake to have offered to help her. He was out in his own garden right now: she could see his head over the fence, bobbing up and down as he hung out some washing. As she watched, he suddenly turned in her direction, saw her at the window and raised his hand. God, was this man psychic? She smiled and waved back. 'Hi there!' she called, although she knew he couldn't hear.

Waiting for the kettle to boil, she sorted through a heap of clean washing. She folded Daniel's little T-shirts and pairs of jeans, knotted socks together and searched for the matching bottoms to his favourite pyjama top.

What kind of pyjamas did he have at Ben's house? She had no idea what he wore to bed there, or what colour his toothbrush was. Lou had bought him a Batman duvet cover, he'd told her that, but Eve didn't know what his bedroom looked like or whether he had any pictures on the wall or which toys were lined up on the floor beside the bed.

At weekends and on every other Wednesday night, Daniel existed in a world she knew nothing about – and it seemed to make him very happy. Sometimes he talked about what happened when he was at that other home. 'Keira and me have a playhouse with red curtains at the window,' he'd told her in the summer. 'We make cups of tea in there for Lou and Daddy when they're sitting in the garden.'

'That sounds fun,' she'd said.

Although it hurt, it seemed important to know about the practicalities of his life with Ben, so occasionally she would ask innocent-sounding questions about the routine in his other home. 'What food do they cook you? What time do you have your bath before bed?' She asked casually, as if the thought had just occurred to her, and his reply didn't matter at all.

There were many other questions she longed to ask, but couldn't – in case the answers hurt too much. Do they make you laugh when they put bubbles on your nose when you're in the bath? Do they hang your pyjamas on the radiator to warm them up before you put them on? Do they leave your bedroom door open at night, just an inch, so you can see the landing light and don't get scared of the dark? Do you think of me and miss me just a tiny bit, my gorgeous boy, when you put your thumb in your mouth and drift off to sleep in that other house?

SEVEN

'We've got an offer, doll. Not quite full price, but it's a decent one.'

'Gav, that's great!' Eve was balancing her mobile under her chin as she stacked yoghurts into a shopping trolley, grabbing some basics before she had to pick up Daniel from school. The supermarket was busy and, as she tried to hear what Gav was saying, she impatiently navigated her trolley around a woman who was blocking the aisle while she studied the small print on the back of a carton of custard.

'We're talking ten grand below the asking price.' Gav's voice was tinny: he must be in his car, talking on speakerphone. 'But they're cash buyers and there's no chain. Think you should accept.'

Eve wasn't sure how Flora was going to take this news, but it would be such a relief to get her flat sold. Whatever equity was in it, would inevitably be swallowed up by the fees for Three Elms, but at least it would see them through the next few years. Eve had no idea what would happen when the money ran out, but at the moment there was no point thinking that far ahead. Flora had no substantial savings, so Eve was making weekly online transfers to pay the care home fees and the amount in her savings account was disappearing faster than water spiralling down a plughole. She didn't resent it, but she really needed to shift that flat.

'Thanks, Gav,' she said. 'I appreciate it. Can you accept it for me?' She ended the call and put her mobile back into her pocket. However much he irritated the hell out of her, there was no denying the man was a master of his craft.

She still couldn't work out how he did it. Gav wore shiny, grey suits with tight trousers that weren't quite long enough to cover his white socks, and he slicked his dark hair back from his forehead with so much moulding wax that he looked like an Elvis impersonator. He was five foot nothing and strutted like a Bee Gee, loudly addressing women – even those he hardly knew – as doll, babe and princess. Yet, he somehow sold more properties than the rest of the staff put together, and Eve was glad she'd taken him up on his offer of handling the sale.

'No offence, love, but you're too close to it to do a good job yourself,' he'd said, when she explained why they were putting it on the market. 'It's your mum's place so you'll want people to love it when you're showing it. How will you react if they laugh at the pictures of kittens she's got on the wall?'

He'd had a point. Flora's décor was tired and old-fashioned and it wasn't going to charm any potential buyers. And it was good of him to say the agency would take on the flat in the first place: it wasn't the sort of high-end property they usually listed on their books.

After finishing the shop and picking up Daniel from school, Eve drove to Three Elms.

'I don't want to be here again!' he yelled from the back seat as she pulled into a parking space.

'I know, I'm sorry,' she said. 'But we won't be long. I just need to speak to Granny about something.'

'I hate this old people house!' shouted Daniel, hurling his water bottle through the gap in the front seats. It struck the dashboard and bounced off into Eve's lap, the top popping off and water soaking into her skirt.

'Daniel, stop it!' said Eve, frantically wiping the material. 'Shit. Now look what you've done!'

'I don't care, I hate it here! Shit, shit, shit.'

'Too bad, we're going in. And don't say shit.'

'You said it?'

'That's different.'

Flora was in the lounge, sitting with a group of other residents. Eve was surprised to see her mother was deep in conversation with the woman beside her; both were nodding enthusiastically, then Flora threw back her head as she laughed.

'Hello Mum,' said Eve, bending down to kiss her cheek. 'You look like you're having a good time.'

As she turned and saw her daughter, Flora's face fell, the sparkle going from her eyes. 'I'm not,' she snapped. 'I hate it here, Eve. It makes me so unhappy. I don't know why you make me stay in this place.'

The woman next to Flora was glaring at Eve as well. 'Me too,' she said. 'This is no kind of life for any of us.'

Before Eve had a chance to say anything, there was a tap on her shoulder, and she turned to find Mrs Donaldson, the manager, standing behind her. 'Glad to catch you,' she said. 'Can I have a word?'

'Yes, of course. Daniel, sit here next to Granny for a minute.' As she followed Mrs Donaldson back out into the corridor, Eve tried to remember when she'd paid the fees. She was sure she'd settled up for last week; well, almost sure. The invoice had been sitting on the kitchen worktop, and it wasn't there anymore. Although that could mean it had fallen onto the floor; oh bugger, maybe it was in the recycling box? She sometimes got a bit gung-ho when tidying up the chaos in the kitchen.

'I'm sorry if I've got behind with payments...' she began.

'We have a problem,' interrupted Mrs Donaldson. 'Your mother is drinking.'

'Sorry?'

'Drinking alcohol. She has been in an unstable state in the evenings, and the cleaners have found a number of wine bottles hidden under her bed.'

Eve frowned. 'No, you must have got that wrong, Mrs Donaldson. My mother doesn't have any alcohol in her room. I brought in a bottle of wine last weekend, but we had a glass together then I took the rest home. She's never been a big drinker.'

'She must have been acquiring it elsewhere then,' said Mrs Donaldson. 'Because this is more than the odd bottle, and I can assure you that your mother is definitely what you might call "a big drinker". The other day she was tiddly by teatime, and ended up singing the *EastEnders* theme tune at the top of her voice in the lounge, when the rest of the residents were trying to watch the programme on the television. We had to take her out. Then, late last night, she was found in Mr Barclay's room, sitting on the end of his bed, drinking his whisky.'

Eve wanted to laugh. 'Well, lucky old Mr Barclay! If he didn't mind, that's not a problem, is it? I would have thought you'd encourage residents to socialise with each other.'

'Mr Barclay was asleep in his bed at the time.'

'Ah.'

'So.' Mrs Donaldson puffed out her chest and glared at Eve. 'We need to look at some damage limitation. I can't allow you to bring in alcohol for Mrs Glover, because she is clearly not to be trusted with it.'

'This is ridiculous,' said Eve. 'I'm sorry if she got a bit

unruly, but she's a grown woman. You can't stop her from enjoying a glass of wine every now and then.'

Mrs Donaldson's eyes narrowed. 'Please don't tell me what I can and can't do in my own establishment,' she said. 'I have to consider the general well-being of all our residents and this is not the sort of behaviour we can tolerate in a reputable home like Three Elms. If the issue can't be addressed, we may need to rethink our ability to provide accommodation for Mrs Glover.'

Eve glared back, her hands clenched into fists by her sides. The words were undoubtedly designed to sting, and they had the desired effect. How would she go about finding another care home for Flora? It was hard enough trying to settle her into this one; her mother would never cope with another move – nor would she, come to that.

'Right, thanks for telling me about this, Mrs Donaldson. I will deal with it.'

'I'd be obliged if you would.' The woman was stony-faced. 'If this continues, I will be forced to take further steps.'

'That won't be necessary,' said Eve. 'I'm sure we can sort it out.' The cheek of the woman; what was she going to do, lock Flora in her room and take away her chocolate digestive privileges? 'My mother is going through a difficult time at the moment, as I'm sure you're aware.' *So, you, Mrs Donaldson, could be a little more understanding.* Eve watched as the care home manager walked away towards the reception area. This wasn't fair: it was bound to take time for new arrivals to get used to their changed surroundings at Three Elms and Flora can't have been the only resident to have struggled to settle in. However, it was worrying if she'd developed such a penchant for Pinot Grigio.

She marched back into the lounge and hustled her mother and Daniel out into the corridor. Had Mrs Donaldson's criticism really just been aimed at her mother? Despite the fact that she'd known nothing about Flora's drinking until a couple of minutes ago, Eve felt like a schoolgirl who'd been caught having a fag in the toilets at break.

'What's all this about you getting drunk?' she whispered in Flora's ear. Daniel had been scuffing the toe of his shoe against the doorframe and now started bunny-hopping away from them towards the dining room at the far end of the corridor. 'Daniel! Come back here!' Eve hissed.

'Honestly, these people! I knew they'd tell you about that.' Flora sniffed and threw back her shoulders. 'Interfering so-and-sos.'

'But Mum, you can't get drunk here!'

'Why not? Anyway, I'm not getting drunk. I'm just having a little drink in the evenings. There's nothing wrong with that.'

'There is, if it upsets the other residents.'

'Rubbish. I don't upset anybody. Anyway, a drink is the only thing that makes my life bearable. It just shows how desperate I am – how unhappy!'

Eve reached out her hand, but Flora shook it off. 'It's all your fault,' she said. 'You've forced me to come to this awful place and you're keeping me here against my will. The only thing that keeps me going – the *only* thing that cheers me up a little bit – is having a glass of something in the evening. Now you're telling me I can't even do that.'

'I'm not saying that, I'm just suggesting you stick to one small glass!'

'It's not fair!' yelled Flora. 'You're horrible!'

'Shh, don't shout at me. Where are you getting the wine from?'

'None of your bloody business.'

'Okay, we'll talk about it later. Anyway, you seemed to be having a good time in the lounge just now, when we arrived? It was good to see you chatting to a few other people and laughing.'

'I make an effort,' said Flora with another sniff. 'But this is not how I want to end my days. And here you are, accusing me of being an alcoholic!' Her lip was wobbling and her eyes were already full of tears.

'I'm not, Mum. I never said that.'

There was a thump from the end of the corridor, and Eve looked round to see Daniel had kicked over a wastepaper basket. 'Stop that! Come here and play on my phone,' she called, digging the mobile from her pocket. 'Listen.' She turned back to Flora. 'We just need to keep everyone happy. I don't mind bringing you a bottle of wine every now and then. But you've got to promise me you'll just have one glass a night, and think about other people.'

Flora had stopped crying again and was standing with her hands on her hips. 'I hate this place, Eve. You have no idea how miserable my life is.'

'You didn't look miserable when I saw you in the lounge a few minutes ago. In fact, you looked like you were having a good time.'

They glared at each other. Eve had never thought of her mother as manipulative, but right now it suddenly felt as if she was being played. Was Flora really as unhappy as she claimed, or was she turning on the tears for Eve's benefit?

Daniel stuck his head under her arm and held out the phone, its screen covered in a garish green cartoon. 'Look Granny, I've got my own Very Hungry Caterpillar who can skate on a pond.'

'Lovely,' said Flora, peering down at him.

Behind her mother's head, Eve could see a large cork noticeboard covered with bits of paper. There were cleaning rotas alongside emergency contact numbers and information sheets for visitors. Right in the centre of the board was an A3 poster, with red lettering and a border of galloping reindeer.

'Look, what's that?' Eve said, desperate to change the subject. 'A concert?'

She took Flora's arm and turned her around, so they were both looking at the poster. '*A joint Carol Concert will take place in December, featuring the residents of Three Elms and the children of St Barnabas Primary School,*' she read. '*Rehearsals to be held each Tuesday afternoon.* That looks interesting. Why don't you take part?'

'Why would I want to do that?' snorted Flora, peering at the poster.

'Well, it might be fun. You've got a lovely voice – it's wasted on the *EastEnders* theme tune. It looks like the children are going to come into Three Elms every week and practise carols with you all. Then you'll put on a performance for friends and family. What a wonderful idea!'

'Sounds bloody dreadful,' said Flora. 'Can't imagine anything worse. Why would I want to spend my time with a load of horrible children? I can't stand them.'

Daniel looked up from Eve's phone. 'That's okay, Granny. Some days I don't like you either.'

EIGHT

M rs Russell was in her classroom, with the door firmly closed. Every now and then a parent came out and another, at the front of the queue, got up and went inside. Eve had now been sitting on this child-sized chair for so long her left buttock had gone to sleep. It seemed as if this was par for the course at parents' evenings: last term she'd waited three quarters of an hour for a three-minute appointment. It was pretty pointless making them book in for a specific time, but if nothing else it must entertain the teaching staff. Maybe next term they'd herd all the parents into the main hall, lock the doors and make them fight it out to see who went first.

'Bit annoying, isn't it?' The man sitting next to her, had a baby strapped to his front in a sling. Her head was resting against his chest, face turned towards Eve, eyelashes fluttering as she slept, tiny bubbles appearing between her lips.

'How old?' Eve asked.

'Four months. My wife has to work this evening, so I'm hoping this little one stays asleep until I'm out of here.'

'Seems like such a long time since my son was that age.'

It really did seem like forever. She had carried Daniel

around in a similar sling, with long straps that always seemed to tangle, however well she tied them. She'd tried to get Ben to use it, but he said he felt weird and insisted it was easier for her to wear it. It was one of the many ways in which he'd seemed so distant from his newborn son, almost disinterested in him during those early months.

She'd known he didn't want a baby, that he wasn't ready for family life. But she was in her late thirties – five years older than him – and her biological clock had been ticking away so stridently she could think about little else. As she walked down the street, her eyes were drawn to every passing pram and buggy; she'd turn her head to peer inside, sometimes striking up a conversation with the proud parents.

She'd never thought much about children until then, but suddenly it was as if someone had flicked a switch inside her and allowed out-of-control hormones to flood through every muscle and sinew; the desire to get pregnant had been immediate and terrifyingly overwhelming. She tried to discuss it with Ben, but he was dismissive, uninterested.

As the months passed, her desperation for a baby became an obsession, but one which she couldn't even talk about with him. So, she'd gone ahead anyway. She had stopped taking the pill, conned him into it. She knew it was wrong, but had expected he'd fall in love with a baby and everything would work out.

So stupid; so incredibly arrogant.

To this day, she remembered sitting on the edge of the bath, watching in disbelief as a thin blue line appeared in the window of the testing wand. Her heart racing, pulse thumping, she had put her hand to her belly, unable to believe there was already a tiny life inside there: the size of a peanut – not even that, the size of a grain of rice.

'But how did it happen?' Ben had asked, when she told him later. 'I mean, you're on the pill. This is crazy!'

She'd shrugged, reaching up to put her arms around his neck. 'Yes, I know, I guess nothing is one hundred per cent safe. But it's wonderful as well, isn't it? Our own baby.'

She'd felt the stiffness of his shoulders, the tension in his back; but had chosen to ignore it.

The baby in the man's sling beside her was now stirring, and he gently rocked from side to side.

'What's her name?' Eve asked, putting out her finger and running it gently down the baby's downy cheek. 'She's just gorgeous.'

'Sophie,' he answered. 'Yes, she's rather amazing, isn't she?' He lowered his face and kissed the top of his daughter's head with such tenderness that Eve had to look away. She had longed to see Ben behave like this with Daniel – to show any kind of affection towards him. There was a loving, warm relationship between them now, but it hadn't come naturally at the start. Had he been different with Keira? She hadn't been close enough to them to know how those early days went, but she guessed he'd bonded instantly with his beautiful blonde daughter. She'd imagined him picking her up as a mewling newborn and holding her to his chest, carrying her around in a sling, just like this one, gazing down at her proudly while women he'd never met before went gooey over the pair of them.

The classroom door opened and a woman came out, her cheeks flushed. She stopped in front of Eve to button up her coat, then brushed her fringe out of her eyes and took a deep breath.

'Golly!' she whispered. 'She's a bit scary!'

The man with the baby got up and went into the classroom, and Eve smiled after him. She tried so hard not to feel resentful that Ben had made a new life for himself – but it hurt that he was so happy, when she was the one who'd ended their relationship. There hadn't been anyone else in her life since then, although she'd been on a couple of dates arranged by friends. The men were nice enough, she'd just never wanted to take things further. It had felt like too much of an effort, when she was already struggling to hold down a job and look after Daniel: she just couldn't be bothered to factor anyone else into the equation. But despite that, it sometimes felt as if she'd been left behind.

And now here she was, waiting to talk to their son's teacher, and why wasn't Ben sitting beside her on one of these ridiculous miniature kids' chairs? She'd given him plenty of warning about this evening's appointment, but his text had only come in this morning:

> Sorry, going to a meeting in London, won't be
> back in time for the school thing.

She had angrily swiped to delete the message, convinced he would have been able to rearrange a work commitment, if he'd really wanted to. *The school thing!* Even if he didn't care about presenting a united parental front to Mrs Russell, surely he should be interested in hearing first-hand how his son was doing?

By the time she went into the classroom for her appointment, she had cramp in her calves and could hardly get up from the tiny chair.

'He's a clever boy,' said Mrs Russell, looking down at pages of handwritten notes, running her finger along a spreadsheet. 'Good progress so far in numeracy, slightly slower with his reading, but nothing to worry about.'

'Oh good!' Eve said. 'I've always thought he was bright.' That sounded arrogant, but so what? She was virtually raising Daniel on her own, she had a right to pat herself on the back.

'He loves PE and there's a definite artistic streak in him.'

Eve couldn't stop herself grinning with pride; Daniel loved

drawing, and she'd always thought the work he produced was good for his age, but it was reassuring to have that confirmed.

'However, there are issues with his behaviour,' continued the teacher. She looked up from the papers in front of her and began to tap her biro against the table. 'He has been a little aggressive in the playground, and we've had incidents where he has been fighting with other children and pushed them over.'

Eve's mouth fell open. 'He never behaves like that at home.'

'This is often something we see at the start of a school year. All the children are coming to terms with a new classroom – and a new teacher – so it's not surprising they try to assert themselves. But by now most of them have settled down, and I don't sense that with Daniel. He still seems on edge and sometimes flies off the handle.'

'Right,' said Eve. 'I see.' This was very strange; it didn't sound like the boy she knew so well.

'He's also very chatty.' Mrs Russell carried on as if she hadn't spoken. 'A little too much at times, and doesn't respond well to being told to quieten down. He takes part in circle-time discussions, but always wants to be the one doing the talking.'

Eve felt her face flushing. 'Well, surely that's not bad, if he has things he wants to talk about?'

'Of course not, but he needs to respect others and learn that they have the right to talk as well.'

'Yes, I can understand that. I'll speak to him about it.'

'He was also quite rude to me earlier this week.'

'Oh?'

'He called me a fat, smelly lettuce.'

Before she could stop herself, Eve snorted with laughter. 'Oh dear, I'm so sorry,' she said, putting her hand up to her mouth. 'It's just... is that really so awful? He's just a little boy! He could have called you something much worse. I mean, of course you're not fat and smelly. Or a lettuce, obviously.'

Mrs Russell was frowning, a muscle twitching under her left eye. 'I don't accept rudeness in this classroom, Mrs Mackay, and I expect parents to back me up on the matter.'

'Yes, of course. Although it's Glover,' said Eve.

'Sorry?'

'My surname is Glover. Daniel is Mackay because that's his dad's surname. But we're not together anymore.' Eve suddenly felt angry. That information had been on the forms they'd filled in before Daniel started school; surely his teacher should be familiar with the family background of her pupils? Being addressed by the wrong name was actually quite insulting. 'I can't believe that's unusual nowadays,' she added. 'You must have other mothers who use their maiden names? Not everyone is happily married.'

Mrs Russell was still glaring at her. It was hard to tell how old she was, possibly only early forties, but she'd always struck Eve as matronly: perfectly suited to helping a class of young children adapt to the demands of school. Now she was seeing a different side to the woman who was spending six hours a day looking after Daniel.

'Please don't patronise me, *Miss* Glover.' Mrs Russell was smiling, but there was no warmth behind it. 'Daniel's family circumstances put him in the majority in this classroom. Less than a third of the children have two parents still happily married – as you put it – or even still together. We have single mums, single dads, gay parents, children who live with grandparents, children who are with temporary foster carers. I spend my time tiptoeing through twenty-first century family relationships and making sure I don't unintentionally offend anybody. For instance, you won't get a Mother's Day card next March – we don't celebrate anything like that, in case there's a child for whom it's not appropriate.'

'Fine,' said Eve. 'I won't expect one of those then.'

They glared at each other before Mrs Russell dropped her eyes back down to the table, flicking a page in her notebook and reading whatever else was written there.

'So basically,' said Eve. 'Apart from being a bit lively, he's doing well academically?'

'There are also problems with his appearance,' said Mrs Russell, looking back up. 'His shoes are not regulation schoolwear; we specifically ask parents not to send the children in wearing trainers – even black ones.'

'Yes, I know. I've been meaning to get him some proper shoes,' said Eve. She really had, but had also completely forgotten about it until this precise second. Although what was wrong with black trainers? From a distance you couldn't tell the difference between those and normal shoes.

'...and a couple of days ago he came into the classroom wearing his PE top instead of his school shirt.'

'I know, that was entirely my fault. You see, I'd had quite a lot going on at work and I'd got behind with the washing...' Eve knew her cheeks were flushing again, as Mrs Russell's gaze bored into her. 'You know how it is, sometimes things just go a bit pear-shaped!'

She laughed, but Mrs Russell didn't crack a smile.

Oh, come on, thought Eve. *Help me out here. Stop making me feel two inches tall.*

I'm just about getting by! she wanted to shout. *I've got too much on at work, I've got no money, my mother hates me because I've put her into a home, my ex thinks I'm useless. Now you're telling me my son is a bully and suggesting I'm a bad mother because he hasn't got enough clean uniform and he's wearing trainers instead of Clarks shoes, which cost fifty quid a pair and will probably only last him six weeks until his feet grow too big for them.*

But the words stayed inside her head.

'I think we're done here,' said the teacher, shuffling her papers into a neat pile. 'I will obviously be monitoring Daniel's behaviour over the next few weeks and will contact you if I feel we need to take further measures.'

Further measures? What the hell was that supposed to mean? Eve was trying to think of a witty retort, but her mind was frustratingly blank. She knew she would come up with something smart and sassy as soon as she was marching away down the corridor.

'He's a good boy,' she said in the end. 'You just don't know him very well.'

As she got up and went towards the door, her heart was racing and she knew she was on the point of tears. She forced a smile as she went past the parents waiting outside the classroom. That bloody woman – there was no need to be quite so abrasive. All that business about Daniel being difficult in the classroom and not getting on with the other children, that was clearly rubbish. But Eve was also cross with herself: some of the other stuff was her fault: she *had* known she ought to get Daniel some proper shoes; she *had* been too exhausted and disorganised to get his washing done on time. Sometimes it felt as if she was running just to stand still.

NINE

The bureau in the corner of the sitting room was packed with old magazines, letters and scraps of paper. As Eve pulled out a bundle of postcards, she dislodged some receipts; they scattered across the carpet, brown with age, the printing so faded it was impossible to tell what most of them had been for.

This was going to be hard work.

'Selling the flat will take ages,' she'd said to Flora, partly to reassure her fretting mother that nothing would change immediately. 'The sales process always drags on, even once you've found a buyer, so there's plenty of time to sort things out.'

But the young couple Gav had found to buy the place, were now pushing to exchange. Their solicitor was being remarkably efficient at sending through the relevant paperwork; a bit too efficient, thought Eve, having found six emails from him when she got into work yesterday.

She'd been involved with hundreds of sales since she started working as an estate agent, in her twenties, and it was impressive to come across a lawyer who actually did what was promised, ahead of time. On the other hand, it was also a bit stressful. She knew she wasn't at her most organised right now, but she had so much on that, every time his name popped up in her email inbox, she felt like crawling underneath her desk, shoving her fingers in her ears and humming loudly. Maybe she was turning into her mother, after all?

'Looks like this one could beat the record,' Gav had bellowed yesterday, as he stood beside her desk. The quickest deal the agency had ever put through had taken place in just under four weeks, from the Friday when the offer was accepted, to the Thursday when the new owners took possession of the keys. 'My finest hour!' Gav had shouted. 'Johnsons out, Burgesses in. Wham, bam, removals van!'

Eve had no desire to turn the sale of Flora's flat into some kind of race so she didn't react to Gav's comments. Given any encouragement at all, he'd have the completion schedule written up on a wall chart and would be standing beside her, with his red Sharpie at the ready, pestering her for hourly updates. But, whenever the sale went through, she would be glad to see the back of this place. The rooms were still full of Flora's furniture, but they now felt strangely empty and unloved. Every time Eve came here, she flung open windows and propped open doors, but the place still smelt musty and slightly damp.

When her mother lived here, she had loved visiting. Now, she had come to dread the way the front door stuck when she pushed it across mounting piles of junk mail. Looking down the hall at the faded blue carpet and the patterned wallpaper, it all seemed so tatty and old-fashioned; there were cobwebs collecting in the high corners of the rooms and carcasses of woodlice were cluttering up windowsills which were well overdue a lick of paint.

But she had no choice but to keep coming back. The furniture must be advertised in the local paper or sent to auction; the pictures and mirrors had to come down off the walls; the books would need to be packed into boxes and delivered to the nearest branch of Oxfam.

In some ways, that was the easy bit: Flora's lifetime of personal paraphernalia was tougher. Not just clothes and shoes, but also photographs, ornaments and toiletries. On the shelves in the sitting room were collections of unused crystal glasses, dusty figurines and blue and white willow pattern plates propped up on display stands. Costume jewellery spilled out of dishes on her dressing table in the bedroom and, when Eve unscrewed the lid on a pot of Nivea, the cream inside was brittle and caked around the edges. The bathroom cabinet was full of decades' worth of yellowing bandages, out-of-date packets of pills and bottles of cough mixture so ancient their contents had solidified.

It was hard knowing where to start, so Eve allowed herself to pick just one thing to tackle on each visit. Today she was sorting out this old bureau. She sat back on her heels and began to put everything into piles, with magazines and yellowing newspapers going straight into a bin liner for recycling, along with the illegible receipts – why on earth had Flora even kept them?

She read a few of the messages on the postcards. They were from names that rang no bells – friends of her mother from decades ago, whom she probably hadn't kept in touch with, and now wouldn't even remember. It was tempting to bin them without showing Flora, but that wouldn't be fair. These weren't the remnants of Eve's own life, it was her mother's history she was holding in her hands.

'You'll regret it, if you don't keep precious memories,' Flora had always told Eve, when she was growing up. 'It may just seem like a birthday card now, but when you look at it in a few years' time, you'll remember so much more than the card itself.'

Teenage Eve had sighed and rolled her eyes, dismissing her

mother's sentimentality. But middle-aged Eve now knew that to be true.

She scooped all the cards into a pile and put them to one side. A couple of weeks ago, she wouldn't have considered sharing any of this with Flora, because her mother's misery at having to leave the flat had been too intense, too raw. Eve would have worried that highlighting the memories would cause unnecessary upset.

But Flora finally seemed to be settling in at Three Elms. For one thing, the frequency of desperate phone calls had decreased. Today there had only been one, just after 9am, when Flora asked for a new face flannel. For the rest of the day, Eve's mobile had remained silent. When she went in to the home last weekend, she'd been surprised to see some framed photographs on display – favourite ones Flora used to keep in the sitting room of her flat; Eve had put them into the ancient suitcase when they came to Three Elms, but Flora had refused to do anything with them when she first arrived. Now they were lined up in a semicircle on the chest of drawers.

'Oh Mum, how lovely you've put those out,' Eve had said. 'It's good to have something of your own in this room at last.'

'Why wouldn't I put them out?' Flora had asked. 'They're my photos. You do say some silly things.'

Moving closer, Eve had realised one of the photographs was upside down. She turned it the right way up, without saying anything.

As she sifted through the contents of the bureau now, she came across more photographs – mostly sepia-tinged ones of long-dead ancestors she didn't remember.

She caught her breath as she came across a photo of herself and Ben. This was a really early one, possibly taken only a couple of months after they'd met in a pub down by the harbour. She and her friend Hannah had gone out for a drink, and she could still remember the thrill of realising that the two good-looking blokes at the next table were glancing across at them. Jon had been the chatty one, moving his chair around and asking to join them. Ben had been quieter, more her type; the bare skin on her arm had tingled when his sleeve brushed over it as he reached for his drink. Jon and Hannah had gone on a handful of dates before going their separate ways, but she and Ben lasted the course. In less than a year, they were living together in a flat in Bedminster; another twelve months after that they had bought their house. Eve ran her finger across the photo: the two of them looked so damned happy.

She put it to one side and ploughed on. There were plenty of pictures of Flora, including a black and white shot of her as a young girl, posing in a professional photographer's studio, and prints of her as a gawky but recognisable teenager. Eve wasn't surprised there were no pictures of her parents' wedding: Flora had always said none were taken.

'It was small,' she'd told her. 'Hardly any guests, registry office. Times were hard. We didn't have the money to spend on anything fancy.'

Eve had only ever seen two photographs of her father, both slightly faded, black and white prints. In one he was leaning his elbows on a gate, looking into the camera, his fringe flopping over his face, his mouth stretched into a wide smile. In the other he was with Flora, his arm draped carelessly around her shoulder, the two of them standing on a beach. This was the photo Flora had kept on her bedside table for as long as Eve could remember.

They had been a beautiful couple. Whenever Eve pictured her mother now, she thought of her as a little old lady, with white hair and skin so weathered that the lines on her face looked like a roadmap. But years ago, Flora had been a beauty, with opaque blue eyes and thick auburn hair that constantly slithered across her face like a curtain, however many times she tucked it behind her ears. She had gone through a stage of piling it up on top of her head, curled into a bun that looked effortlessly casual; when she saw pictures of Flora like that, Eve always thought she looked like Audrey Hepburn.

Now she picked up a snapshot of herself and her mother, their heads tilted towards each other, raising glasses to the camera. They both looked much younger, and it must have been taken years ago at some family celebration, but she couldn't remember which one. There was a striking similarity between them – the shape of their noses, the nub of their chins, their slightly lopsided grins – and they both looked so happy.

The bureau was now almost empty; the bin liner bulging with ancient certificates, invoices and bills from utility companies.

'Why did you keep all this crap, Mum?' she muttered. 'What was the point?'

There was an old shoebox tucked away at the back of the bottom shelf, and, dragging it out, she opened the lid. God, yet more Christmas cards and letters, the messages inside from people Eve couldn't remember.

Would be super to see you in the New Year! Love Terry and Joan

Hope all's well, yet another Christmas – where does the time go? Maureen

She looked through a few more cards – there were dozens of them on top of what looked like a pile of letters at the bottom. But she was exhausted and had done enough sorting for now. The prospect of a long soak in the bath and an early night was so much more enticing than another couple of hours going through the contents of the flat. She could come back at the weekend to carry on with all of this, and perhaps tackle the musty coats, shoes and handbags that had lain untouched for years at the back of the wardrobe.

Eve pushed the lid back onto the shoebox. She would take it home and look through it when she had more time, select a few cards to share with Flora.

TEN

'Bugger!' muttered Jake. He got the mower restarted and pushed it forward, but it cut out again almost immediately. 'Bugger! Bloody thing.'

Eve had been looking forward to today. When they'd arranged this, she'd pictured herself raking cut grass with ease as Jake manfully manoeuvred the strimmer; she would hand him a beer, then they'd sit together on the patio, admiring their handiwork. They would chat about the children, and maybe their work, looking proudly at what they'd achieved with the overgrown garden. She had been thinking about planting some rosebushes and was going to ask his advice. There was a pretty rambling rose clambering up his side of the fence, so it was likely he knew a bit about them – he'd have to know more than she did.

But the afternoon had gone wrong early on. Jake had arrived wearing a baggy pair of faded jeans, the waistband secured by a length of string tied in an enormous knot at the front. Eve tried not to stare. It looked as if he was wearing a plain blue T-shirt but, when he turned around, she saw there was a caption printed on the back, above a silhouette of a group of women running: *Moreton WI Over-50s Run-a-Thon 2019*, she read. *Proudly sponsored by Tena Lady.*

'Nice top,' she said. 'Did you, er, take part in that run?'

Jake looked confused, then shook his head and laughed. 'Not me. I'm not very good at physical stuff like running. When I move too quickly, it looks like bits of my body are about to drop off.'

It had taken him a while to start the strimmer but, once it roared into life, he'd spent a few minutes sweeping it in wide arcs, the machine buzzing like a swarm of bees as it snapped through the tall grass, stalks collapsing onto the ground in its wake. Eve had stood on the patio, watching. He was surprisingly muscular; tendons standing out like taut rope in his lower arms and she could see the swell of his biceps disappearing into the rolled-up sleeves of the sweatshirt. No one would have guessed he had a half-decent body hidden under all that weird clothing. Maybe he worked out?

But then, there was a crack and the engine died.

'Cord's gone,' he'd said, wiping sweat from his forehead with the back of his hand. 'Never mind, I'll put the mower on its highest setting. Should be fine.'

It wasn't. The machine roared into life, but the long grass clogged up the blades.

'Bugger!' Jake yelled again now, as the mower stalled for the sixth time.

'Let's call it a day,' Eve said. 'We've made a start, which is great...'

'Not giving up on it yet,' said Jake, teeth gritted as he crouched over the mower. There was a patch of sweat breaking out between his shoulder blades, darkening the words *Moreton WI.*

She couldn't watch, it was too painful: like looking on while someone repeatedly bashed themselves on the head with a mallet. As he pushed the roaring mower back into the knee-high grass, she went into the kitchen, knocked back half a bottle of beer and took a Tesco Finest cake out of its packaging – lemon drizzle this time; never let it be said she was predictable. She'd intended to bake something herself but, after waving Daniel off with Ben earlier this morning, had discovered she had no self-raising flour and no eggs. There was a packet of caster sugar, but the contents had solidified into a crystallised brick. So, she'd slung it in the bin and done an emergency dash to Tesco.

There was a worrying silence; the mower had stalled again.

'Here!' she called, holding out a slice of cake as she went back onto the patio. 'Please stop now, Jake. You've done a great job, but I think I need to get someone in to deal with this, with some proper equipment.' She only realised how insulting that sounded, as the words left her mouth. 'Not that your equipment is no good. You have great equipment! I mean, your gardening stuff obviously. Sorry, that came out all wrong too.'

Jake just glared at her, wiping trails of sweat out of his eyes with fingers which were now bright green and covered in clumps of grass. He marched across to the fence and threw the broken strimmer back into his own garden.

'I really appreciate what you've done,' she said, as he pulled the mower out of the long grass. 'You've made such a good start.'

Once the mower was free, he turned it over and knelt beside it, peering through the blades, which were matted with grass.

'No idea what's going on here,' he said to himself, as he poked a screwdriver up into the body of the machine. 'Never had this happen before.'

'It's my fault for letting the grass get so long,' said Eve. 'I should have done something about it ages ago. I hope it hasn't broken your blades?'

'It's broken something,' he muttered.

'God, I'm sorry. Let me pay for the damage, if you can't

mend it yourself, I mean. Not that I'm suggesting you're not capable of mending it – I'm sure you are! But if it's too complicated, and you need to take it somewhere...'

Jake stood up and hauled the mower upright again. He wiped the palms of his hands down the legs of his jeans, leaving a long green stripe on either side. The sweaty patch on his back had now spread to include the words *Over-50s*.

'It's ridiculous,' he said, shaking his head. 'I only got it serviced a few weeks ago. I just can't work out what's gone wrong.' He looked so depressed, his arms hanging by his sides. 'Sorry,' he said. 'What a fiasco.'

He turned and wheeled the broken machine down the path towards the side of the house. Eve trotted along behind him, wincing as the metal edge of the mower scraped against the brickwork.

'Jake, please don't go. I didn't mean to insult you – or your mower. You're both great. You more so than the mower, obviously.'

'That's fine, don't worry about it,' he called, the machine rasping down the path, as if it was taking the top layer of gravel with it. Neither he nor the mower sounded fine at all.

'How about a beer?' she asked his retreating back. 'They're nice and cold, they've been in the fridge.'

He didn't answer.

'Piece of cake?' she asked, holding up the plate, as he opened the side gate. 'It's lemon drizzle?'

'I'm gluten-free,' he muttered over his shoulder, before disappearing around the front of the house.

ELEVEN

'This is my friend, Barbara,' said Flora. 'She moved in here quite recently.' She was sitting in the lounge beside the woman Eve had seen her chatting to, the other week.

'She's got two new hips and has had valve replacement surgery as well,' Flora continued. 'She's eighty-two, but says she feels like a new woman.'

'I do,' said Barbara, nodding. 'My body works better than ever now. My surgeon says I'm an inspiration.'

Barbara had protruding front teeth and large hips. She dressed in a beige jumper and brown tweed skirt and made Eve think of Sid, the sloth in *Ice Age*. It was one of Daniel's favourite films.

Flora tapped her finger on the Scrabble board, set out on the table between them. 'Come on then, your turn.'

Eve couldn't believe how cheerful her mother was. Flora's mood had been improving for the last couple of weeks, but today she was positively jolly.

'Right, how about this one then?' Barbara leant forward and put a handful of letters down onto the board, rearranging them around a word that was already there.

'Oh yes.' Flora nodded. 'That's very clever. How many points?'

'I think it's thirty-two,' said Barbara. 'There's a double word score under there as well. So, let's call it eighty.'

'Well done,' said Flora, writing the score on a notepad beside her. It looked like she'd written sixty-three, but the numbers were so wobbly it was hard to tell.

'I think I'm winning now, aren't I?' asked Barbara, as she neatened the tiles she had just placed on the board. They spelt out SHARELP.

'Is that a word?' asked Eve.

Barbara glared at her. 'Of course it's a word!' She looked at Flora and raised her eyes to the ceiling.

'Barbara was a county-level Scrabble player in her youth,' Flora said. 'She knows what she's doing.'

Eve wasn't used to being allowed to sit in the communal lounge and watch the comings and goings. Usually, if Flora was in there when her daughter arrived, she shooed her out and insisted they went into the garden or back to her room. But today she was so engrossed in the game, she didn't seem to care that Eve was sitting watching them.

'My husband and I used to play Scrabble,' she was telling Barbara. 'He was much better at it than I was. He came up with all these clever words. But I was good at finding the triple word scores.'

'That's what will win you the game,' said Barbara, sagely. 'Here you go, another big one for me.' She added A and T after a stray S. There were no double or triple score squares anywhere in sight. 'I think that's forty-eight.'

Eve made it three.

There was a tap on her shoulder. Nathan was hopping from one foot to the other, blotches of pink across his cheeks. 'Sorry,' he whispered. 'Can I talk to you?'

Eve followed him into the corridor.

'This is really embarrassing,' he started saying, before they were even out of the room. 'They've asked me to speak to you, because I'm working on Mrs Glover's wing, and they're saying this is something I should have been aware of much earlier, although that's unfair because it's not always easy to know what's going on when there are so many residents, and some of them are difficult to communicate with, as you'll be aware, so things do get past us...'

'Nathan, slow down!' said Eve. 'What is it?'

'Gin,' he said, his eyes wide, but looking into the middle distance somewhere off to the left of Eve's face. 'Your mother is on the gin.'

Eve stared at him.

'She's drinking gin at night and her behaviour is getting worse.'

'Hang on a minute,' said Eve. 'Just the other day I got told off because she was somehow smuggling in wine, and disturbing the other residents. Now you're saying she's moved on to gin? Where the hell is she getting that from?'

'Barbara,' said Nathan. 'The lady she's playing Scrabble with.'

Eve turned and looked through the open door of the lounge at the two women, their white heads huddled together over the table. Flora was picking out handfuls of unused tiles from the bag and putting them down randomly on the board, while Barbara had taken the paper and pencil and appeared to be altering the scores.

'Oh dear,' said Eve. 'That's not good.'

'No,' said Nathan, shaking his head vigorously. 'It's not good at all. They get very loud and start singing, and Barbara told one of the other residents to get stuffed last night. If this continues, I think both of them will be given official warnings and Mrs Donaldson is talking about asking them to leave.'

'Shit,' said Eve, thinking of the *Sold* sign outside the window of Flora's flat, and the numerous bulging black bags she'd delivered to the charity shop or thrown into the non-recyclable container at the local tip.

'So, will you have a word?' asked Nathan.

'Of course,' Eve said, nodding. 'I'll speak to both of them about it.'

The tension in the boy's cheeks visibly relaxed. 'Sorry,' he said. 'It's my first time doing anything like this. I'm studying for my Diploma in Elderly Care and Mrs Donaldson says that, if I'm going to have any chance of passing it, I need to develop some backbone.'

When Eve sat back down in the chair beside her mother, the two women were giggling.

'We're not going to tell you what we're talking about,' said Flora. 'It's a secret.'

'That's fine, I don't want to know,' said Eve. She did, but wasn't going to give them the satisfaction of asking; they were smirking at her, like a couple of naughty teenagers. 'Look Mum – and you too, Barbara: sorry, I know I've only just met you, but this concerns both of you. I've been talking to Nathan, and the staff are concerned about your drinking.'

The two women stopped smiling and stared at her.

'Apparently you're drinking gin together in the evenings and getting a bit rowdy.'

Neither said a word.

'This has got to stop,' Eve continued. 'It's fine for you to have the odd drink, but it sounds as if this is more than one or two.'

Barbara nodded. 'Much more,' she said. 'What on earth would be the point in just one gin?'

'The thing is, if you carry on like this it's going to cause trouble. For a start it's not fair on the staff – they're here to look after everyone; they haven't got time to deal with the pair of you, if you're getting drunk and behaving badly.'

'Well, we certainly aren't doing that!' said Flora, drawing herself up straight in her chair and pulling the edges of her cardigan tightly across her chest.

'They say you are.'

'Well, they're lying,' said Flora. 'They just don't want us to have any fun in this place. I bet they'll even try to stop us going to Alton Towers.'

'Flora!' shrieked Barbara. 'Don't tell!'

Flora slapped her hand in front of her mouth. 'Oh dear, sorry. That's our secret, Eve, the one we've been planning. But you mustn't tell anyone.'

'Not a soul,' said Barbara. 'Otherwise, they would try to stop us.'

Eve wanted to laugh, but the two wrinkled faces were deadly serious. 'But how can you go to Alton Towers? It's hundreds of miles away, how will you get there?'

'Aha!' said Flora, triumphantly. 'That's the bit of the secret we're not going to tell you. But it's going to be a grand day out. We'll go on those dipper things, and the big cups that spin around.'

'I want to go on the ghost train,' said Barbara. 'There was one on the pier at Brighton, and I used to go there as a girl.'

'There's something called Oblivious,' said Flora. 'Barbara's granddaughter told us about it. And another one called Demented.'

'Nemesis,' said Barbara. 'You go upside down, a bit like this...' She put her arms out on either side of her body, closed her eyes, threw back her head and screamed. The resemblance to *Ice Age* Sid was now uncanny.

The care assistants across the room looked up. Eve gave them a reassuring wave. 'Don't worry!' she called. 'Barbara's just showing me something.'

'You've got to stop this,' she whispered to the women. 'I thought you wanted to keep it all a secret?'

Flora was laughing so hard there were tears at the edges of her eyes. 'Oh, Eve,' she said, dabbing at them with her handkerchief. 'I am so excited. It will be such a grand day out.'

'Wild,' said Barbara. 'It will be wild. As will we!'

The two women looked at each other and cackled.

'Steady,' said Barbara, jiggling up and down on her armchair and crossing her legs. 'Any more of this laughing and I'll not make it to the bathroom in time.'

TWELVE

'Daniel, do you want to go and wait in the car? I just need to talk to Daddy about something.'

She needn't have worried about him overhearing – the little boy was already on his way down the path to the car, flinging open the door and turning back, a stricken look on his face. 'Where's Keira? Why isn't she here?'

'She's at home, buddy,' said Ben. 'She's got a bit of a cold, so I didn't bring her with me today. But you just hop in and we're going straight home to see her. Actually...' He turned back to Eve. 'There's something I wanted to talk to you about as well.'

'Me first,' she said. 'This is quite serious. I went to that parents' evening at school. The one I told you about? The one you couldn't make?' She hated herself for point-scoring, but if Ben had been squatting beside her on a child-sized chair in the classroom, she might have felt less vulnerable and handled Mrs Russell's criticisms more effectively. 'Anyway, Daniel's teacher – she's a grumpy old cow, can't say I warmed to her – said he's causing a bit of trouble.'

'What kind of trouble?'

'He's pushing other kids in the playground, getting into fights and refusing to listen when he's told off.'

Ben looked confused. 'That's not like him at all? He's such a gentle little lad. He's so good with Keira, and we never have any problems disciplining him.'

Eve felt the sting of the *we*, which clearly referred to himself and Lou.

'Nor do I, he's perfectly behaved when he's here with me,' she snapped. Why did Ben always manage to press her buttons like this? 'Anyway, for some reason, he's playing up at school. I haven't spoken to him about it, apart from asking if he's happy there. He says everything's fine and I know he's got some good friends, especially Robbie. I just don't understand it – there was nothing like this last year, when he was in Reception. I'm not sure what to do about it.'

Ben had dug his hands into his trouser pockets and was nodding, his face inscrutable behind the designer sunglasses. 'What did the teacher suggest?' he asked.

'Nothing really. She says they'll monitor the situation. But if Daniel says there isn't anything wrong, I don't want to upset him by bringing all this up.'

'He may just be settling in,' said Ben. 'Finding his place in a new environment with a different teacher? I'll keep an eye on him though, when he's with us, and try to chat to him about it. I'll get Lou to have a word with him as well. They've got such a great relationship and they're really close. Maybe, if there's something worrying him, he'll feel he can talk to her about it, even if he doesn't want to tell us.'

No! shrieked a voice inside Eve's head. *Don't you dare! She's not his mother. I'm the one he should be speaking to, not her.*

'Whatever,' she said, trying to sound as if it didn't matter. 'Although to be honest, Ben, I think it might be better coming from you and me.'

Having started to move towards the car, he turned around again. 'Oh, I nearly forgot. There's something I need to speak to you about, too.'

Eve waved at Daniel, in the back seat of the car, and blew him a kiss.

'There are a few changes happening at work,' Ben was saying. 'We're opening a new office in Glasgow in the spring and there are some opportunities for relocation. It's been in the pipeline for a while and it now looks as if it's all going ahead. If so, I've been asked if I'd like to go up there.'

'What, to oversee the move?'

'Well, partly. But to be based there once the office is operational. It would be a promotion – quite a lot more money – and the job would be interesting. It would be a real challenge for me. Apart from anything else, it would be good to be back up there again.'

Eve's brain was trying to process what he was telling her. Ben was from Stirling and his parents and older sister, Josie, still lived there. When they first met, he used to talk about moving back to Scotland at some stage, although she'd never believed he was serious. Once they were living together, he mentioned it less, and seemed content with trips to visit his family a couple of times a year. Then, much later, when he married Lou, Eve had presumed he was settled in the south for good.

It was strange, thinking about Ben's family now; she used to get on well with Josie, but hadn't seen or heard from her for years. His whole family had been at Ben's wedding – at that stage Eve was stalking him regularly on Facebook, and she'd pored over the photos, enlarging them so she could study all the guests in the group scenes. There was Josie, throwing rose petals outside the church, laughing as the newly-weds tried to duck away from the fragranced shower. There was Ben's best friend, Mark, and his wife, who'd spent so many weekends staying with

Eve and Ben in the house in Bedminster before Daniel was born. There was Ben's dad, Graham, with his arm thrown across Lou's shoulders, half turning towards her, looking at her so fondly. Eve had always got on well with Graham; such a lovely man. He used to look at her like that.

Flicking through the dozens of photographs was like picking at a scab. She hated herself for it, but couldn't stop doing it time and time again over the days and weeks that followed. It didn't get any easier. One evening, about six months after the wedding, buoyed by the best part of a bottle of wine, she unfriended Ben. She regretted it as soon as she'd done it, but also knew it was the right thing to do. The grown-up thing. Otherwise, the temptation to spy on his perfect new life would have been overwhelming and she'd never be able to move on. Which she really had to do, now he was married. She often thought about sending him a new friend request, but pride wouldn't let her do it.

That had been more than three years ago, and thinking about Ben's family now felt strange – like a distant memory that had happened to someone else. But a move to Scotland? That was a such big deal for him.

'It sounds good,' she said. 'Especially if it's a promotion.'

He nodded. 'We've not made any definite decisions yet, but Lou has talked to her partner, who would be prepared to buy her out. She was feeling ready for a change anyway, so the idea is that she'd open another florist's up in Glasgow. She's got so much experience, and a great reputation for what she does, I'm sure she'd make a go of it and we've been investigating lease options for retail premises in the city centre.'

'How long have you been thinking about all this?' Eve asked. For some reason it seemed important to know that; to hear how long they'd been planning this major life change. It was clearly more than a vague idea that was being floated around. She had no right to be involved – Ben's life was his own business – but this would have a big impact on all of them.

'I mean, it's great news,' she continued, not waiting for him to answer. 'And if Lou's happy as well, then I'm pleased for you. But we'd obviously need to think about the effect it would have on Daniel. He's used to having you living nearby, and spending a lot of time with you. I guess he'd have to come up during school holidays? But he's too young to travel on his own – I wouldn't be happy about putting him on a plane alone, even though I think the airlines have that system where they look after kids. So, I'd need to go with him, and that would get expensive.'

Ben took off his sunglasses and started polishing them on his shirt. 'Well, actually we've been...'

'I suppose we could come up by train,' said Eve. 'But it's all going to take a lot of organising and I wouldn't necessarily be able to get the time off work. Do you think you'd ever come back down to the Bristol office for meetings? That would make life easier. I'm happy for you, of course I am. But we'll need to think really carefully about all this, before we say anything about it to Daniel and tell him you'll be moving.'

Ben was still rubbing the lenses of his glasses, not meeting her eye. He looked pained, almost sheepish. 'The thing is, Eve, I'm not suggesting anything like that. Lou and I have talked about this, and we both think it would be really hard for Daniel to only see us a few times a year – even if it was for longer periods. He's so close to Keira, he just adores her – you've seen them together. It would break their hearts if they weren't able to be with each other.' He put his glasses back on and cleared his throat, digging his hands into the front pockets of his jeans. 'So, what we're thinking, me and Lou, is that Daniel could come with us – move up to Glasgow?'

In the silence that stretched between them, Eve could hear

her own heart thumping like a drum. Over Ben's shoulder, the branches of the horse chestnut tree down the road were waving softly in the breeze, just a handful of persistent leaves still clinging on. She'd always loved that tree: each autumn Daniel gleefully filled his pockets with shiny brown conkers that he would later line up on the windowsill in his bedroom.

'We could do a trial period,' Ben was saying now. 'If we go up in January and take a couple of months to settle into a new house, we could get him booked into a local school after Easter and see how he likes it. He's such a friendly little boy, I'm sure he'd adapt really easily. Lou won't be working at first, while she sorts out the logistics of the new shop, so she'll be able to spend lots of time with him and make sure he's okay.'

There was still a straggling row of conkers up on Daniel's windowsill, carefully arranged in order, from the biggest, most-prized specimen, to the smallest, most insignificant, no larger than a marble. Possibly thirty of them in all. They were past their best now: most of them drying up, their skins wrinkling in the heat thrown out by the bedroom radiator. But Daniel was refusing to let her throw them away. Just the other day he'd taken one of her dusters from the cupboard under the sink and Eve had watched through the open bedroom door as he sat polishing the mahogany shells until they shone.

Ben was still talking; she wanted to put her fingers in her ears or turn away, but she kept her eyes fixed on his lips as they moved.

'There are some great schools in Glasgow,' he was saying. 'Lou's been doing some online research and the reports are impressive.'

She wanted to butt in, to say something. But she didn't know what. There was a roaring sound in her ears, like waves crashing across the pebbles on a beach.

'It sounds like the timing is spot on for all this,' Ben was saying. 'Daniel isn't settling in well at school here, as you've just pointed out. We don't know what's going on, but he obviously can't be happy if he's behaving badly. So maybe a new start is what he needs?'

THIRTEEN

There was a bunch of carnations on the doorstep, the stems wrapped in garish pink tissue paper, a card poking out from the folds.

Sorry I was grumpy last week. Peace offering? J.

Eve smiled as she took the flowers inside and hunted in the kitchen cupboard for a vase. She'd been feeling guilty about Jake's unsuccessful attempts to tame her wild garden, but hadn't known what to do about it. She'd gone to Homebase to buy a replacement cord for the strimmer, but the trip had revealed they came in numerous different sizes, colours and shapes, and she stood for ages in front of the relevant shelf, with no idea which was the right one.

She'd been working up the courage to go and see him, but the whole thing felt awkward so she hadn't got round to it. Instead, she'd spent the last few days working her way through the remains of the lemon drizzle cake and sneaking in and out of the house, keeping her eyes firmly averted from next door.

Thank God he'd made the first move.

'Sorry.' He grinned as he answered her knock at his front door. 'I behaved like a stroppy teenager.'

'It's fine.' She smiled back. 'You were only trying to do me a favour. And I'm sorry my grass broke your strimmer. Can I pay for that?'

'No, you can't,' he said. 'But you can come in and have a cup of tea.'

Eve had never been inside his house before. They'd only chatted over the fence or called out pleasantries as one or other of them rushed off to work. The layout was, unsurprisingly, exactly the same as in her own house, with a sitting room off to the right and the kitchen at the back, running the width of the house. Jake's bike was balanced against one wall just inside the front door, and she caught her shin on the pedal as she followed him along the hall towards the kitchen.

She peered up the stairs as she went past: the walls were an insipid peach, the carpet a dull burgundy. She preferred her own décor, even though the magnolia walls and cream carpet in her home were now covered in the sort of spills, stains and sticky fingerprints that can only be created by a small child on a mission to destroy all domesticity.

She was relieved to see Jake's kitchen was as messy as her own. Most of the cupboard doors were open and a tea-towel was on the floor, along with a patina of muddy footprints that suggested this wasn't a 'shoes off' household.

'I don't know what got into me,' he was saying now, as he filled the kettle. 'I'm not usually so impatient. But I really wanted to help you out and I guess I was embarrassed I'd made a mess of it.'

'Jake, you didn't. It was kind of you to offer to help,' she said. 'It's my fault for leaving things so long. I never seem to have the time to keep the garden under control, so every now and then I do a little bit, but it all grows back again and runs away with me. Ben was the one who loved gardening...'

She faltered, embarrassed. Did Jake even know what had

happened between her and Ben? When they were still living next door together, they'd never shouted at each other in a way that would have attracted the neighbours' attention; instead, their relationship had worn itself out in a welter of frosty silences and cold-shouldered reproaches. But Ben hadn't lived here for years now, and Jake couldn't have failed to notice the twice-weekly visits to pick up and drop off Daniel.

Ben. Occasionally, over the last couple of days, she had gone for an entire hour without thinking about the conversation they'd had, especially at work when her mind was on so much else. But then something would remind her, and she'd start to go over the whole bloody mess again.

At first, she'd told herself Ben wasn't serious about the job in Glasgow. Why would he uproot his family and make such a dramatic move? He and Lou were settled in Bristol; they must have good friends here, a great quality of life. But, deep down, she knew it was entirely believable: he loved Scotland, and the appeal of being back there was strong enough on its own, even without the added attraction of a promotion, an entire office to manage and a big salary hike.

But how could he possibly imagine she would be happy for him to take Daniel with him? After he'd driven away on Saturday, she had gone back inside the house, shaking, the shock of what he'd suggested causing her head to thump and nausea to build up inside her throat. He couldn't take away her baby boy. He just couldn't. She'd gone upstairs and lain down on Daniel's unmade bed, howling into the Spider-Man pillowcase.

Hours later, her cheeks still sticky with tears, she had dug out some folders and gone through all the legal papers they'd signed when they separated: the agreements about maintenance and custody. Daniel had stayed with her because they'd both been happy for that to happen – Ben hadn't wanted his son living with him at the time. And she'd done a good job of raising him – almost single-handed at first – there was no way Ben could disagree with that. Granted, he'd played a bigger part in Daniel's life over the last few years, but Eve was still his mother, his main carer. She would stop this from happening; she would refuse to even discuss it. Bloody Ben could take a running jump.

But the initial bravado died away swiftly and after that she hadn't been able to stop going over it all in her mind: what if Ben refused to back down about taking Daniel to Glasgow? What if he took her to court? He was a good father and he had rights. If he challenged her over custody, whose side would a judge take?

Standing here now, in Jake's kitchen, she felt her pulse race as Ben's words flickered through her head again. Jake was looking at her, waiting for her to finish her sentence as the kettle bubbled beside him.

'Anyway, now I'm on my own with Daniel,' she continued. 'I'm afraid the garden comes way down my list of priorities.'

He smiled as he flung teabags into a couple of mugs. 'Same here,' he said. 'Life's too busy.'

They both turned at the sound of the front door opening and slamming so hard that the pictures rattled on the walls.

'Hi Katie!' called Jake.

There was no reply, but footsteps stomped up the stairs and, after a moment's pause, a door on the landing was slammed shut.

'Oh dear,' he said. 'That will either be the boyfriend who's in trouble, or me. I really hope it's him. Let's take these mugs next door and hide in the sitting room.'

The curtains were still drawn from the night before and, as Jake pushed them open, she saw an empty beer bottle, an open newspaper and a used bowl and plate on the coffee table.

'Sorry,' he said, scooping it all up. 'I've got into bad habits. With Katie hardly ever here, it feels like I'm living on my own. It means I can be a slob and don't have to bother clearing up. But that's not the way to impress a woman.'

Eve wasn't sure how she was meant to react. Did he want to impress her? She perched on the edge of the sofa, resting her mug on her knees. She wished she hadn't come in now. What were they going to talk about? She hardly knew this man and, although he was nice enough, they probably had nothing in common; it felt like she was intruding.

'What do you think of these curtains?' he was asking. 'I've had them up for years and was wondering if it was time to replace them. But I struggle with things like this, because I'm colour-blind.'

'Really?'

'Yup, I can't distinguish between greens and browns. Purples and blues can be a bugger as well. So, it's not safe to let me out alone to shop for soft furnishings.'

Eve almost laughed: this probably explained his bizarre clothing sense! Today Jake was wearing a faded red shirt and a pair of purple tracksuit bottoms which were too small for him and ended way above his ankles, exposing a couple of inches of skin and mismatched socks – one black, the other green. Colour-blindness couldn't excuse the Tena Lady T-shirt, but it went a long way towards accounting for everything else.

'So, how does that work?' She was fascinated. 'Do all those colours look the same to you, or are they just different shades of grey?'

'It's hard to explain,' said Jake. 'I've never known anything else. But what usually...'

The sitting-room door burst open and Katie marched into the room. 'Oh,' she said, seeing Eve. 'What are you doing here?'

'What she means is, hello Eve, how lovely to see you,' said Jake.

Katie glared at him. The weak shafts of sunlight coming in through the windows picked out the dark blonde highlights in her hair and, standing there with her hands on her hips and chin jutting out, she looked just like her father.

'We haven't got any batteries,' she said.

'Really? Well, you might have to go and buy some from the corner shop. My wallet's in the kitchen, take some money.'

'For God's sake, why do we never have the right stuff in this house!' The girl huffed and turned on her heel, slamming the door behind her with practised efficiency.

'Sorry,' said Jake. 'She's not exactly a little ray of sunshine at the moment. The teenage years are hard work. I'm hoping this phase will pass and I'll get my daughter back by the time she's eighteen. In the meantime, a stroppy, hormonal alien has taken possession of her body.'

Eve laughed. It would be rude to agree with him, but this was one bolshie girl. It was impressive Jake was being so laid-back about her behaviour: if it was up to her, she'd stand up to Katie and tell her not to be selfish and rude. She hoped Daniel wouldn't turn into the kind of sixteen-year-old who answered back and slammed doors so hard they threatened to come off their hinges. Mind you, if he did, he might be living hundreds of miles away from her: by that stage, it would be Lou's job to cope with his mood swings and irrational tantrums.

Before she could help herself, a sob fought its way up through her throat and, as she tried to choke it back, another followed too swiftly. Suddenly her eyes were full of tears and her hands were shaking so badly she had to put the mug of tea down on the carpet at her feet. 'Sorry,' she whispered, burying her face in her hands.

She felt the sofa cushion move beside her and an arm went across her shoulders. 'Hey, what's the matter?' asked Jake. 'Tell me what's happened?'

As she leant against him, she stopped fighting the sobs, opened her mouth and howled.

FOURTEEN

Eve got out of the car and locked it, her mind miles away, running through the list of chores she had to do on the way home. As usual, she needed to get a few bits from Tesco before she picked up Daniel later, and she must get some petrol – the warning light had been blinking at her since yesterday. One of her jackets needed picking up from the dry cleaners – it had been there such a long time they'd probably given up hope of her ever coming to collect it. What happened to all the forgotten skirts and suits in Johnsons? Maybe they had a massive clear-out every few months and took a clothing mountain to one of the local charity shops. Hopefully things weren't at that stage yet; she quite liked that particular jacket.

As she turned towards the front door of Three Elms, she saw a flash of blue out of the corner of her eye and noticed two figures making their way down the gravel drive. Two very familiar figures. A pair of white heads were bobbing, above a pair of bottoms waddling towards the gates, handbags slung across forearms. One of the figures gave a shriek of laughter.

'Mum?' Eve had just taken a step after them when Nathan

came flying out of the door, his eyes wide, breathless as he bounded down the steps.

'Have you seen them?' he gasped. 'Someone just told me they've made a run for it!'

Eve gaped at him, then pointed down the drive, where the figures had reached the gate.

'Stop them!' he yelled. He set off down the drive, gravel scrunching beneath his trainers, and Eve ran after him, wishing she wasn't in the stupid high heels she'd been wearing for this afternoon's viewing.

'Mrs Glover!' Nathan was calling. 'Mrs Harrison! Please come back!'

But the two women were upping the pace. They turned right and headed along the pavement that ran on the other side of the Three Elms's railings, their elbows pumping like speed walkers, handbags bouncing against their hips.

'Mum, stop!' shouted Eve, as she came out of the gate, skidding to a halt in front of a young girl with a pushchair.

Up ahead, Nathan had almost caught up with the women. He was waving his arms and shouting, and passers-by were gawping. As Eve gained ground, she could see that both women were wearing their carpet slippers, Flora's old beige ones flapping off her heels as she waddled along. Eve hadn't seen her mother move this quickly in years: it was extraordinary.

Barbara had produced a newspaper from somewhere and was holding it open in front of her, clearly hoping it would provide anonymity. It backfired. As Nathan raced alongside them, Barbara veered sharply to the right and walked straight into a postbox.

'Ow!' she shrieked. 'Look what you made me do.'

Nathan grabbed her and reached out towards Flora. Eve finally drew near enough to take her mother's other arm.

'Get off me!' huffed Barbara, slapping at Nathan's hand.

'Young man, this is common assault. I will report you to the authorities.'

'Mum, what are you doing?' panted Eve.

'We are going out for a cup of tea!' said Flora. 'What on earth is wrong with that? For goodness' sake, Eve, there's no need to make a spectacle of yourself – your face is all red and your hair is messed up.'

'That's because I've been chasing after you!'

'Take your hand off me!' shouted Barbara, swatting at Nathan with her newspaper, as if his fingers were a fly on her arm.

'Excuse me,' said a man, standing nearby. 'But should you be treating these ladies like this? There's no need to be quite so rough with them.'

'Call the police!' yelled Barbara, over her shoulder.

'Please don't!' said Nathan, turning to the man. 'They live at Three Elms, just along the road here. They're not meant to be out without us knowing. They're my responsibility.'

'Pah!' said Barbara. 'We don't need anyone's permission to go out for tea. We are free agents, and we should have the right to go wherever we please, whenever we please.'

'Yes, but you need to tell me!' said Nathan, leading both women back the way they'd come. 'I'm responsible for you, Mrs Harrison. If you leave without letting anyone know, then I'll get into trouble. What if you fell over or had some kind of accident?'

'Well, that isn't going to happen,' said Barbara. But her tone was less strident, and both women were allowing themselves to be led back towards the gates. Following, Eve saw that her mother's skirt had twisted around and the tweed was riding up above the lining. She bent forward and tried to pull it down again as Nathan marched them up the drive.

'Eve, stop that!' said Flora, trying to turn around. 'What are you doing? Honestly, people can't keep their hands off me today.'

'You must be freezing out here!' said Nathan. 'I can't believe neither of you has a coat on. It's December, you'll catch cold.'

'Is it December already?' asked Flora. 'Well, I never; where has this year gone?'

Barbara was out of breath now, dragging behind slightly as Nathan led both women up the stairs to the front door of Three Elms. 'Goodness, that was a bit of a workout,' she puffed.

Eve wondered if she ought to be helping, but the spark seemed to have gone out of them and Nathan clearly had the situation under control.

'We don't want to cause any problems for you, Nathan,' said Flora. 'You're a lovely boy.'

'Thank you,' said Nathan.

Mrs Donaldson was waiting in front of the reception desk, her arms crossed, her mouth set in a line. 'What on earth is going on? Ladies, we cannot have this sort of behaviour. We are here to look after you. Please go back to the lounge and I will come and speak to you shortly. Nathan, in my office. Now.'

'It's not his fault,' said Eve, but the manager had turned on her heel and was disappearing through a door.

'Now look what you've done!' Eve said, taking Flora's arm and guiding her through into the communal lounge. Barbara followed meekly. 'If you get that poor boy sacked, I'll be furious. What a way to behave!'

'But we only wanted to go out for a cup of tea...'

Flora looked so upset that Eve immediately felt guilty. 'I know. But you have to tell people and maybe they'll be able to arrange for someone to go with you?' She sat Flora down, and stroked a wayward strand of hair back from her mother's forehead. Sitting in the armchair, she suddenly seemed very small and frail. Her eyes were darting about her, looking at Barbara, then up at Eve. She seemed completely bewildered.

'I'm sorry,' she said. 'We didn't want to cause any trouble.'

'It's fine,' said Eve, wishing she hadn't snapped. 'No harm done. At least you're both back safe and sound. That's the main thing.'

Barbara had sat down on the chair beside Flora and was glaring around her as if challenging anyone to remark on what had happened. But her hands, clutched in her lap, were shaking.

'Let's find you both a drink,' said Eve, getting up. 'And some biscuits.'

The mission wasn't easily accomplished. The trolley was nowhere in sight; clearly it wasn't the done thing to ask for a hot drink at 2.30pm, when the regular afternoon tea round didn't start for another half hour.

As Eve came out of the communal lounge, Nathan scampered out of Mrs Donaldson's office.

'Is everything okay?' asked Eve.

He nodded. 'Think so. She's fuming. But there should have been someone on reception to stop them going out, and that's not my fault.'

'You were great out there; you handled it really well.'

'Thanks.' The boy grinned and puffed out his chest slightly. 'All in a day's work, you know. Anyway, it's just as well they weren't out for much longer: we've got St Barnabas coming in this afternoon.'

Eve's confusion must have shown on her face.

'You know, the schoolchildren who come in to sing carols with our residents? They're practising for the concert.'

'Of course.' Eve had forgotten all about that. 'I tried to persuade Mum to do that, but she wasn't keen. It's a shame, because it sounded lovely.'

'Oh, she's doing it all right,' said Nathan, staring at the usual spot, several inches to the left of Eve's face. 'She's been coming along for the last few weeks. She's one of the best we've got, and she loves the children – they all get on like a house on fire!'

As he headed back up the corridor, Eve turned and stared through the door of the lounge, watching Flora as she delved around in her handbag, pulling out crumpled tissues and several pairs of glasses. How strange that she hadn't mentioned she was taking part in the weekly rehearsals. She'd seemed so dismissive of the whole thing.

With an exclamation, Flora pulled a lipstick from her handbag and drew a wobbly fuchsia line around her mouth. Once done, she smacked her lips together; there was a smudge of bright pink on both her front teeth. She turned to Barbara and handed her the lipstick, leaning forward and watching intently as her friend turned her lips the same colour. Barbara wound down the lipstick and popped it into her own handbag and the two women grinned at each other as they sat back in their armchairs.

Looking up, Flora saw Eve standing in the door and waved energetically, as if noticing her for the first time. 'Hello darling!' she called. 'What are you doing here? This is a lovely surprise.'

FIFTEEN

There was an almighty crash upstairs. Followed by an ominous silence.

'What's happened?' Eve called.

Silence.

'Daniel, what have you done?'

As she ran up the stairs, she could hear cupboard doors shutting, the boys talking in agitated whispers. Pushing open her bedroom door, she found them sitting side by side on her bed; Daniel was beaming up at her, his best friend Robbie looked terrified.

'Nothing! It's nothing. We haven't done anything,' said Daniel.

'Well, clearly you have.' Eve looked around the room. 'I heard something break. What was it?'

'Nothing!' sang Daniel again.

But Robbie's lower lip was wobbling. 'It wasn't our fault,' he whimpered.

Eve's eyes came to rest on her chest of drawers, against the far wall, and she suddenly realised that the photo which usually stood on it was missing: the big colour picture of the three of them. It was a selfie Ben had taken on the beach at Weston; Daniel had been a few weeks old and, despite their sleep-deprived exhaustion, they had decided they'd go out for the day.

The sun had blazed down from a cornflower-blue sky, the gulls had screeched, other people's children had cried and laughed and shrieked, the pebbles on the beach had rattled as they'd staggered across them, Eve holding Daniel tightly to her chest as he bounced around in the sling. They'd had a drink outside a pub, then sat beside the sea, eating ice cream while Eve tucked the baby under her T-shirt and fed him. It had been a near perfect trip; the sort of day she'd dreamed they would regularly share as a family, but – as it turned out – one of the few they would actually have. Ben had held out his phone, capturing their two smiling, bronzed faces, cheeks pressed together, with Daniel's tiny, sleepy face between them.

She had gone out and bought a frame for the photo immediately, and it had stood on her chest of drawers in the bedroom ever since: a happy memory at first and, for the last few years, a reminder of better times.

But now it had disappeared.

She marched across the room and looked in the bin and then behind the chest, dragging it away from the wall. Nothing. She went across to the built-in cupboards on the opposite wall. Wrenching open the doors, she saw the shards of shattered glass on the floor amongst her shoes, pushed into a messy pile around the empty frame, the photo bent in two beneath it.

'Daniel!' she said. 'How could you?'

'It wasn't us!' yelled Daniel, his cheeks pink. 'It just fell over all by itself. We didn't touch it. We didn't go anywhere near it when we were doing our special kick-boxing training.'

'For fuck's sake!' snapped Eve, kneeling down and picking up the crumpled photograph. 'Get out of my room, both of you. I can't believe you've done this.'

Robbie really looked as if he was about to cry now, but she didn't care.

'Get out!' she screamed.

The two little boys fell off the bed in a tumble of legs and arms, pushing each other towards the door, pulling it shut behind them and thundering down the stairs.

She sat back on her heels and flattened out the picture, running the tip of her finger across Daniel's tiny, squashed newborn features. Her own eyes were stretched wide, almost sparkling in the sunlight, despite the tiredness she could still remember so well: an exhaustion so all-encompassing that at times it had been an effort to walk and talk at the same time, her bones as heavy as lead.

And Ben. He looked very handsome in this picture: his smile wide, his face tanned, the skin around his eyes crinkled as he grinned up at the camera.

Something lurched in the pit of her stomach as she looked at his face. She could still remember falling in love with this man. Ten years ago, as they first sat opposite each other in the pub, she had been aware that she was talking too loudly, laughing too easily, everything brought into such sharp focus by the presence of this dark-haired stranger.

As they worked their way through the first bottle of wine, Hannah and Jon had been disagreeing about something they'd both read in the paper, already bickering in the flirty, light-hearted way, which would set the pattern for their brief relationship. But Ben was just looking at her, grinning, raising his eyebrows as the other two sparred. She had glanced down at his hand, watching him twist the stem of his glass between his thumb and forefinger, then looked back up at his face, realising he hadn't taken his eyes off her for what felt like a very long time. It was as if every nerve ending in her body was tingling. He liked her, that was obvious. She smiled at him and hoped it was just as obvious she felt the same, dozens of imaginary butterflies flittering around in her loins.

Now there was just an empty ache deep inside her, as if someone had kicked her in the gut. She honestly didn't have those sorts of feelings for him any longer: hadn't done for years. But she missed the Ben she'd fallen in love with. How had she messed up everything so badly?

She put the photo frame to one side and began to pick up the shards of glass, piling them onto one hand until they were balanced so precariously it felt like the whole lot would spill onto the carpet again. She emptied the glass into the bin and went downstairs to get a dustpan and brush, realising as she did so that it was too quiet. The boys were nowhere to be seen.

Then, looking through the kitchen window, she saw them sitting at the end of the garden, squeezed side by side onto the plastic swing that hung from the high bough of a tree that stretched over into her garden from next door. For the first time it occurred to her that she should have asked Jake if he minded her using his tree. She knew you could pick apples from a neighbour's tree if it overhung your garden, but she wasn't entirely sure about swing rights.

Even from this distance, she could see Robbie's eyes were red and blotchy. *Shit.* She shouldn't have yelled at them. Plus, she'd dropped the F-bomb in front of Robbie – Juliet was definitely not the sort of parent who swore in front of her children. Would he tell her? She opened the back door, slipped on her wellies and waded through the long grass towards the swing.

'Boys, I'm really sorry I shouted at you,' she said. 'It was horrible of me. I know you didn't mean to break the photo frame. Of course you didn't. It's just that it's one of my favourite pictures of you, Daniel – and it's definitely the best one I've got of you, me and Daddy together. That's why I was so upset to see it had gone.'

The boys sat, heads bowed, swinging slightly, their feet scuffing along the ground. Eve knelt in front of them and put one hand on each of their knees.

'I'm so sorry,' she said again. 'Robbie, please don't cry. I know it wasn't your fault.'

The little boy looked up at her and sniffed, trying to smile. She couldn't remember ever having shouted at him before and was deeply ashamed of herself. Would Juliet send her an angry text or back her into a corner outside the school gates, demanding an apology and saying she'd never let her son come over to play at Daniel's again? Surely not: Juliet would understand she had been upset and frustrated. But they were friends and she didn't want this to come between them. Bribery and corruption should put things right.

'Let's go and get a Happy Meal for tea!' she said. 'Do you want chicken nuggets or a cheeseburger?'

'Burger!' shouted Daniel.

'Nuggets!' whispered Robbie.

'Okay, get your coats and we'll go now,' she said, getting up from where she'd been kneeling on the grass, damp patches spreading across the knees of her jeans. The boys jumped off the swing and raced into the house and, as she followed them, Eve decided she'd tell Juliet what had happened as soon as she dropped Robbie back, just in case he said something about it later. She would mention the photo frame, which of course had been broken by accident, and hint the boys were so upset by what they'd done that she'd taken them for a Happy Meal to cheer them up. There was probably no need to mention the fact that she'd yelled at them. Or used the F-word.

She could hear them laughing in the hall while they put on

their coats and there was a trail of muddy footprints leading along the carpet towards the front door.

'Can we have juice instead of water?' Daniel was asking, as he jumped up to open the latch. 'I know you always say I have to choose water, but this is different because Robbie's coming with us and he really likes juice, don't you, Robbie?'

'You can have whatever you like,' said Eve, picking up her car keys and her purse. 'Coke, 7Up, chocolate milk.'

The two boys stared at her, open-mouthed, then looked at each other and screeched as they ran down the path towards the car. It was such a relief to see them happy again, and it wasn't really bribery at all, Eve thought, as she slammed the door behind her. Two Happy Meals and a hefty dose of sugar were a small price to pay.

SIXTEEN

Everything that could have gone wrong so far this morning, had done. There was no milk left for their cereal, the iron wouldn't heat up so she'd had to dig out her least creased blouse to wear to work – and her wheelie bin hadn't been emptied.

'Bugger,' she muttered, as she slammed the lid back down. She knew the binmen had been, because she'd heard the lorry grinding and whining its way slowly past the house at the crack of dawn. One of the guys was a whistler: every Thursday he treated local residents to his rendition of eighties hits. This morning he had been murdering *Sweet Dreams* (*Are Made of This*) as he came through Eve's gate. She had shoved her head under the pillow, prepared to put up with the whistling since he was doing her a favour and removing her rubbish. Although apparently now, he hadn't even done that.

The neighbour over the road waved as she came down the path to collect her bin.

'I wouldn't bother,' called Eve. 'They haven't emptied them!'

The woman lifted up the lid and peered inside her bin.

'They've done mine!' she said, as she turned and began to pull it back towards the house. 'Have a nice day.'

Eve's mouth dropped open and she glared at her own bin.

She was shattered this morning. She hadn't been sleeping well recently, and last night had been worse than usual. She'd woken several times and, on each occasion, found her mind alert and racing through different scenarios involving Ben. Maybe he wouldn't get the Glasgow promotion – or the whole office relocation wouldn't come off. Or maybe Lou would decide she was happily settled in Bristol and didn't want to uproot Keira and start all over again in a strange city? None of those things were likely; Eve knew she was clutching at straws.

She hadn't spoken to Ben about the move since their initial conversation, mostly because it was easier to stick her head in the sand and pretend it wasn't happening. But that didn't stop her overactive imagination conjuring up a future for them all in which her son was living hundreds of miles away, and she was rattling around on her own in this empty house, missing major milestones and gradually becoming a minor part of his life.

She hadn't spoken to Daniel about what might happen either, although Ben and Lou may have talked about it when he was with them. But she couldn't bear the possibility that, if she asked him about the move, he'd tell her he wanted to go and live with Daddy.

Ben was right, Daniel adored Keira and always came back buzzing with excitement at the things they'd done together. Being at Ben's was fun: there was a PlayStation 5 console and a huge telly with a Netflix account. Ben took him to football matches and in the summer they'd gone kayaking. Even if they just went out for a pizza or to spend time at the park, there were four of them: a proper family.

Here, it was just her and Daniel. However hard she tried,

she couldn't make her little boy's life as exciting or as busy as when he was with his father.

She kicked the wheelie bin. 'Bloody thing.'

'Talking to yourself again?' Jake was lifting his bike out through the front door. He was wearing a lime-green cycling helmet with red go-faster stripes, and tufts of his hair were sticking through the holes in the sides. She couldn't remember seeing him wear this helmet before; it must be new. He looked a bit ridiculous. Why would anyone in their right mind buy such a weird thing?

'The dustmen haven't emptied my bin,' she said.

'What did you put in it?'

'Rubbish. What do you usually put in a bin?'

'Of course, but have you contaminated it?'

Eve wasn't in the mood for this. 'What does that mean? I've just put my rubbish in black bin liners, put the bin liners inside my wheelie bin and left the sodding thing out on the pavement to be emptied. Which hasn't happened. I'll have to ring the council and complain.'

Jake balanced his bike against the fence and walked over to her. He lifted up the lid of her bin, looked inside and nodded sagely. 'That's what I thought. Contaminated. You've put some biodegradable material in here.'

He was pointing at the handful of weeds which Eve had thrown into the top of the bin last night. She'd been dragging it down to the kerb and had pulled the weeds out of the path on her way past, opening the lid of the bin and putting them in as she went, pleased with herself for doing two jobs at once.

'But that's rubbish too?' she said.

'Nope.' Jake shook his head. 'It's classed as biodegradable, so it shouldn't go to landfill, which means the binmen are within their rights to refuse to empty this.'

On any other morning, when she'd had a good night's sleep,

enough milk to put on her cereal and was wearing a properly ironed blouse, Eve would have seen the funny side. But today her sense of humour had been lost in action.

'Well, that's just stupid. What is the point in us paying for services when they don't provide them? Contaminated waste! I've never heard anything so ridiculous. Now I'm going to have to find the time to load all this into the car and take it to the tip. Otherwise, if I leave it, the bin will get full of maggots. That's just brilliant.'

Jake grinned. 'You won't get maggots at this time of year, it's too cold.'

'Oh, fantastic!' she said sarcastically. 'Thank you so much for that one piece of good news.'

She was so angry, everything inside her head felt taut, like a stretched rubber band. This was all so unfair; she had a busy day ahead and didn't need to add anything else onto the long overdue to-do list which was sitting on the kitchen worktop. She wanted to lash out at someone, anyone. Jake happened to be closest.

'Where did you get that awful helmet?' she asked, watching as he fiddled with the strap, twisting it under his chin. 'I've never seen anything so naff. Even a child wouldn't wear something like that!'

'Is it that bad?' He looked surprised. 'It was on offer down at Halfords. I needed a new one and I thought it would make me stand out in the traffic.'

'That's true, no one could miss you in that,' said Eve. She bit her lip. Oh God, why was she being so cruel? It was none of her business what sort of helmet Jake wore. 'Well, as long as it does the job and keeps you safe,' she added, trying to make her voice brighter.

'It does that all right!' He grinned. Either he had a very thick skin or he was deliberately ignoring her rudeness. She felt so mean.

'Right, I must get to work. Have a nice day,' she said, grabbing the wheelie bin and turning it round.

'You too,' he said. 'Got anything planned for tonight?'

'Oh, just the usual,' said Eve. 'A bowl of pasta pesto, half an hour's vacuuming, online bill payments. I might cheer myself up later by turning on the *News at Ten* and finding out that the world is going to hell in a handcart.'

'The thing is,' he continued, 'I've got a couple of tickets to see the show tonight at The Comedy Box, you know that place on North Street? I've been before and it's always a good evening.'

Eve stared at him.

'So, I just wondered if you fancied coming with me? It starts about 7pm I think, and I'm sure I could get Katie to come over and look after Daniel. It might cheer you up to get out and do something a bit different?'

Her mouth dropped open as her brain scrabbled to keep up. Shit, he was asking her out. Or was he? Maybe someone else had blown him out and he had a spare ticket. She might be getting the wrong idea – but what if he really was asking her out! Why hadn't she realised this was what he was saying when he asked what she was doing tonight?

She frantically tried to think of an excuse, a reason she couldn't make it. How stupid to make that remark about staying in with a bowl of pasta – that made it obvious she didn't have any other plans. She saw something flicker across his face, and realised she was taking too long to answer, aware her own face wasn't showing the right kind of expression.

'Look, don't worry about it,' he said. 'It was just a thought. I'll find someone at work who wants to come.' He turned away and walked back towards his bike, still fiddling with the strap of his garish helmet.

'Jake!' At last, she found her voice. 'I'm sorry, that would have been lovely.' She realised she still hadn't come up with a reason why she was turning him down. Could she think of something else she had planned – which needed to be fitted around the pasta, vacuuming and television watching? Whatever she said now, it would sound as if she was lying. 'Maybe another time? It's very kind of you to think of me.'

He didn't turn around, just waved as he wheeled his bike down to the road and launched himself onto it, picking up speed as he headed away between the rows of parked cars.

Eve stared after the lime-green-and-red helmet for a few seconds, then put her head in her hands. How awful: she must have seemed so rude. She hadn't meant to knock him back; she'd just been taken by surprise. He'd looked really hurt when she didn't say anything, as if she'd smacked him in the face. She'd clearly got it wrong – poor, kind Jake had just been offering her a night out, knowing she was unhappy and trying to cheer her up. Now she'd offended him and put them both in an awkward position.

'Oh, Eve,' she muttered to herself. 'You grumpy bitch.'

SEVENTEEN

She didn't want to tell Gav where she was going – it would have meant explaining what was going on with Ben, and she had no intention of sharing something that personal. So, right now, it was easier to tell a little white lie.

'I've got a doctor's appointment after lunch,' she'd said. 'They've called me in for a smear.'

'Ahhhh.' Gav looked horrified, as she'd known he would.

'Sorry about the short notice, they're running an extra clinic. You know how it is with smears, the last one wasn't very clear so they want me to go back and...'

Gav's face was very pink. 'Ah, yes indeed, fine, okay. No problemo, princess. Take as much time as you want.' He was shuffling papers on his desk and not meeting her eye. He wasn't the sort of man who dealt well with anything vaguely gynaecological.

Her appointment at Bell & Simpson was booked for 1.30pm. Before that she had to do a viewing for Mr Timpson, the owner of the overpriced Victorian semi on the outskirts of the city, which had been languishing on the market for weeks. A young couple had finally asked to look round – Eve was so relieved she could have kissed them when she met them on the pavement outside – but Mr Timpson insisted on accompanying her as she showed them through the house, hopping from one foot to the other and pointing out features he was convinced would secure a sale.

'Fully double glazed!' he said, as she walked them into the sitting room. 'Television aerial sockets in all the bedrooms!'

'Mr Timpson, you must let me handle these viewings,' she said afterwards, as the young couple beat a hasty retreat. She knew she wouldn't hear from them again. 'I realise you're keen to help, but most buyers prefer to look at a property without the vendor being there.'

'But you're missing out important information!' he'd said. 'You didn't mention the architraves!'

When Eve arrived at Bell & Simpson, she was five minutes late and in a foul mood.

'The thing is,' she explained, 'I have custody and, when we split up, we agreed access arrangements, and everything has worked out well so far. Ben has certain times when he sees Daniel, but we're both flexible and I never mind if he wants to change the day.'

'That all sounds very positive,' said the girl sitting opposite her, who looked too young to have finished her GCSEs, let alone be a fully qualified solicitor.

'But if Ben wants Daniel to go with him to Glasgow,' said Eve, 'can he make that happen?' She had decided that, rather than lying awake worrying every night, she would get a professional opinion on her situation. This young solicitor and her firm had come highly recommended by someone on a local Mumsnet forum. She wasn't entirely sure that was a good thing, but it seemed a better starting point than sticking a pin in the Yellow Pages.

'It is permissible to modify a custody agreement if there has been a change in circumstances,' said the girl. 'A relocation such as this would come under that category, because it would mean it wasn't possible for you all to continue with your existing access arrangements.'

She had beautifully manicured nails and long, elegant fingers, which she now spread out on the desk in front of her. She clearly didn't have to do much domestic drudgery; Eve hid her own hands in her lap – she'd torn a fingernail on the door of the washing machine this morning, and the plaster she'd wrapped round it was already flapping off.

'But if I decided to fight it, would a judge look on me more favourably?' she asked. 'Ben is a great dad, and I'd never claim he wasn't. But Daniel is happy with me and he's settled at school.' That bit wasn't true, but there was no point going into it right now. 'I just couldn't bear to see so little of him. I know he'd have to go up to Scotland in the holidays and maybe for the odd weekend, but he's only six – it would be so disruptive for him to do more than that.'

'A judge would make a decision based upon whatever is in the best interests of the child,' said the girl. 'But the process can be stressful for all concerned and it shouldn't be necessary to have to go back to court to get a settlement. It seems to me that, if you and your former partner have a good relationship, it should be possible and would make more sense to come to an arrangement together? We do offer mediation services and, if both of you are agreeable, I could arrange an appointment with a member of our specialist team?'

Leaving the solicitor's office, Eve felt drained. She collapsed into her car and leant back against the headrest. That hadn't been a total waste of £120: it sounded as if a judge wouldn't automatically insist Daniel be uprooted, if there was nothing wrong with his existing living arrangements.

But what if Ben mentioned the problems at school? She

really should have done something to address that, but there was so much else going on, and it felt easier to wait for Mrs Russell to get in touch again. Which the dragon woman would undoubtedly do, if there were further problems.

She had half an hour before she needed to pick up Daniel, so there was just time to go and collect that bloody jacket, which was still at the dry cleaners. She scrambled around in her handbag for the receipt. There was so much rubbish in here, why could she never keep her bag tidy? Maybe a smaller bag would help – if she couldn't fit so much stuff into it, she'd be forced to keep it tidy. She threw a Mars Bar wrapper onto the passenger seat, along with a used tissue and a very bruised apple that ought to have been eaten days ago. There was a sock of Daniel's, caught up in the spokes of the small umbrella she always carried around, but never remembered to use. Right at the bottom of the bag was a folded piece of paper; pulling it out she realised it was a letter Daniel had brought home from school a couple of weeks ago, about a trip to Bristol Zoo in a couple of weeks.

'Eve, you're bloody useless,' she muttered, realising she hadn't signed the permission slip. The letter was also asking for parent volunteers. Maybe she ought to put her name down? She never did anything to help at school, and this would also be a chance to see Daniel with the other kids, look out for any signs of wayward behaviour. Despite Mrs Russell's stinging feedback, she was still finding it hard to imagine her little boy in the role of playground bully. She found a pen and filled in her details; she'd drop the form into the school office this afternoon.

As she drove towards the dry cleaners, she wondered whether Ben would agree to some sort of mediation. God knows when he'd fit it in; he struggled to find five minutes to attend his own son's parents' evening, so she couldn't see him setting aside hours to sit in a solicitors' office, thrashing out the details of their access arrangements. Hopefully it wouldn't come to that, and they would sort it out between them. But she would have to stand firm.

'Moving our son to Scotland won't do him any good at all, Ben,' she said out loud. 'You need to think about what's best for him, not you. He's happy where he is and it would be unfair to uproot him.'

But it was one thing being firm and decisive when she was talking to an empty car, quite another when she had to pluck up the guts to say those things to her former lover's expensive sunglasses.

EIGHTEEN

There was an ambulance parked outside Three Elms, its rear doors gaping, a stretcher standing beside it on the tarmac. Eve's heart flipped, before she saw an elderly man being led down the steps, care assistants on either side, their hands grasped so firmly under his stick-thin arms that they were virtually carrying him.

She shot them a sympathetic glance as she walked past, and ran up the steps, embarrassed at the relief that was flooding through her.

There was no reason why anything should happen to Flora; at the moment she seemed relatively fit and strong for her age, despite her increased confusion. But that didn't stop Eve expecting the worst. If the care home's number came up on her mobile, a jolt of dread pulsed through her, and she answered tentatively, hoping a stranger's voice wasn't about to break bad news. She was being paranoid, of course she was. But although Flora seemed to be settling in at last, and accepting her new life, at the back of Eve's mind there was still the constant fear that her mother might somehow manage to carry out the threat she'd made on her first day at Three Elms, and do herself harm.

As she walked in through the main doors today, she was hit by a blast of noise. Two rows of children were lined up in the foyer, their excited chatter bouncing off the walls, strangely incongruous in this place that was usually so still and quiet. The children were possibly a year or two older than Daniel, both girls and boys, dressed in grey uniforms with scarlet blazers.

'Okay everyone, listen up!' called a man, walking past the disorderly rows. 'We're going to go quietly out of the door and down the steps. Keep to the right and hold your partner's hand.'

The man was wearing a tweed jacket over a pair of bright red trousers and he made Eve think of Jake, although she had no idea why – physically they were nothing like each other. Maybe it was their taste in clothing.

She'd been trying not to think about Jake over the last day or so. She cringed every time she remembered the hurt expression on his face when he'd invited her to The Comedy Box, the perfunctory wave as he wheeled his bike away. Had he been asking her out? She still couldn't decide, but longed to be able to wind back time and rerun those few minutes.

She would wipe the astonishment off her face, smile sweetly, thank him for thinking of her and come up with a believable excuse for not taking his second ticket. Poor Jake; he was such a lovely guy. The more she thought about it, the more she wondered why she hadn't just said yes. So what if it was a date? It would have been fun to do something different.

The children began to move forward and Eve stepped back and smiled at them as they went past.

Barbara and Flora weren't in the lounge, and she eventually found them in the library, sunk into a pair of deep armchairs, Flora sitting so far back that her toes weren't touching the carpet.

'I've read that one,' Barbara was saying. 'And that one.' She had a pile of books on her lap and, after looking at each one, she tossed it onto the floor beside her chair. 'This one is rubbish!' she said, holding it up and showing it to Nathan, who was picking up the books as fast as she discarded them. 'Worst thing I ever read. Stupid story.'

'Please don't throw them like that, Mrs Harrison,' begged the boy, his arms full of books. 'If you don't want to read them, leave them on the table and I'll put them back onto the shelves.'

'Why haven't you got anything decent in here?' Barbara said. 'I don't want to read the boring Brontës or yawny old Charles Dickens. Have you got any Jilly Cooper?'

'I don't think so,' said Nathan, looking confused. 'I don't know who that is.'

'You don't know who Jilly Cooper is?' Barbara was almost shouting now. 'What do they teach young people in school nowadays? Jilly Cooper should be in every library in the country. The woman's a genius! Her equestrian knowledge is phenomenal and she knows quite a lot about sex as well.'

'Oh goodness,' said Flora.

'I'll see if I can find some of her books for you,' said Nathan. 'But please stop throwing everything else around. You'll break the spines.'

'He's right,' said Flora. 'Books should be treasured, Barbara.' She looked up and saw Eve standing in the doorway. 'Hello darling. Have you got any Jilly Cooper books?'

'Um, I'm not sure,' said Eve.

'Doesn't just have to be Jilly,' said Barbara. 'Have you got Fifty Shades of Grey? I'm told it's very good indeed. Highly educational.'

'I'm certainly not getting you a copy of that,' muttered Nathan as he went to the shelves at the side of the room and started slotting books back onto them.

'I saw the children from St Barnabas just now,' said Eve. 'They must have been in here for the carol concert rehearsals?'

'Oh yes, they've been around all afternoon,' said Barbara. 'Irritating little sods. Most of them can't sing to save their lives, and they're so noisy! Even when they walk past the door they're chattering away like a bunch of monkeys.'

Eve moved across the room and perched on the arm of Flora's chair, leaning over to kiss her on the cheek. 'I bet their singing is wonderful,' she said. 'I can't wait to come to the concert. It's a great thing to be doing, linking Three Elms with the school. I hear you've been taking part in the rehearsals, Mum! I'm so pleased – you've got such a good voice, and you've always loved carols.'

'Oh no, dear,' said Flora, shaking her head. 'I'm not doing that. It's not my kind of thing at all. Barbara's right: they're too loud and naughty, those children.'

Barbara had discarded most of the books now and was tapping her palms on the arms of her chair. 'It's a social experiment,' she said. 'This carol concert business. What they're doing is gathering together the very young and the very old – the two groups that cause the most problems in society – then locking them all up and throwing away the key. It's the kind of thing you read about in the *Daily Mail* – I think they call it ethical cleansing.'

Flora rested her hand on her friend's arm and stroked it reassuringly. 'Don't worry, dear,' she said. 'I know where they keep all the keys, on that big board behind the reception desk. They won't be able to lock us up for long.'

Eve looked up and almost caught Nathan's eye as he put the last few books back onto the shelves. He grinned into the middle distance and raised one eyebrow.

'No one is going to lock you up,' said Eve. 'Listen Mum, I just wanted to let you know that the sale is completing tomorrow.'

'The sale of what?'

'Your flat?'

'Oh, jolly good.' Flora nodded, absently.

'It should all go through at midday and then the new couple are coming into the office to collect the keys from me.'

Flora's face fell and she looked at Eve in confusion. 'But what about all my things? My furniture? They can't have that. We need to go over there and get it all.'

'I've done that, Mum. I told you. I've sorted through everything and the furniture you didn't need has all been sold.'

Flora was shaking her head vigorously from side to side.

'We talked about this a few weeks ago,' said Eve, dread creeping into the pit of her stomach. 'You said you were happy for me to sell it all. There's no room for it here, and I can't fit in anything else at my house.'

'But I'll need to have it there when I go home!' said Flora. 'What will I sleep on if you've taken my bed away? What will I sit on to watch the telly if my sofa's gone? I've always loved that sofa: your father helped me choose it. Burgundy was his favourite colour.'

Eve knew full well that the sofa had post-dated her father: she'd helped Flora order it from Marks & Spencer about ten years ago.

'Mum, this is ridiculous,' she said, before she could stop herself. 'We've talked about this so many times, and I've kept you informed about all of it. Maybe you're just a bit tired this afternoon, so you've forgotten?'

Flora looked like she was on the point of tears now. *Damn it.* Eve knew this wasn't the way to deal with her anxiety. She tried to be patient, but got so frustrated with these increasingly frequent memory lapses. It was exhausting having to repeat herself time and time again, go over the same things whenever she came to visit Flora.

It should have made her feel better knowing she wasn't the

only one in this position, but it really didn't. The other day she had eavesdropped on a woman of about her own age, sitting in the communal lounge beside her elderly father: over the course of ten minutes, they'd had the same conversation time after time.

'Has my car gone? My old Audi?'

'Yes Dad, you sold it a long time ago.'

'The blue one – the blue Audi?'

'Yes Dad, you sold it to that man from Birmingham.'

'But I'd like my car back, Susie. That old Audi I used to have.'

'I know, Dad, but you can't have it back because you sold it years ago.'

'What, the blue one?'

'Yes Dad.'

'Has it gone then? My old Audi?'

Eve had caught the other woman's eye, briefly, and they had smiled at each other, both understanding the frustration and acknowledging the cruelty of this role reversal: middle-aged children having to take on the care of their own parents, whose minds were returning to a childlike state.

Now Flora's voice was rising. 'I don't want you to get rid of my sofa, Eve. I love that sofa. Why are you doing this to me?'

'It's fine, we'll sort it out,' said Eve quickly. 'I'll make sure everything is where you need it to be. Don't get upset.'

Flora's shoulders relaxed a little and she nodded at Eve, raising up one hand to run it down her daughter's cheek. 'Even my lovely burgundy sofa?' she asked.

Eve nodded, a lump in her throat: all this lying was so awful. 'Yes, even the sofa. Everything will be fine.'

'Thank you,' whispered Flora. 'Thank you for taking care of me, dear Eve. What would I do without you? I think I'd like a cup of tea now. Shall we go and find that girl with the trolley? It must be nearly teatime. Barbara, are you coming for a chocolate digestive?'

'Not just yet,' said Barbara, leaning down and picking up one of the books from the carpet. 'I've got some more reading to do.'

Eve helped Flora out of the chair and guided her towards the door, her hand in the small of her mother's back.

As they went past Nathan, he turned towards her. 'She joined in with the children from St Barnabas again, today,' he whispered. 'She sang her heart out.'

NINETEEN

E ve had completely forgotten about the shoebox. After bringing it back from Flora's flat all those weeks ago, she had taken it upstairs and slid it under her bed. She only found it again now because she'd knocked a tube of cream off the bedside table, and was down on her hands and knees, scrabbling around under the bed trying to find it. At this level she could see a thick layer of dust, along with a sock, some ear plugs and a blue biro which had leaked into the cream carpet: when was the last time she'd cleaned under here?

She pulled out the shoebox and brushed off the lid before opening it and seeing again the layers of cards and letters. There was probably nothing of value in here, but she felt she ought to go through it all before throwing it out. It was really too late to do this now: she'd been about to get into bed. But once she started, she couldn't stop. She sat back on her heels and flicked through a few Christmas cards, many so old that the white paper had turned sepia at the edges.

Further down were birthday cards, including one she'd made for her mother's fortieth birthday. She opened it and recognised her own teenage handwriting, with long sweeping tails on the G's and Y's and little hearts drawn over each I.

To the greatest mum in the whole wide world.
Happy 40th birthday and thank you for doing so much
for me. We're the best team! E xxxxx

There was a picture on the front: a pencil sketch of a horse galloping through countryside, its mane and tail flying backwards in the wind. She had no memory of drawing this picture, or of writing the message inside. What had Flora done to celebrate her milestone birthday? Maybe she'd gone out with friends or the two of them had done something together. Eve smiled at the strangely misshapen back legs of the horse: art had never been one of her strengths.

She did remember why she'd written that message though.

'You and me,' Flora used to say. 'We're a dream team.'

'The best team!' a young Eve would shout in response.

It had become a mantra, something they chanted at each other when they were celebrating: Eve's exam results, Flora's promotion at work, a fun holiday.

She put the birthday card to one side; maybe she'd keep it to show Daniel at some stage, hide it somewhere safe along with the cards he'd made for her over the years – she'd kept all of them, even the most recent one where she was smoking in a bikini and Ben was a dashing young George Clooney.

Now that she had taken out a great pile of cards, she could see the bundle of letters at the bottom of the shoebox, held together with an elastic band so old it snapped apart when she picked up the envelopes. Strangely, when she flicked through them, she realised none had been opened. They were all addressed to the same person: *Mr A. D. Baker* was written in her mother's neat handwriting, above an address in Brighton. Scrawled across the front of each envelope were the words: *Return to sender*.

The bedroom door burst open and Daniel tumbled into the room, nearly colliding with her as she sat on the floor.

'Mummy, there's a spider!' he yelled. 'A really big, huge spider in my bedroom! It's as big as my hand.'

By the time she'd tracked down the spider – it was the size of her thumbnail – and put it out of the back door, Daniel was insistent he couldn't sleep in his own bed that night. 'It's going to come back in the house and kill me!' he screamed.

Eventually she gave in, and settled him into the other side of her double bed, pulling the duvet up over his shoulders and watching as he fell asleep almost immediately, his thumb sliding slowly out of his mouth as his breathing softened.

She climbed in beside him and lifted up the bundle of letters. They were clearly written by Flora, but why had she carried on writing when previous letters had been sent back? She counted the envelopes: twenty-two in total. All addressed to the same man. All unopened. She looked at the postmarks on the front and realised the letters were in chronological order. The first one written more than forty-five years ago, the last sent four years after that.

This was none of her business.

She turned to look at Daniel and stroked his hair, feeling the warmth radiate from his sleeping body.

It was really none of her business.

As she slid her finger under the flap of the first envelope, the old paper crackled as it ripped. She pulled out the letter inside. It was written on thick quality notepaper, pale blue with a *Basildon Bond* watermark imprinted across the centre.

My dearest darling A, I have some news I need to share with you. I don't have a number, so I can't telephone you, but I'm hoping this will reach you, even if you're not staying in Lewes Close anymore.

Eve glanced back at the address on the front of the envelope, then carried on reading.

This summer has been so wonderful, and I've loved spending it with you. I feel so lonely now you're no longer here. I've got some news, and I don't really know how to break it to you. I know it will come as a shock, but I've found out I'm pregnant...

'Bloody hell!' said Eve. Beside her Daniel stirred and rolled towards her, and she sat for a couple of seconds, holding her breath, waiting to make sure he was still asleep before she carried on reading.

I know we thought we'd been careful, and I have no idea how it happened. I'm now six weeks and feeling pretty awful, sick for hours when I wake up every day. I've decided I'm going to have the baby, but I'm hoping you will want to be involved. I know this wasn't how we saw the future and I'm so sorry for the shock this will cause you. Dearest Alan, please get in touch and let me know when you can come back. We need to talk and decide what we're going to do. All my love, Flora x

Eve's heart was beating so fast she could hardly breathe. She read the words over and over.

'Alan,' she whispered out loud. 'Oh my God.'

Her father had been called Alan: Alan Derek Glover. She

looked at the front of the envelope again; it was definitely addressed to A. D. Baker – what the hell was this all about?

She read the letter again, and then a third time. There was a date at the top – just over seven months before she'd been born. So, Flora had been pregnant with her when she wrote this letter: she, Eve, had been an accident. How strange she'd never known that? Nowadays that wasn't a big deal – but it might have been frowned upon back then, in the seventies. From the way her mother talked, Eve had always presumed her parents had been happily married and settled when she was born. But this letter suggested they must have got married when Flora was pregnant. Or even afterwards?

She reached for the second envelope and ripped it open, unfolding another sheet of Basildon Bond and skimming through the words. Then she read them again, because they didn't make sense.

Dearest A, I can't bear it that I haven't heard from you. I don't want to ruin your life, or be a burden. I'm having this baby whatever happens. But I'm writing to you again because I think you have a right to know.

That letter was written three months after the first.
Eve tore open the third envelope, her head thumping.

Dearest Alan, four days ago I gave birth to a beautiful baby girl, our daughter. I'm calling her Evelyn – but she'll be known as Eve. She weighed 7lbs 5oz, and the labour took twelve hours – apparently that's quick! She's the most gorgeous thing I've ever seen. I can't tell if she looks like either of us yet. I was in hospital for two days and Eve and I are now back at home. Please call me or write to me. I need to know that you're getting these letters.

There was a photo tucked inside the envelope: a black and white shot of a newborn baby. It might have been her, but Eve hadn't seen it before and didn't recognise herself.

She tore open the other envelopes, one after the other, throwing them onto the carpet and skimming through each letter in turn. Over the next four years, Flora wrote to Alan every few months, telling him about Eve's christening, her first birthday, her first words. The letters were full of detail, about Flora's life and the baby, and the tone was always upbeat, although clearly she had received no reply to anything she had sent before.

Eve skim-read each one, greedy to find out what it contained, before going back to the start and rereading, hearing her mother's voice in her head, speaking the words she had written.

The last letter was dated September 1983 and, as she unfolded it, another photo fell out onto the duvet. It was a colour print of a little girl, standing outside a house, beaming into the camera. She was wearing an outsized school uniform, the skirt coming halfway down her calves, with a big satchel hanging from one shoulder. Eve had seen this picture before – or one very like it. She could almost remember the physical weight of that bag, and the smell of the new leather. She had been so excited to be starting school: Flora had bought her a fluffy pink pencil case and she had filled it with her Caran d'Ache pencils, the ones that came lined up in colour order in a long, flat tin with a picture of a snow-covered mountain on the front. Eve had wanted to take the tin with her on her first day at school, but it hadn't fitted into the satchel. She could still remember bringing the pink pencil case out of her bag and putting it onto the table in front of her in her new classroom, the thrill of it all so intense that she could hardly breathe.

I thought you'd like to see how beautiful our little girl looked today, on her first day at school. She was so excited about going, and I felt so proud of her. We got to the gates and she ran on ahead of me without looking back!

The ache in Eve's head had moved to the front now, a dull throbbing that stretched across her forehead, weighing down the skin above her eyes. Her mind was racing so fast she could hardly keep up. These letters were from Flora to her father, Alan – Baker or Glover or whatever his name was. But none of them had even been opened. Had he never received them? Or had he recognised Flora's handwriting and returned them unopened?

Either way, Flora had carried on writing, for more than four years, to the man who got her pregnant. Despite getting no response, she had updated him about Eve, told him what his daughter was doing, how she was growing up. She had sent photos and without fail – voicing no resentment or anger – had signed each one of her letters, *All my love, Flora x.*

As she lay back against the pillow, Eve realised her forearm was damp. Looking down, she saw smudges across the ink on the top sheet of paper, and became aware that tears were streaming down her cheeks, dripping onto the pile of letters which had been written with so much hope and love, but had never been read.

TWENTY

'This can't carry on. These aren't one-off incidents, they are turning into a pattern of behaviour.'

Eve glared at Mrs Russell. Clearly there was a problem: but this horrible woman was making it sound as if it was all her fault.

'If Daniel can't control his temper and treat his fellow pupils with respect, then we will have to consider our options. Both myself and the head have spoken to him on several occasions, but he is always unwilling to explain his behaviour.'

'But he hasn't got a temper!' said Eve. 'I'm not trying to be difficult, Mrs Russell, and I'm sorry there have been problems. But I don't know what to say to you, because the boy you're describing here isn't the boy I see at home. He's very easy-going and loving. He can be high-spirited, but he isn't a bully, and he isn't deliberately naughty.'

Mrs Russell pursed her lips and tapped her pen on her notepad. 'I'm sure you believe that to be the case, Mrs Mackay, but that isn't what we're seeing here at school.'

'It's Glover,' snapped Eve. 'My surname is Glover.'

Mrs Russell carried on as if she hadn't heard. 'Most of his

anger seems to be directed at one boy in particular, Liam Boxall. I have also spoken to Liam's parents but, to be honest, he isn't the one initiating the fighting. The Boxalls are upset that their son is being targeted, which is understandable because, from what I have seen, it is all coming from Daniel.'

The wall behind the teacher's head was covered in large cut-out snowflakes, a child's name written across the centre of each one. Some of the shapes were much neater than others, and Eve couldn't help glancing up at them, searching for Daniel's name. There were a couple of neat, more sophisticated snowflakes at the far end of the wall, towards the door: Eve screwed up her eyes, trying to read the names, hoping that Daniel's would be one of the more impressive ones.

Mrs Russell sat back in her chair and slotted the lid onto the end of her pen. She was clearly waiting for Eve to say something.

'Listen, I'm sorry that he's been involved in these incidents, as you call them, and I'll definitely talk to him about it. But I'm just very confused by what you're telling me.' Eve tried to control the anger in her voice, the impatience. She wanted to storm out, slamming the classroom door behind her. This was all so unfair: there was no way Daniel was the nasty little bully his teacher was describing.

She was also furious that she was here alone, taking the flak. Yet again. Ben should be sitting beside her in the classroom, listening to these accusations and complaints, offering some support. When she got the call from the school, earlier this afternoon, Eve had texted to ask if he'd go with her: *This is something we need to deal with together, Ben.* But she hadn't been surprised when his reply pinged in: he had meetings all day with an important client, no one could cover for him, and wasn't it rather short notice? The inference was that he was far too busy and important to have to deal with something like this, which was infuriating considering Eve had already told him there were problems at school, so this was clearly serious. Daniel should be his priority as well as hers. Yes, he worked full time, but she wasn't exactly sitting around on her backside baking cupcakes and crocheting blankets for kittens.

'I wonder if it might be beneficial to send Daniel to see someone?' Mrs Russell was saying.

'What sort of someone?'

'A child psychologist, perhaps. With experience in dealing with children with these sorts of behavioural issues.'

'What?' Eve couldn't believe what she was hearing.

'The school has access to psychologists who work with the local authority, and who might be able to...'

Eve stood up, the child-sized chair scraping across the floor before falling over behind her. 'I don't think that's necessary,' she said. 'I will speak to Daniel, and to his father, but I can't see that we need to go down that route.'

A psychologist! Incensed, Eve swung open the door and marched out of the classroom and back down the hallway. Her son didn't need to see a shrink. The bloody cheek of the woman.

Daniel was waiting for her in the reception area by the school office. His head was bent over her phone, and he was playing a game, the tinny pings echoing around the confined space. When Eve came through the door, the school secretary glanced up from behind the sliding glass window, then looked pointedly across at Daniel.

'We don't allow phones or iPads on the school premises,' she said.

'I know, sorry,' said Eve. 'But he's only been here five minutes.'

'Rules are there for the general well-being of everyone and they can't be ignored,' said the woman, shuffling some papers into a neat pile in front of her. 'If parents allow their children to flout them, it sets a bad example to the other pupils.'

'Well, school has finished for the day,' said Eve as she grabbed Daniel by the hand and led him towards the door. 'So, there aren't any other pupils around to be led astray, are there?'

The secretary glared at her as she buzzed them out through the door, and Eve glared back. *He's not exactly corrupting anybody*, she wanted to say. *He's just sitting, waiting patiently, while his mother gets a dressing down from his teacher and is made to feel like the worst parent in the world.*

They walked through the empty playground and she pulled her boy towards her, leaning down to kiss his tousled hair, which smelt of school dinners and stuffy cloakrooms. God, the small-mindedness of officialdom; it made her want to scream.

'Listen sweetheart,' she said, as they drove home, 'Mrs Russell says you're still not very happy at school.'

Daniel's face was turned away from her, as he stared out of the side window; he shrugged.

'Is it just that you don't like some of the other children? Or is it the work?'

Silence.

'We need to talk about this, because I can't help you if I don't know what's wrong?'

The boy didn't respond and she couldn't see the expression on his face.

'Daniel, are you listening to me? It isn't good when I get called into school to talk to your teacher like this, and Mrs Russell isn't happy about your behaviour. I need to understand what's going on, so we can work out what to do about it?'

He crossed his arms in front of his chest and jutted out his chin, still staring out at the houses and crowded pavements as the car crawled past them.

Eve tried again. 'Whatever's going on, we can do something

about it. You, me and Daddy. But you have to talk to us, so we can decide how we deal with it.'

Still nothing.

Eve sighed and they drove the rest of the way without speaking.

Maybe this conversation would be better coming from Ben? Daniel might feel he could tell his father what was worrying him, or explain the incidents with Liam Boxall. But the trouble was, if Ben couldn't spare the time to go to the school, he would end up talking to Daniel at home. His home; with Lou listening in. Maybe Lou would be sitting there beside him, reaching out to take Daniel's hand as they brought the subject up. Maybe she would even be the one to mention it? *Daddy says you're not happy at school, Daniel. Do you want to talk about it?*

The possibility of Lou getting answers from her son that Eve couldn't squeeze out of him herself, was almost too much to bear. As they pulled up outside the house, she tried again. 'You know you can tell me if something's bothering you? It's not always easy being with other people and fitting in. But if something's making you really unhappy while you're at school, please tell me what it is and maybe I can help?'

Daniel shook his head vigorously from side to side.

'Is it to do with this other boy, Liam? You haven't mentioned him before. Have the two of you had a fight about something?'

Daniel turned and glared at her. 'Shut up!' he yelled as he tugged on the handle of the door and pushed it open. 'Just go away and leave me alone. I hate you!'

As he tumbled out of the car and ran up the path, pushing through the side gate into the garden, Eve stared after him, open-mouthed. He had never spoken to her like that before; her heart was racing and she tried not to cry. She sat, wondering what to do. This was so unlike Daniel; what on earth was going on inside that little head?

After a few seconds, she got out of the car and followed him through the gate. He was sitting with his back to her on the edge of the patio outside the kitchen window and didn't hear her approaching. He'd taken his teddy out of his bag and had it balanced on his knee, holding it tightly by the arms. Eve stood beside the corner of the house.

'It will happen very soon,' she heard him say to the teddy. 'Daddy says maybe after Christmas. And when we live with Daddy and Lou, everything will be better. We won't have to go to that school anymore. We'll go to another one and Daddy says I'll have new friends and they'll like me and they'll all want to play with me.'

TWENTY-ONE

Squinting through the gap in the sitting-room door, Eve could just see the back of Daniel's hair. She'd given him some Smarties and every now and then his head dipped as he shook the tube and emptied a few more onto the carpet in front of him. It was a game he always played with Smarties: he would eat all the yellow ones first, then the orange, then the green, putting the rest back in the tube each time and shaking them up before rolling them out again like multicoloured dice and picking the ones he wanted.

The programme changed on the television and Daniel began to sing along with the theme tune. Eve leant against the doorframe and closed her eyes. There was too much inside her head; too many thoughts and questions pushing and shoving against each other, desperate to burst out. How could her son be so unhappy? How had she let this precious boy become so miserable without even noticing there was a problem?

Bad mother, screamed a voice inside her head. *Bad, selfish, neglectful mother. This is all your fault, Eve.*

She pushed open the door and went into the sitting room,

perching on the edge of the sofa behind Daniel and putting out her arms to pull him towards her into a hug.

'It's *Andy's Safari Adventures!*' he said, twisting round to look at her. 'I *love* this one. I've seen it before – they've got zebras. Can we get a puppy soon, Mummy? Like the one I put on your birthday card?'

She smiled and ran her fingers through his hair to tame the fringe that was getting too long. He'd always had such lovely thick hair, like Ben.

'But what will happen if you go away with Daddy?' she said. 'If you're not living here, what will I do with a dog?'

Why was she even having this conversation? They wouldn't be getting a dog whether Daniel stayed with her or went to live with Ben, so she wasn't being fair. But she could feel herself clutching at straws: maybe Daniel would go off the idea of moving away if she promised him a puppy? He was bound to have talked to Ben and Lou like this as well; they might even have said he could get a pet if he moved with them to Glasgow.

'You could bring it up to see us?' he said. 'Or if we get it soon, I could take it with me? Daddy says we might go after Christmas.'

She smiled, to stop her bottom lip trembling. But he had turned away from her again, his eyes back on the colourful images on the screen in the corner of the room. She rested her chin against the top of his head, glad he would never know how much those words had hurt her.

He hadn't noticed her earlier, standing at the corner of the house, watching him talk to his teddy. Half a minute later, he had tossed the toy down onto the patio beside his rucksack, and ran to the end of the garden, throwing himself belly first onto the plastic swing, pushing away from the ground and lifting his legs high as he swung backwards and forwards, looking as if he was flying through the air.

Eve had watched him on the swing for a few seconds and then had gone back round to the front of the house to unlock the door, his words still ringing in her ears.

She had known Ben and Lou would have mentioned the move to Daniel – of course she had. But although she'd been thinking about little else, she herself hadn't spoken to him about it. That would have been the sensible thing to do, the grown-up thing to do. But that would also have made it real and, in her mind, she had been fighting against this whole scenario, persuading herself it wasn't going to happen so it was all right to stick her head in the sand and ignore what was going on. But now the cold realities were pushing themselves into her brain from every angle. Not only did Ben want their son to move away with him, but it seemed as if Daniel wanted to go too. He wanted to leave everything he was familiar with – his home, his friends, his school – and make a new start hundreds of miles away. Not only that, but he wanted to leave her.

She had watched him on the swing as she filled the kettle. By that time he was sitting on the plastic seat and pushing himself round and round so the blue ropes knotted themselves together. Then, when the twist of blue was tight above the top of his head, he lifted his feet off the ground and threw his head back as the swing rewound the other way, spinning him so fast that the hood of his coat flew out behind him.

There had been a swing very like this one, with a red plastic seat, in the garden of the house they'd moved to when Eve was eight years old. She remembered sitting on it for hours, twisting and pushing herself away from the ground like Daniel was doing now. She would stand up on the seat and grab the ropes tightly, lifting herself up and trying to somersault in the air, like they did in gym sessions at school. Flora was always terrified she would fall, and Eve remembered her running out from the house, 'Evelyn Glover! Get off that swing right now!'

Her heart jolted as she thought about her mother, as it had done ever since she'd read those letters the other night. Was she really Evelyn Glover? Might she have been Evelyn Baker if things had turned out differently? She still couldn't take it all in, and she certainly couldn't think about it at the moment. There was too much else jostling for space in her head.

They had now been home for half an hour and sitting here, in front of the television, Daniel seemed fine. His normal self. It was as if their row in the car and his angry comments to his teddy, had never happened. When he came in from the garden earlier, he'd pushed open the back door and bounded across the kitchen, demanding Smarties and a drink, throwing himself into her arms for a hug. She envied him the ability to forget his worries so swiftly.

On the television, the presenter was describing how snakes shed their skins, running his hands along the smooth scales of a brown and black python that had draped itself around his neck.

'Wow!' breathed Daniel. 'Look, Mummy!'

It clearly wasn't just the prospect of living with Ben and Lou that was appealing to him – it was also the fact that a new life with them would mean he could get away from whatever was upsetting him at school.

The trouble was, without knowing what that was, she could do nothing about it. The voice inside her – the one that was refusing to face up to reality – started again: even if she couldn't get to the bottom of what was going on, maybe he could change schools? It wouldn't be easy: she knew, from listening to other parents talk outside the gates, that all the good local primaries were heavily oversubscribed. But she must try. She would get online tonight, once he was in bed, and do some research.

She kissed the top of his head, briefly buoyed by the thought that she might be able to do something about all this. But she knew she was kidding herself. Whether Daniel went to his current school, or another one a mile down the road, it wouldn't change the fact that Ben was leaving and wanted to take their son with him.

TWENTY-TWO

It took a while, but eventually she found it, tucked into the back of an old manila folder she'd brought away from the flat when she cleared out Flora's personal possessions. There had been half a dozen of these folders piled up in the wardrobe in the back bedroom of the flat, and Eve had sat on the carpet there and looked through the first two, finding they contained bank statements, insurance forms, NHS records and various other official records of Flora's life. Many of the documents were faded and illegible, most were out of date, and all of it could probably be thrown away. Presuming that the rest of the folders contained a similar mix of irrelevant records, Eve had piled them up and taken them home to sort through at a later date.

Now the piece of paper lay in front of her on the kitchen table and she ran her palms across it, flattening it out, pressing down on the creases that had been there for years. She had studied it so intently over the last ten minutes, that the faded black ink and words felt familiar, even though she had never set eyes on her birth certificate before this evening.

Her full name was at the top – *Evelyn Mary Glover* – along

with her date of birth and the name of the hospital where she'd been born. Under the section titled *Mother*, was Flora's name, followed by her place of birth and her address. But the section for *Father* was blank.

Eve kept looking at it, wondering how Flora had felt when she registered her baby's birth. Was she embarrassed at having to leave this empty space on the form? Was the lack of a husband and father for her child made all the more painful, by having it recorded and publicly witnessed?

Eve's mobile rang and Gav's name lit up on the screen. She couldn't face speaking to him now, so ignored the call. But he was a persistent bugger: when the phone rang for the third time, she gave in and picked it up.

'Hey doll, no need to snap my head off,' shouted Gav. 'Just wanted to let you know that the meeting with Gleesons has been moved forward tomorrow – they'll be in at 8.30. See you then!'

He rang off and she swore at the handset. Gav knew she couldn't make it into the office that early – even if she threw Daniel through the school gates as soon as the caretaker unlocked them, distance and traffic meant she'd be doing well to get to her desk by 8.45am.

She put the phone down again and looked at her birth certificate. Why had she never seen this before? Probably because there had been no need. Flora had applied for a passport on her behalf when Eve was fifteen, before the two of them went on their first foreign holiday to France. From then on, her passport was the only official proof of identity Eve had ever needed when she applied for a driving licence, opened bank accounts and submitted job applications. She and Ben had never married, and she hadn't needed to produce her own certificate when she registered Daniel's birth. So, this creased, faded piece of paper had stayed hidden away for forty-five years – which was probably just as Flora had intended.

Eve went upstairs and poked her head around the door of Daniel's bedroom, listening to the regular rise and fall of his breath. It would be so good to get these problems at school ironed out. She'd left a voicemail yesterday for Ben, but was still waiting to hear back from him. She probably should have said what it was about, but was it really too much to expect him to communicate with her and return her calls? All she wanted was someone to help share this load, to agree with her that Daniel was a normal little boy and his miserable old bat of a teacher was blowing the whole thing out of proportion.

She went back downstairs and poured herself a glass of wine, then sat at the kitchen table studying the birth certificate again. There was a hollowness inside her chest and a deep fatigue that seemed to be affecting every muscle in her body. She wanted to crawl up to her bed, pull the covers over her head and stay there – well away from all of this. Not just the worry about Daniel, but the mystery about her father. For a day or so after reading her mother's letters to Alan, she'd felt shocked – unable to process this new information that so dramatically affected her. She was the same person she'd been in the days, hours and minutes leading up to that night when she sat in bed surrounded by discarded envelopes, but she also felt entirely different. How could anything be the same now? How could *she* be the same?

But after a while, even this extraordinary discovery began to feel less strange. It was a bit like bereavement, she realised: the initial horror and shock gradually lessened but, as acceptance took their place, a whole new gamut of emotions needed to be addressed. Thinking back to the words her mother had written, she began to feel overwhelmed by the predicament of a young woman who had been left on her own to deal with pregnancy, childbirth and parenthood. What an awful burden for her mother to have carried, all by herself. Eve knew how hard single motherhood could be, and Flora had been forced into a situation where she went through it too.

There was anger stirring inside her now as well. Whoever Alan Baker was, or had been, he didn't fit the image Flora had created of her father. That man had been six feet tall with dark brown hair. His birthday was on 4th March and he'd grown up in London and worked for the civil service. He liked cricket and rugby. He didn't smoke. He loved the theatre and the first film he'd taken Flora to see had been *Mad Max*. He was a good card player and his favourite band was The Rolling Stones. The meal he always ordered when they ate out was roast beef; his favourite colour was blue; he was a dreadful dancer. He drove a dark green Rover; he wore size ten shoes.

These were just some of the things her mother had told her about the man she didn't remember. Was any of it true? Maybe all those characteristics and traits also applied to Alan Derek Baker – or had done during the brief summer when he and Flora had been together. But however perfect he sounded on paper, the man her mother had fallen in love with – who then got her pregnant – didn't have the decency to answer any of her letters or offer to support her while she carried his child.

As a result, it seemed that – in his absence – Flora had created a picture of the perfect husband and father. She turned Alan Derek Baker into Alan Derek Glover. That was clever, Eve realised: it meant Flora didn't have to change her surname; she was already Flora Glover, so she just told everyone she was a Mrs instead of a Miss. She then created a character who had adored them both, but had been tragically taken away from his loving family too early, dying in a car crash when Eve was eighteen months old.

At least that part of the story was total rubbish: Flora

obviously had no idea what had happened to her lover, but had invented an accident because it was a neat, tidy ending – as well as vaguely glamorous. Plenty of famous people had met their end in a similar way – James Dean, Grace Kelly, Princess Diana... well okay, not plenty, only a handful really that Eve could think of. But it was still a more interesting way to kill off an imaginary husband, than a heart attack.

Over the years Flora had told her so many snippets and stories: places she and Alan had visited together, jokes they'd shared, things Alan had done with baby Eve. According to Flora, he had sung to her, danced with her, read to her at night. He had dabbed bubbles on her nose to make her laugh in the bath, he had chosen and bought her very first pair of shiny black shoes with silver buckles. He had pushed her around the park on a little tricycle with a long handle at the back.

Flora once told her that the three of them had been away for a long weekend in the Gower, a few weeks before the accident that took his life. They'd stayed in a hotel in The Mumbles, and sat on the beach nursing newspaper parcels of fish and chips. Flora had told Eve she'd only been walking for a few months so was still unsteady on her feet, staggering across the sand, picking up shells and bringing them back to show her parents. Alan had teased her with chips: holding out one at a time, a dab of ketchup on its tip.

Obviously, none of that was true. The man hadn't even been around.

Eve folded up the birth certificate and slid it inside the brown envelope. She didn't need it, so for now it could go back where she'd found it in Flora's manila folder. At some stage she might put it in her desk in the corner of the sitting room, beside Daniel's birth certificate. But for now, the mere sight of it was too painful. She wanted it to be hidden away, so there was no chance of her coming across it again by accident.

She went next door and collapsed onto the sofa with her glass of wine. There was a property programme on the television: a couple had been persuaded to spend thousands on upgrading their existing house, rather than move.

'It's amazing!' the woman was saying, as she walked around her new kitchen. 'I never imagined I'd live in a house like this!'

The place was a sea of vast plate glass windows, smooth speckled granite, self-closing drawers and cupboards with no handles. It reminded Eve of the apartment overlooking the Suspension Bridge.

She couldn't concentrate, and went across to the desk in the corner of the room and took out Daniel's birth certificate, rereading the familiar details. She could vividly remember everything about the day she and Ben had gone to register his birth. She'd been looking forward to it, because it felt like an important occasion, one which marked the official start of this young life. They'd booked an appointment for midday and were intending to go out to lunch somewhere afterwards. She had imagined them sitting in a little bistro, treating themselves to champagne, clinking glasses across the table as their tiny son dozed in his car seat beside the table.

But Daniel had been fractious and whiny all morning, and by the time they left the register office he was howling so plaintively that her breasts were leaking milk in sympathy. It was pouring with rain so they sat in the car while she fed him, then they got soaked walking to the restaurant, where the smell of fried food turned her stomach and made them both short-tempered and snappy. It had been one of those days which should have been so wonderful but which, yet again, went wrong and ended with her and Ben driving home in resentful silence.

But even if his parents weren't still together, at least Daniel would grow up knowing and seeing both of them, and being reassured they loved him and that his life wasn't based on a series of stories fabricated by his mother. That was what was hurting Eve most of all, right now: the fact that everything she had grown up believing, everything her mother had ever told her about the father she'd never met, had turned out to be a lie.

TWENTY-THREE

The day started badly: by the time Eve rushed into the office, Gav was shaking hands with the man from Gleesons and showing him out of the door.

'Sorry!' panted Eve. 'Dreadful traffic.'

Gav tutted, turned his back and walked away, going into his office and slamming the door behind him. She felt like running after him and kicking it open again, reminding him that her contracted hours were 9am to 3pm. But there was no point: Gav didn't have children or a partner, or even a cat to worry about. He was never late to work because the only things he had to sort out every morning were himself, his lacquered hair and his extremely shiny suit.

Half an hour later, things brightened up considerably.

'Eve,' growled a voice on the other end of the phone. 'It's Mike Sewell. Now listen, that penthouse of yours in Clifton. I wasn't keen myself, but we haven't seen anything else that's better and my Steph has fallen in love with the view. We'd like to make an offer.'

Eve had never expected to hear from the Sewells again. After she'd squeezed through the window of the utility room of the luxurious apartment and landed heavily on the floor, she had looked up to see the couple standing side by side in the doorway, staring at her with as much horror as if she had just stripped naked and danced on the fancy sun loungers overlooking the Avon Gorge. They had left shortly afterwards, without a backwards glance.

Now, she bent over her desk and clenched her fist in delight as she tried to keep the excitement out of her voice. His offer was a decent one, but Eve suspected he could afford more.

'The thing is, Mr Sewell, it's great to hear you like that apartment, but I've got another couple who are interested in it. I mean *very* interested. I'm expecting a call from them later today and – between you and me – I know their starting offer will be higher.'

It wasn't exactly a lie: she had shown the flat to someone else the week before. She hadn't heard from him yet, but that didn't mean she wasn't going to. Mike Sewell caved immediately, as she'd hoped he would, and upped his offer another £50,000 to just below the asking price.

'I'll do my very best,' Eve told him. 'No promises. But I'll see if I can get that lovely place for you and Steph.' As soon as he was off the phone, Eve phoned the owner of the Clifton apartment to pass on the good news.

'Hey, guess what? I've sold 47a Sion Hill!' she called out, standing up from her desk and doing a victory dance around the centre of the office. Caroline cheered and started applauding. The door to Gav's office was now open again, but he was on the phone and just waved at her dismissively before turning away. Eve knew he'd be pissed off: this would be excellent commission, which was a relief – the latest bill from Three Elms was sitting on the worktop at home, waiting to be paid. The money from the sale of the flat would be in Flora's bank account shortly but, in the meantime, Eve was robbing Peter to pay Paul and, having subsidised the care home fees for the last couple of months, her small savings pot was nearly empty.

At lunchtime she went out to get a sandwich, still bubbling with excitement at the sale, enjoying the sharp clack of her heels as she strode down to the café on the corner. Just inside the door, she stood behind an elderly man who was bent over a rollator, which he shoved forward as the queue moved, taking shuffling steps behind it. Maybe this is what Alan looks like now, she suddenly thought. Flora had been thirty-two when she got pregnant, and she'd always told Eve her father had been a similar age. But what if that wasn't true and the real Alan had been a few years older than her? If so, he might not even be alive now.

Eve had still done nothing about this mystery man. Part of her yearned to trace him – not just to find out what he was like, but also to ask him why he'd treated her mother so badly. The problem was, of course, that if he'd ignored Flora's attempts to get in touch with him, he clearly hadn't wanted any contact with her or her child. So, there was nothing to suggest he'd be pleased to hear from either of them again now. He would also probably have had a family of his own in the intervening years. So, Eve might have half-brothers and sisters? But the more she thought about it, the more certain she was that Alan must already have been married when he met Flora that summer. Why else would he suddenly disappear from her life, and not be known at the address he'd given her in Brighton?

But, she kept reminding herself, if he had no longer been living in Lewes Close, maybe he had never known she'd written the letters – in which case someone else had scrawled *Return to sender* across the top of each envelope. He might have moved away for work, or had some sort of family crisis. In that case, surely he had a right to know – even after all these years – that he had a daughter?

She veered backwards and forwards: one minute determined to try and track down Alan Derek Baker, the next convinced it would be pointless and only cause herself – and everyone else – unnecessary stress and potential upset.

Even if she did go ahead, it was a daunting task: one evening she had typed his name into Google, watching as the search engine produced 24,175,644 results in 0.23 seconds. A quick look through the first two pages made it depressingly obvious that she would have to know an awful lot more to narrow down the search.

She had also typed the address on the envelopes into Google Maps; when the location came up, she'd zoomed in, as if looking at it more closely would throw up some clues about the sort of people who lived there. When she changed to street view, she saw there was a mixture of housing on the road – some modern blocks to one side, larger detached houses on the other, set back behind small neat front gardens. Had her father been in one of these houses? Was this where he'd lived with an entirely different family?

But all the online research was pointless, because it felt like Alan Derek Baker was a needle in a very large haystack. She had to speak to Flora: her mother was the only person who could throw some light onto any of this. Eve might be opening a can of worms, but she wasn't going to get anywhere unless she tried. *Just don't get angry,* she told herself. *Whatever you find out, stay calm and be understanding.*

She mustn't make Flora feel guilty either. She just needed to know more about what had happened: how her mother had felt when Alan didn't make contact, how she'd coped with the silence – and why she'd hidden the truth from her daughter and lied to her for all these years.

After work she drove to Three Elms and, picking up the bundle of letters from the passenger seat, went in search of

Flora. Today, Barbara was nowhere to be seen, and her mother was sitting in the chair in her own room, watching an auction programme on the small TV in the corner. She took her eyes off the screen briefly when Eve came in.

'Hello darling. This man is about to find out that he's bought a house but all the wooden floors are rotten!'

'Oh, that's not good.' Eve sat down on the bed. 'Didn't he have a survey done when he bought it?'

Flora looked at her in confusion. 'I don't know what that is. He's a bit stupid though, because the voice has been telling him there's a problem with the floorboards since he moved in.'

'The voice?'

'You know, the voice that comes out of the television to tell us what's happening.'

'The presenter, you mean?'

Flora shrugged. 'This silly man should have been paying attention. It's his own fault really.'

Eve sat watching the screen for a couple of minutes, unable to feel much sympathy for the property developer whose dry rot might bankrupt him. She had the bundle of letters in her lap, and realised there were butterflies churning in the pit of her stomach. Was there a right way to bring this up?

'Mum, there's something I need to talk to you about,' she said, eventually. 'When I was clearing out the flat, I found some letters, and I wanted to ask you about them.'

Flora turned to her, frowning.

'There are lots of them,' said Eve, holding out the top envelope. 'They hadn't been opened, but I took a look inside and read them. I'm sorry, I know they weren't my letters to read.' God, this did sound awful: she'd opened her mother's private letters and read them and was now expecting Flora to not mind.

'I was being nosy, I'm so sorry. I know they weren't mine to look at, but I'm glad I read them, and I want you to know that I'm really sorry for everything you went through, when I was a baby.'

Flora had turned back at the screen, chuckling as the property owner stamped on his floorboards, his foot smashing through the wood with a crash. 'Oh, dear me!' she said. 'Well, that serves him right for not listening to the voice.'

Eve reached out and touched Flora's arm to get her attention. 'Mum, will you look at these?' She unfolded one of the letters and put it into Flora's hand. 'Just take a look, please?'

Flora squinted at the piece of paper and shook her head, tutting. 'I don't know what this is about, Eve. It's not addressed to me.'

'No, Mum. You wrote it. Don't you recognise your own writing?'

Flora moved the letter closer to her eyes, then shook her head and held it out towards Eve. 'You're wrong, this is nothing to do with me. I'm not sure why you brought it here.'

Eve pushed the letter back towards her. 'Look again, Mum. It's your handwriting. This was a letter you wrote years ago, when you found you were pregnant. This is the first of the letters you wrote to Alan, my father.'

Flora's head snapped up and she stared at Eve, her eyes wide. 'I only ever wanted to do what was best for you!' she said. 'That was all that mattered.'

'Of course you did,' said Eve. 'You've always done what's best for me.'

'I had to look after you. I had to make sure you were happy.' Tears had welled up in Flora's eyes, and her lips were quivering. The colour had drained out of her cheeks and she looked as shocked as if someone had smacked her across the face.

'I know that. You did such a good job of bringing me up on your own. You were so strong and brave.'

'None of it was your fault, you were just a baby!' Flora's voice was rising. 'I just wanted to protect you, make everything all right for you.'

'Mum, I know that,' said Eve, leaning forward to put her hand on her mother's arm. 'But I just wondered if you'd remember sending these letters? There are more than twenty of them and they were...'

'Stop it!' shouted Flora, suddenly. 'Stop talking about this!' She threw the letter onto the floor and clamped her hands over her ears. 'I don't want to hear any more! Don't say anything else!'

Eve put the rest of the envelopes onto the bed and knelt down beside Flora's chair. 'Don't cry. I'm so sorry, I didn't mean to upset you.'

'Stop it!' screamed Flora. 'No more!'

'Mum, please. I'm sorry.' Eve put her hand back on Flora's arm but the old lady pushed her away and began battering at her with her fists.

'Get away from me!'

Nathan appeared in the doorway. 'What's the problem, Mrs Glover?'

Flora had picked up the framed photo on her bedside table and now threw it at Eve. It hit her foot and when she bent down to pick it up, she saw there was a small crack in the bottom corner of the glass.

Flora fell back in her chair and put her hands up to cover her ears again, starting to rock backwards and forwards, sobbing.

'She got upset, all of a sudden,' said Eve. 'It's my fault, I'm sorry, Nathan. I showed her some old letters, but I only wanted to ask her about them – I didn't expect her to react like this.'

Flora was moaning now, low wails of pain that cut through Eve's skull. Her own hands were shaking as she held them out towards her mother.

Nathan moved across and knelt down on the other side of the chair, putting his arm around Flora and hugging her to his chest, making soothing noises as if he was calming a baby. 'Hey now,' he said. 'What's all this about?'

Flora was gasping for breath and looked up at him, panic scrawled across her face. 'I don't know what she wants,' she whimpered.

'You'll be fine, Mrs Glover,' he said. 'Take some nice, deep breaths for me. That's right. You're quite safe here, with us.'

He looked back towards Eve. 'What could have upset her like this? She's normally such a calm lady. That's good, Mrs Glover, keep breathing in and out, I've got you.'

'I showed her these,' said Eve, pointing to the envelopes on the bed. 'They're some old letters she wrote years ago. I didn't know they were going to upset her so much.'

Flora's sobs were softening, although her hands were still shaking. She put them on Nathan's arm, as if clinging onto him for support. 'No more,' she whispered. 'No more.'

'I tell you what,' said Nathan. 'Why don't you take all those away for the time being? There's obviously something there she doesn't want to talk about, so let's not force it. Come on, Mrs Glover, I'm going to help you get onto the bed and you can have a lie-down. Your daughter will come back and see you another day.'

Eve scrabbled the envelopes into a messy pile and got up, backing away as Nathan helped Flora up from the chair and gently guided her towards the bed.

'That's it, just hop up here,' the boy was saying. He eased off Flora's slippers and lifted her legs up onto the bed.

'Mum?' said Eve.

Flora was lying quite still and had closed her eyes, her chest rising and falling unevenly as her sobs subsided.

'She'll be fine,' said Nathan. 'But I think you ought to go now. Maybe you can come back tomorrow?'

Eve nodded. She moved to the door and turned back to look at them. Nathan had pulled the chair up to the side of the bed and was sitting on it, leaning forward and gently stroking Flora's forehead with one hand, holding her quivering fingers with his other.

'I'm sorry,' Eve whispered, so softly that neither of them heard.

She walked slowly down the corridor, realising she was still holding the photo frame as well as the letters, but not wanting to go back. It was awful, but part of her didn't mind being sent away: thank God Nathan had arrived and taken over. She had never seen Flora so hysterical; it had been terrifying. If she'd known she would react like this, she would never have brought the letters. Or she would at least have worked out another way to bring up the subject. She'd been so thoughtless. Mind you, what other way could she have tackled this? Flora had been fine until Eve tried to make her mother remember something that was clearly so disturbing that she'd filed it away at the back of her mind.

When she got home, her hands were still shaking, her head thumping. She couldn't get her mother's face out of her mind: her mouth twisted into a scream, her cheeks hollowed by the trauma.

Daniel was at Robbie's for tea and, by the time Juliet dropped him back, Eve had opened a bottle of wine and was on her second glass. She was furious with herself – she was a bloody appalling daughter.

TWENTY-FOUR

There was something wrong with her eyes: they felt sticky, as if her eyelids were glued together. When she did manage to open them, blinking rapidly, everything was blurry and cloudy at the edges, like she was looking at the bedroom through the bottom of a milk bottle.

An insistent beep was coming from nearby, but Eve couldn't work out where. Her hand scrabbled around under the duvet and knocked against something hard: the edge of her phone. She brought it to her face, realising her alarm was going off, but not sure how to stop it. As she stabbed at the screen with her thumb, the door burst open and light flooded into the room from the landing.

'Mummy! I haven't got any pants in my drawer – where are all the pants? Where are they? Where are the PANTS?'

Daniel threw himself on top of her, and she knew with sudden, horrifying clarity, that she was going to be sick. She pushed him away and staggered into the en suite, colliding with the doorframe so hard that, even through the fog of a hangover, she knew she would later have a purple, flowering bruise on her shoulder. As she knelt over the toilet bowl, Daniel was still bellowing at her from the bedroom.

'No pants! No pants! No pants!'

When the retching came to an end, she wiped her mouth with loo roll and leant back against the wall; there were prickles of sweat breaking out on her forehead and her heart was beating so fast, she was short of breath. Shit, what had she done?

'I want breakfast!'

'Go and get some,' she called out, her voice too loud in her own head. 'I'll be down in a moment.'

But she couldn't move. Her stomach was churning and the room was on a slant: the walls tipping up and down at either end. It reminded her of a fairground ride she'd been on, years ago when she first met Ben. They'd stood around the inside edges of a big empty barrel which began spinning until it was going so fast that, when the floor dropped away, centrifugal force kept them pressed against the sides. She'd screamed so loudly she thought she might burst her own eardrums. It was a mistake to think back to that ride: she rolled over towards the toilet seat and threw up again so violently that her stomach muscles felt they were being ripped apart.

When the spasms finally stopped, she hauled herself up to the basin and scrubbed at her face with a flannel drenched in cold water. Looking in the mirror, she saw her skin was so pale it was almost grey, and her hair was matted against her face.

'Eve, you bloody idiot.' She suddenly realised why everything was blurry, she still had her contact lenses in. She couldn't remember the last time she'd forgotten to take them out before bed; mind you, she couldn't remember the last time she'd got this trolleyed. Her eyes were so dry she had to dig a fingernail under each lens to lever it out.

Right; this was good, she was making progress. Now she had to get to the kitchen. She breathed deeply, in and out, and started to go down the stairs, stopping and sitting still a couple of times until everything around her stopped spinning. When she eventually walked into the kitchen, putting both hands onto the table and supporting herself on it, Daniel was mashing Frosties into a bowl with a yoghurt, most of which seemed to have gone on the floor.

'Mummy, your breath smells horrible!' he said. 'You've got to get ready because we can't be late today – you know that. But I haven't got any pants. Find me some pants!'

'Why can't we be late?' whispered Eve, tasting the fur on her tongue as it rasped against her teeth.

'For the zoo!' yelled Daniel, banging his spoon against the side of the bowl like a gong. 'We're going to the zoo!'

Fuck. Today was the class trip to Bristol Zoo.

'Noooo.' She collapsed into a chair.

'Yes!' said Daniel. 'It's going to be brilliant. I'm sitting with Robbie on the coach, and you're coming too!'

There was absolutely no way she could go on a school trip today. Eve didn't even know if she could make it back upstairs to her bedroom, let alone have a shower, get dressed and put on make-up. She certainly couldn't drive her son to school or sit on a coach with Mrs Russell and thirty frenzied six-year-olds. Her head was pounding, her stomach churning, her legs so wobbly she wasn't sure they could hold her up. Fighting down waves of nausea, she forced herself to think.

'Daniel,' she whispered. 'Go upstairs and get my phone for me, please. It's on my bed. I need to call Robbie's mummy.'

An hour later, Juliet was at the door, being so wonderfully sympathetic that Eve felt like a fraud.

'You look dreadful,' she said. 'Go back to bed. I'll find Mrs Russell and explain. Do you think you ate something dodgy last night?'

'I think I must have done,' said Eve, sitting at the bottom of the stairs, watching Daniel struggle with the Velcro straps on his shoes, but unable to lean forward and help him. 'Maybe some prawns?' She hoped Juliet would keep looking at her and not down the hall into the kitchen, where two empty wine bottles were lying on the floor by the back door.

'Prawns can be nasty,' said Juliet. 'Hope you feel better soon, I'll drop him home later. Come on, boys!'

Daniel ran back to give Eve a hug. 'Sorry you're sick,' he said. 'I wish you were coming to the zoo, Mummy.'

The look on his face made her eyes fill with tears. 'Me too,' she whispered. 'I'm so sorry.'

Back upstairs, curled in a foetal position under the duvet, she began to cry: huge heaving sobs of humiliation and self-loathing. Keeping her eyes closed to stop the room spinning, she imagined Daniel arriving at school, and the look on Mrs Russell's face as Juliet explained that his mother wasn't going to make it. Why did this have to happen today, of all days? She hadn't exactly been looking forward to spending a day at the zoo with a bunch of manic children, but at least she would have been giving something back: stacking up a few parental Brownie points. Now, in the eyes of Mrs Russell – who already disliked her anyway – she would always be the mother who let them down at the last moment.

She groaned and buried her head in her pillow, smelling her own rank breath.

But worse than that, she'd let Daniel down. He'd been so excited when she announced she was going on the trip: off-the-scale excited. He'd ran into the garden shrieking and bunny-hopping down the lawn toward the swing. 'Mummy's coming to the zoo!' he'd yelled. 'My Mummy. Is. Coming. To. The zoo!'

Daniel was due to stay at Ben's tomorrow night; please let him not mention this to his father. Ben wouldn't guess she'd been laid low by alcohol, rather than a sick bug, but she had failed her son in a massive way and the last person she wanted to hear about this was Ben. Right now, she needed to be as good a mother as she possibly could in his eyes.

Although, in her own defence, he wouldn't win any awards for the world's greatest father. He still hadn't returned her call. What a shit. Maybe she should have explained what it was about, but she shouldn't need to do that in order to make sure he got back to her. If she left him a message, it was only ever going to be about Daniel; she'd long ago given up trying to pretend they could have normal conversations about their lives or work or anything that was happening in the world.

Eve stared at the glass of water on the bedside table: she really ought to make herself drink some of it, but her guts flipped at the thought. She would call Ben again later today, when she was feeling a bit more human, tell him about the child psychologist thing. They needed to decide what to do, how to deal with whatever was affecting their son's behaviour.

She knew her priorities had been all wrong over the last few days; her mind had been full of Flora's letters, but she must prioritise Daniel. She was still shocked at the conversation she'd overheard him having with his teddy – even though he'd seemed to recover more quickly than she had from the upset of that afternoon.

At some stage she must tell him she'd heard what he was saying, so they could deal with it and move forward, but so far cowardice had won through, and she'd said nothing. Every evening she tucked him up in bed, kissing the soft skin on his cheek and wrapping her arms around him as he drifted off to sleep, full of guilt that she hadn't addressed all this stuff yet again. But what was the point? Daniel would just tell her that Ben and Lou were forging ahead with their plans to move, confirming that all their futures were about to change dramatically.

Eve looked at the clock beside the bed: it was nearly 10am. The class would be on the coach en route to Bristol Zoo, maybe even there already, with Mrs Russell lining up the children and reminding them to stay in their pairs and pay attention.

As she rolled over again in bed, her head thumped, but at least she wasn't feeling sick anymore. There were paracetamol in the bathroom cabinet, in a minute she would force herself to get up and take some. Outside, she could hear a lorry driving down the street, car doors slamming, the muted voices of people laughing and talking as they went about their business.

She pictured the empty wine bottles downstairs in the kitchen. She never normally drank that much, especially during the week: a glass or two of wine was her limit. Well, this would teach her. The irony of it all wasn't lost on her: she'd been reproaching Flora for drinking at Three Elms, for behaving badly and disturbing the other residents. But sitting on her own last night, feeling sorry for herself, Eve had done exactly what she'd been telling her own mother was unacceptable.

TWENTY-FIVE

By early afternoon, she was feeling more human. She had slept for a couple of hours, then forced herself to get up and shower. She certainly wasn't firing on all cylinders, but the world had stopped spinning and her stomach had settled. She sipped at a cup of sweet tea and nibbled a biscuit, and could feel the sugar working its magic.

Daniel wouldn't be back from the zoo trip until early evening, so she had several hours to herself. She ought to do something constructive, like wash windows or shampoo carpets – something to atone for her bad behaviour. But all she wanted to do was see her mother: she couldn't get the image of Flora's screaming face out of her head. Even though she had been calmer and quieter by the time Nathan persuaded her to lie on the bed, Eve was still horrified at the reaction she'd caused.

She got in the car and drove – very slowly, she was probably still over the limit – to Three Elms. As she walked into the foyer, she heard singing and realised the children from St Barnabas must be in again.

The woman behind the desk saw her pause, and smiled. 'Lovely, isn't it?' she said. 'They're having an extra rehearsal this afternoon because the kiddies can't come in next week, they've got their nativity play. I love listening to them!'

Standing in the door to the lounge, Eve saw the teacher at the far end of the room, his arms swinging up and down as he conducted the singing. The children were sitting cross-legged on the carpet in front of him, and the residents were behind them on armchairs and sofas that had been dragged into a semicircle.

'*Four French hens, three calling birds…!*'

There was an extraordinary range of voices, from croaky tenors to shrill sopranos, but everyone in the room was singing – even the care workers standing at the back.

'*Two turtle doves, and a partridge in a pear tree!*'

'Fantastic!' called the teacher. 'Give yourselves a round of applause.'

As everyone clapped and a bubble of chatter spread around the room, Eve saw Flora sitting by the window. She was perched on a sofa, smiling broadly and leaning forward to speak to one of the children, a little girl with a mass of auburn curls. They were talking about something, the girl stretching her arms wide and throwing her head back, as if singing to the stars. Flora laughed and clapped her hands together in delight, then drew the child towards her in a hug.

Eve slipped in at the back of the room.

'Wonderful, isn't it?' whispered the care worker standing beside her. 'I love seeing them all so happy.'

There were two more carols. *Away in a Manger* went relatively well, but no one could remember the words for the last verse of *We Three Kings* and the children were starting to fidget on the carpet, some yawning, others chatting.

'Right, I think that's enough for today,' called the teacher. 'Well done everyone, this is going to be fantastic. Children, say goodbye and line up by the door.'

Eve made her way over to where Flora was sitting, and smiled at the auburn-haired girl, who was taking a long time to say goodbye.

'...And because I'm a shepherd, I'm going to wear a cloak and have a stick with a hook on the end,' she was telling Flora. 'My friend Lauren is going to be an angel and she's got a halo that her mummy made from tinsel.'

'That sounds perfect,' said Flora, glancing sideways and seeing Eve. 'Oh hello, darling. This is Olivia. She and I are singing together in the concert. Olivia, this is my daughter, Eve.'

'Hello,' said Eve. 'That's a lovely name.'

'Thank you,' said the girl. 'Yours is lovely too. It's like Christmas Eve, which is my favourite day of the year.' She turned and waved at Flora. 'See you soon!' she said and ran to join the other children by the door.

'What a sweetheart,' said Eve.

'She always sits near me when they come in,' said Flora, beaming. 'We have an understanding, Olivia and I. Isn't she delightful? She was very shy at first, would hardly say a word to me. But now we chat away like old friends.'

With the children gone, a clanking and rattling heralded the arrival of the afternoon tea trolley, and Eve helped the care workers push the furniture back into its usual place, around the edges of the room.

'How are you feeling today, Mum?' she asked, sitting down next to Flora.

'I'm fine, thank you, dear.'

'I'm so sorry about yesterday. I really didn't mean to upset you. Were you all right after I left?'

Flora was looking at her in surprise. 'Yes, of course. I was fine. Why do you ask?'

'Well, you were upset when I showed you those letters. It was so stupid of me, and I feel awful about it. I should have talked to you first, rather than just bringing them in here. Please forgive me.'

Flora shook her head, smiling up at a girl who was handing her a cup and saucer. 'I don't know what you're talking about, Eve. I'm absolutely fine. I don't know why I need to forgive you. Excuse me...! Have you got any bourbons today?'

'Do you really not remember?' Eve was amazed. She knew many small things slipped Flora's mind, but what happened yesterday afternoon had been so traumatic. How could she already have forgotten about it?

Flora shrugged. 'I don't think so, darling. There was a lot going on yesterday. They do keep us busy in here, you know.'

'It was letters you'd written,' persisted Eve. She should probably stop; she didn't want a repeat of yesterday. But maybe if she could just spark off a memory somewhere in Flora's head, other things might come back to her? 'You wrote them to Alan, do you remember him?'

'Of course I do!' Flora said with a sniff. 'Your father. Why would I not remember him? Don't be so silly, Eve. He would have loved that little singing session we had with the children just now. He had a marvellous voice, you know, he could always hold a tune. You used to sing with him when you were still tiny, before you started walking – he'd bounce you on his knee and you'd sing all sorts of things together.'

Eve held out the photo frame. 'Here. I took this by mistake, yesterday. It's the one you have on your bedside table.'

Flora peered at it. 'Oh, I don't want that old thing anymore,' she said, tutting. 'You keep it.'

'Ah, there you are!' Barbara appeared and collapsed onto the sofa, the cushions shaking so much that the cup and saucer rattled in Flora's hands. 'I haven't missed the trolley, have I?'

'No, dear,' said Flora. 'You're just in time. They've got bourbons today.'

Eve studied her mother's face, looking for a glimmer, some flicker of memory at the mention of Alan's name. But there was nothing. Flora was smiling, relaxed and calm; her mood today a complete contrast with the hysteria of yesterday. Was this all a show? Maybe Flora knew exactly what Eve was asking and was deliberately choosing to feign ignorance? Overnight she would have had time to calm down and gather her thoughts together – decide how she was going to deal with her daughter's impertinence.

No, that couldn't be the case: if Flora hadn't been able to control her reaction yesterday, she wouldn't be able to do so today. Without even being aware she was doing it, she had simply managed to file away their disturbing exchange in some distant part of her brain, where it could stay hidden and not upset her any further. If there was anything positive to be said for dementia, it was this ability to forget distress.

'I like a bourbon,' said Barbara. 'You can pull the biscuits on the outside away from the chocolatey bit in the centre. I do the same with custard creams.'

Eve looked at the two women, sitting side by side. They made an odd couple: one short, skinny and pale, the other taller and dumpy with ruddy cheeks and bright red lipstick slashed across her protruding teeth.

There had been no more mention of the trip to Alton Towers, which was a relief: Eve couldn't imagine what would happen if they really did try to take themselves off to Staffordshire for the day. But you had to give it to them: that sparkle had been admirable.

She'd been furious with Flora when the two women made their bid for freedom through the front gates of Three Elms, but also surprisingly proud that, despite the confines of increasing dementia and physical infirmity, her mother was still a feisty old thing. Hopefully that flicker of gutsiness would never fade.

'Are you not taking part in the carol concert, Barbara?' asked Eve.

The woman looked at her aghast, as if Eve had suggested she put on a pair of trainers and do star jumps in the garden. 'Good Lord, no. Why would I want to do that?'

'Well, it seems like fun, in the run-up to Christmas?'

Barbara tutted and raised her eyes to the ceiling. 'I am absolutely not taking part in anything involving children. Can't stand them. They are irritating, noisy and generally disruptive. I would rather stick knitting needles in my eyes than sing carols with a bunch of small children.'

Eve's mouth dropped open: she didn't know what to say. But, as Barbara turned to wave and get the attention of the woman who was serving up cups of tea, Flora leant towards Eve and whispered, loudly enough for everyone nearby to hear, 'The truth is, darling, she's got the most dreadful voice. Can't sing for toffee. The rest of us are relieved she's not taking part: when Barbara sings it's like sitting next to a foghorn.'

TWENTY-SIX

As she came around the end of the aisle, Eve saw Jake right in front of her. He had a packet of cheddar in each hand and was peering down at them.

Shit! He was the last person she wanted to bump into right now. She turned back the way she'd come, spinning her trolley so quickly that it lurched onto two wheels and clattered against the corner of the aisle, sending a pot of double cream ricocheting into several others.

She put her head down and slunk away, mouthing *Sorry* at the member of staff glaring at her from behind the fish counter. She found herself back with the yoghurts. She'd already been down here – in fact she'd been up and down several times, because she was invariably dogged by indecision and forgetfulness in the supermarket – but it was too bad, she would have to lurk here for a few more minutes.

She picked up an Activia four-pack, then put it down again and wandered further along, pretending to study the small print on the back of a pot of Greek yoghurt, which was exactly the same as the one she already had in her trolley.

Why the hell did he have to be here? It was 3.30pm on Sunday afternoon – how irritating that he was as disorganised as her and had left his shopping until now. This was the first time she'd seen Jake in the flesh since the morning he'd asked her out. That was because, for the last couple of weeks she had done her utmost to avoid him.

Once she'd been on her way to work but had ducked back inside the house, when she saw him coming out of his front door; another evening she'd pretended not to notice him cycling up the road on his bike as she was parking the car. She still wished she'd reacted differently to his offer but, as the days went by, the embarrassment had begun to fade. She'd started thinking that, at some stage, she was bound to bump into him, but when it happened she would just pretend there was nothing wrong. She would be so bright and chatty that neither of them would feel the slightest bit awkward about it. 'Hey stranger!' she imagined herself calling out across the fence. 'Haven't seen you for ages. How are you?'

Except that, now the real Jake was a few feet away from her, trying to read the nutritional information on a packet of extra-mature cheddar, all her good intentions disappeared. Her stomach was jiggling and she could feel a muscle in her neck pulsing. She ought to go up and speak to him: just say hello and act as if nothing has happened. That would be the grown-up, sensible thing to do. But instead, she spent another couple of minutes lurking in front of the pots of Petit Filous that Daniel refused to eat. She was being such an idiot.

A message blasted over the loudspeaker, informed customers that the store would be closing shortly. This was ridiculous: she needed to finish the shopping and get home for when Ben dropped Daniel back.

She tentatively poked her head around the end of the cheese aisle; Jake was nowhere to be seen. Breathing a sigh of relief, she hurtled forward with the trolley, scooping up some brie and a string bag of Babybel. Five minutes later, she had everything she needed and was waiting at the checkout, bent over the trolley, rummaging around beneath the boxes, jars, cans and packets she'd carelessly thrown in there, to try and find all the reusable bags she shouldn't have left at the bottom in the first place.

'Hello,' said a voice.

She leapt up, hitting her elbow on the metal bars.

'How are you?'

Eve tried to look surprised as she turned around, so that he wouldn't know she'd been avoiding him for the last twenty minutes. 'Jake! What a lovely surprise.' She tugged down her jumper, which had risen up over the waistband of her jeans.

'Thought it was you,' he said. 'You ran away from me earlier when I was choosing cheese.'

She felt her cheeks flush. 'No!' she started to say. 'I had no idea. I didn't see you... was that you?'

He had that funny lopsided grin, which made him look about sixteen years old.

'Okay, I did see you,' she said. 'Sorry. I was a bit embarrassed. I thought you'd probably rather not bump into me.'

'Why?' He looked genuinely confused.

'Because I turned down when you asked me to the comedy thing. I didn't mean to be rude when you asked, I was just surprised. But I've felt awful about it ever since.'

He threw back his head and laughed, and she realised he'd had a haircut since she'd last seen him. The sides were shorter and neater: it suited him.

'...But it was so kind of you to offer me a ticket, and I'm really sorry I said no,' she said.

'You didn't exactly say no,' he pointed out. 'You didn't say anything!'

'I was just a bit surprised,' she said. 'I wasn't expecting it and...'

'And you couldn't think of an excuse quickly enough?'

'No! Well, yes. But not in that way. I like comedy, and it would have been fun. I just wasn't sure why you were asking me – I didn't want you to get the wrong idea.'

He put his head on one side. 'The wrong idea about...?'

'Well, about me. About us. I wasn't sure if you were asking me because you just had a spare ticket. Or because... Oh, for goodness' sake, Jake. You know what I mean!'

He laughed again. 'Eve, you are my next-door neighbour, and – hopefully – my friend. I just thought it would be nice to spend the evening with you and, I have to admit, I would be quite happy if we did get to know each other better. I think you're lovely, and I'm pretty sure we'd enjoy each other's company. But I wasn't planning to trap you in the back row of The Comedy Box and ravish you.'

She grinned back. 'That's probably just as well,' she said. 'It's been so long since I was last ravished, I can't remember what I'm meant to do in that kind of situation.'

'In that case it sounds like you need the practice,' said Jake. 'I may have to put your name on my list for the future. I've got quite a lot of ravishing planned over the next few weeks, with a whole bunch of different women, but you never know, I may get a last-minute cancellation. If I do, I'll be in touch.'

He winked at her, then turned and wheeled his trolley towards the entrance. Standing staring after him, she realised that today he was wearing relatively normal clothes: a dark blue fleece over grey combat trousers and a pair of trainers. All were clean and appeared to be a perfect fit. But as he walked away, she noticed a flash of red at his ankles. She laughed out loud, then stopped herself as the girl behind the checkout looked up and stared at her. It was actually reassuring: Jake wouldn't be Jake if he conformed completely. At least he was wearing matching red socks, rather than one orange and one pink.

Driving away from the supermarket, she began to hum along to a song that came on the radio. Funny how her mood seemed to have lifted. She hated to admit it, but it was down to Jake. It was partly the fact that she didn't have to worry about accidentally bumping into him anymore; she could stop leaping into doorways and burying her head in the footwell of her car when she saw him. But there was something else as well. It had been nice to see him; she didn't know this man well at all, but he felt strangely familiar, and she loved the fact that, whenever she saw him, he made her laugh.

Back home, she had just unlocked the front door and carried the bags into the hall, when Ben's car pulled up outside. Daniel jumped out and raced up the path, turning to wave as the Audi glided away again.

'Mummy, guess what!' he shouted as he followed her down the hallway into the kitchen. 'I've got something exciting to tell you!'

'What's that?' She smiled down at him, as she lifted the shopping bags onto the table. 'How was your time at Daddy's? Did you go anywhere nice?'

'Yes, but that's not my exciting news.'

'Oh, okay. Tell me then.' She pulled out a bag of apples and ripped it open, ready to tip the fruit into the bowl on the table.

'I'm going to have a new baby brother!'

Her hand froze in mid-air.

'It's so brilliant!' he yelled, jumping around the kitchen table.

Eve was staring at the label on the packet: *Royal Gala Premium Apples: crisp, sweet and juicy.*

'Did you hear me, Mummy?'

There were six apples in this bag, but she probably ought to have bought more than this. They both loved apples, and went through them so quickly. Daniel sometimes had two a day.

'Mummy, listen! Why aren't you saying anything? Isn't it brilliant – Daddy and Lou are having a baby!'

TWENTY-SEVEN

She'd had to drag Daniel back into the office again, after school. He didn't want to be there, and it was almost impossible for her to concentrate when he was sitting by the window, kicking his heels against the chair. But it was nearly a week since Mike Sewell's offer had been accepted on the Sion Hill apartment, and both sides were on her back to get the contracts drawn up. Eve wasn't usually so slow with this sort of thing, but at the moment it felt as if she was constantly chasing her tail. She'd promised Gav the documents would go in tonight's post, but it was nearly 5pm so that wasn't going to happen. God, why was life so manic?

'Mummy, I got four hundred and sixty-three points!'

'Well done.'

It would have been so much easier to call Juliet, or one of the other school-gate mums, and ask them to pick up Daniel and hold onto him for a couple of hours. But it felt as if she was always the one asking favours, and rarely returning them. So instead, her son was sitting in the office playing on her phone. She had turned the volume down, but could still hear tinny squeaks and bangs and, every now and then, he'd shout out in triumph as he got onto the next level of whatever mind-rotting rubbish his crap mother was letting him play.

'Yesssss! Killed them all!'

'Keep your voice down for me, Daniel,' Eve said, smiling apologetically across the office at Caroline, who grinned back: *Don't worry,* she mouthed. She was such a sweetheart; thank God Gav was out at a viewing, he always made it clear he wasn't happy about small children being in the office. 'Company policy, Eve!' he'd bellow. 'Over-eighteens only! And even then, if they spend time in here, they have to be able to sell houses!'

But Gav's disapproval was way down her list of priorities at the moment. Anyway, she was glad she'd picked up Daniel today: he'd been subdued when he came out of the gates, dragging his backpack along the ground behind him, scuffing the toes of his shoes. Other children had been racing past, pushing and jostling each other, screaming and laughing, throwing themselves at their waiting parents. But her little boy's head had been down and he'd refused to smile at her, even when she put her arm around his shoulders and tried to tickle him.

'Bad day?' she'd whispered in his ear.

He nodded, leaning towards her, resting his head against her coat.

'Well, it's over now,' she'd said. 'Come on. I've got KitKats in the car.' Chocolate wasn't going to make everything better, but it was all she had to offer.

By 6pm, Eve and Daniel were the only ones left in the office, and she still hadn't finished the contracts. The streets outside were dark and the shapes of people scurrying home in the drizzle flashed past the windows. Rush hour was in full swing, and cars, taxis and buses were crawling along the road, the glare of headlights picking out the spatter of raindrops on the firm's A-board on the pavement. There was no point leaving now: it would take them over an hour to get home. Maybe they should just stop at McDonald's on the way – she had filled the fridge with food yesterday, during her Jake-infused supermarket trip, but it would take so long to prepare something and they were both tired. She watched Daniel swinging his feet backwards and forwards, trying not to get irritated by the clank every time his heels connected with the metal bar at the back of the chair.

Her mobile started to vibrate and Ben's name flashed on the screen. About bloody time: it had taken him three days to return her call last week about Mrs Russell, then he'd been vague about finding a time to meet up. 'I'll get back to you tomorrow,' he'd said. She was irritated but not surprised when he didn't, and she hadn't had the chance to talk to him yesterday because he'd dropped off Daniel and driven away again without bothering to say hello. What could be so important that he couldn't find the time to discuss how unhappy his son was at school? Work presumably: that was the usual excuse.

Or Lou. His beautiful wife Lou, who was pregnant with his next child. Lou, who might be feeling tired and ill, and in need of being looked after. Would Ben be rushing to her side when she asked for anything? Would he be insisting she took it easy while he looked after Keira and sorted out supper? Would he be stepping up in the way so many husbands did at this time, shouldering more of the burden so his pregnant wife could rest while their tiny scrap of a baby grew inside her? Stepping up in the way he had never done while she was pregnant with Daniel.

Thinking about Lou and the baby made something sting deep inside Eve. It was an ache of jealousy and she knew she was being mean-spirited. But their happiness felt very brutal and horribly unfair. The hardest part was that she couldn't share this feeling with anyone else – least of all Ben. As she lifted her mobile to her ear, she dug the nails of her left hand into her palm, watching as indentations in the shape of half-moons turned her skin red.

'Hi Ben,' she said, her voice bright and cheery. 'Thanks for calling back. Everything okay with you?'

She didn't care about the answer, and realised she was listening to the tone of his voice, rather than what he was saying, straining to catch every nuance. Did he sound happier than normal? Excited? Was there a new kind of elation in his voice, at the fact that he was going to be a father again?

TWENTY-EIGHT

Eve was looking at the letters again. She got them out nearly every night now, after Daniel was in bed – even though she knew most of them by heart. For some reason she needed to keep reading and rereading Flora's words. It was probably because she knew this was all she was ever going to have now. Her mother clearly didn't remember anything about the letters – why she'd written them, or who she'd been writing to. She didn't even recognise her own handwriting, so she was never going to be able to help Eve solve this mystery.

In some ways, there wasn't a mystery to be solved. Flora had been let down by the man she loved and left to give birth to and raise their baby on her own. Either Alan Baker hadn't known that this girl he'd spent the summer with was pregnant, or he'd chosen to ignore a regular flow of letters from her. But either way, he hadn't been there for Flora or her baby.

As the baby in question, Eve was still considering trying to find this mystery man: since she'd discovered her mother's well-kept secret it had felt as if her life was one big loose end which needed to be tied up, and tying together the flailing anchorless extremities of her existence could only happen once she'd tracked down her father. But, as time went on and the initial shock of her discovery waned, she was feeling less optimistic about her chances of finding him. If Alan Baker hadn't wanted to be found forty-five years ago, it was unlikely she'd be able to track him down now – even though it was now so much easier to find out information about people than it had been back in the seventies.

She'd also realised that, if she wanted to track him down, it made no difference whether he'd deliberately ignored Flora's letters, or had just moved on from the Brighton address without knowing anything about them. Eve had no idea what part of the country he was from, how old he was, or what he did for a living. She doubted very much that he had been the respectable civil servant in Flora's version of events but, with so little to go on, there was no starting point.

Although she knew the quest was an impossible one, she still couldn't help feeling he might be lurking somewhere amongst the 24,175,644 results for Alan Derek Baker which had been thrown up by her internet search.

During lulls at work, or at home in the evenings, she often logged on to Google and clicked through some of the search results. She had got as far as the twenty-seventh page. There were Alan Derek Bakers across the world, doing all sorts of fascinating things.

She found birthday wishes to them in local papers, impressive run scores achieved by them in cricket matches. There was an Alan Derek Baker who had written books on seismological movements in the Western Seaboard, and another who ran a successful veterinary practice in Cape Town. An Alan Derek Baker in Scotland had apparently patented a leaf blower that ran on vegetable oil, while another in Kent had a painting hanging in the National Gallery. A. D. Baker was listed by Companies House as the director of a company that made exercise equipment, and yet another A. D. Baker was a driving instructor based in the East Midlands.

It was incredibly unlikely that any of these men were her father, but invariably there wasn't even enough information about them for her to look into it any further.

A couple of nights ago, she had found an Alan Derek Baker who was living in Worthing and linked to Sussex University, in Brighton. Her pulse raced as she typed in the new information, excited by the coincidence, desperate to find out more. Maybe her father had become a lecturer? A career in the civil service might have led him into politics or the law, from where he had moved into education as he neared retirement. He could now be an emeritus professor at Sussex: his gowned portrait on the wall of some department.

She eventually found out more. This particular Alan Derek Baker was a PhD student in the department of engineering and design. And he was thirty-eight years old.

'This is so stupid,' she'd said out loud, slamming shut her laptop and putting it on the sofa beside her, next to the shoebox full of letters. 'Just bloody stupid.'

She was going to have to think of another way. Part of her was tempted to get in the car and drive to Brighton, but that was a crazy idea. It was a six-hour round trip for a start, so she'd have to wait until the weekend when Daniel was with Ben; even if she did go, how likely was it that the current resident of 17 Lewes Close had any connection with whoever had lived there in 1979? Some people did stay in their homes for a long time – Flora had been in her flat for more than fifty years – but plenty of others moved on as the years went by: downsizing, upsizing, moving to a different area for work. Alan Baker was almost certainly long gone – if he'd ever been there in the first place.

Maybe she could talk to Flora again? Despite her mother's hysteria the other week, nothing seemed to have happened as a result. Flora wasn't depressed or more confused than usual. She certainly didn't seem to have suffered any psychological trauma as a result of her daughter's thoughtlessness.

'She's doing well!' insisted Nathan, every time Eve asked. 'She's happy, she's busy, she's getting to know more of the other residents. She even took part in our afternoon bingo session the other day – despite refusing to join in last week and telling me she's always hated bingo.'

If Flora really was fine, maybe Eve could ask her about the letters again? She would just have to choose her moment this time, and think of a gentle way of bringing up the subject. She got up from the sofa and carried the shoebox into the hall, putting it on the stairs so she'd remember to take it back up to her bedroom later.

Turning around, she caught sight of the small, framed photo on the hall table. She had only put it there a couple of days ago, so was still slightly surprised every time she saw it. She picked it up now and studied the two figures, standing side by side, their heads bowed towards each other, the beach stretching out in the background behind them.

They were such an attractive couple: Flora's dark hair tumbling across her shoulders, Alan several inches taller than her, his arm around her shoulders, pulling her close and radiating affection for her – even through this slightly faded black and white photograph. Surely this man hadn't just knowingly walked away?

TWENTY-NINE

They'd arranged to meet at 7pm but he was late, and Eve sat at a corner table sipping a glass of wine, trying not to look as if she'd been stood up. She had made an effort before she came out tonight, straightening her hair and putting on eyeshadow and lipstick. For the life of her, she didn't know why she'd bothered. Bloody man; it was so typical he was keeping her waiting like this.

'Sorry, sorry,' he said, striding up to the table and shrugging off his coat. 'Awful traffic. I don't usually come over to this side of the city after work.'

This side of the city. The way he said it made it sound as if she lived in a corrugated iron shack in a slum with open sewers. But just a few years ago, Bedminster had been *his* side of the city too.

'Want another one of those?' he asked, pointing to her glass, which was now nearly empty.

Eve watched him lean against the bar, pointing out the brand of bottled beer he wanted, reaching into his back pocket for his wallet. Even after all this time, something jolted, deep in the pit of her stomach, as she saw him smile and flirt with the barmaid.

She didn't love Ben anymore – most of the time she didn't even like him very much – but their shared history had left its mark on her. He was a good-looking man, that hadn't changed. If anything, he looked more handsome now than he had done when they met ten years ago. There were tiny flecks of grey in his hair, and the laughter lines on either side of his eyes were deeper – but none of that made Ben, aged forty, less attractive than the younger version she had fallen in love with. Why was it that men didn't need to care about the signs that their bodies were on the downhill straight, whereas women ran themselves ragged dying their roots, bleaching their facial hair and trying to disguise spider veins and stretch marks?

She looked down at her hands and ran her finger across a brown mark that was too large to be a freckle so might be officially classified as a liver spot. She half expected it to disappear as the skin settled back into place again, but it was still there, yelling *old woman's hands* at her.

Ben was walking back, carrying a drink in each hand, with a packet of crisps between his teeth. From a certain angle he really did look a little bit like George Clooney: if you squinted and made everything slightly fuzzy.

'Why are you doing that weird thing with your eyes?' he asked, dropping the crisps onto the table and passing her a glass of wine. 'God, what a day I've had. One boring meeting after another; didn't get anything done. Then I had to find something constructive to do with two new interns. Two! I ask you, how come I'm the mug that gets two of them in his department? One would be bad enough. I know they need to be trained up, but it takes so bloody long to run through everything with them, it ends up taking twice as long as it would if you'd just got on and done the work yourself.'

Eve had been looking forward to this evening. Although they weren't meeting for an ideal reason, she'd enjoyed the prospect that they were going out and it would be just the two of them. This hadn't happened in such a long time; years in fact. The last time must have been when they finalised all the maintenance details after the separation. They'd met in a pub very like this one, sitting across the table from each other and making notes, agreeing that the whole thing was awkward, but congratulating themselves that they were handling everything like grown-ups.

But now she was sitting inches away from her former lover, she was remembering all the things about him which she didn't like so much. There had always been an arrogance there; a self-centred obsession with his work and his own importance. Ben had been a young, nervous intern once; he would have been the one taking up the precious time of someone much more important, as he learnt on the job. But he wouldn't thank her for reminding him about that. Any more than he'd take the time to ask how she was, or how her job was going. Or maybe tell her she looked nice, or that her new haircut suited her. He wasn't being deliberately cruel or thoughtless; he just didn't care.

'So,' he said. 'What's been going on with Daniel then? I know you said he's still not settled. I just can't understand it – this doesn't sound like him. He's such a relaxed, happy little chap when he's with us.'

She bristled and bit the inside of her lip, reminding herself not to be oversensitive. 'He's the same when he's at home with me,' she said. 'I've never seen him getting really wound up or angry. He's high-spirited sometimes, but I don't know a single six-year-old boy who isn't.'

'What exactly is he doing wrong?' asked Ben, reaching forward and tearing open the packet of crisps.

'It sounds like it's mostly to do with one other boy, called

Liam something or other. I can't remember his surname. Mrs Russell said that Daniel has been fighting with him but I don't really know any more than that. She said he'd been disruptive in the classroom as well and hadn't calmed down when he was told off, but I don't know if Liam was involved that time.'

'You don't sound like you know much about it,' said Ben, pulling his phone from his pocket and scrolling through some messages as he put it on the table in front of him.

'Well, of course I do! That's ridiculous.' Eve took a deep breath. *Keep calm; don't react.* She mustn't let him wind her up, they weren't here to fight. 'It's just that Daniel won't tell me what's going on and Mrs Russell isn't the easiest person to talk to. She's a bit abrasive.'

'Did you ask her what the school have done to try and sort it out?'

'Yes, I did! Honestly, Ben, I'm not a total idiot. It's just that she's quite prickly and I don't think she likes me very much – actually I don't think she likes me at all. And it's always awkward going in to see the teacher in those sorts of situations. You feel on the defensive and it's only afterwards that you think about all the questions you could have asked. You know how it is.'

He didn't; he hadn't gone with her to any of these sessions where parents were grilled, roasted and hung out to dry by an antagonistic teacher. Eve was waiting for a response, but Ben's phone pinged and he looked down and grinned as he read a text.

'Anyway,' she carried on. 'It would have been helpful if you'd been there as well, because we ought to present a united front at the school. We need to show them that, just because we're not together, it doesn't mean we don't both have Daniel's best interests at heart.'

'Well, of course we do! What a ridiculous thing to say,' said Ben, finishing his beer. 'I need another one. You okay with that?'

He didn't wait for an answer and got up and walked back to the bar, waving at the pretty barmaid.

Eve sat back in her chair: this wasn't going to plan – why were they bitching at each other already? This shouldn't be about the two of them, it was about their son. But she did have the right to point out that Ben was less than supportive when it came to attending parents' evenings – or anything else related to the school. He was never outside the gates waiting to pick up Daniel – even on Wednesdays when he had him overnight – and she could only remember him meeting the Reception teacher once during the whole of last year, and that had been at an end-of-term concert. She didn't want to pick a fight, but it wasn't fair that she was the one doing all the heavy lifting here.

'Right,' said Ben, sitting back down. 'Let's forget the detail and look at the bigger picture. The problem is that Daniel is clearly unhappy. I don't think it's about him being a bully or just behaving badly for the hell of it, because he's not that kind of child.'

Eve nodded, that was true.

'So, we need to find out why he's miserable. The subject hasn't come up when he's been staying with us, we've never had any need to talk to him about it because he's always a happy lad. If he hadn't been, then either Lou or I would have made a point of sitting down with him and finding out what was going on.'

'He's happy with me, too,' said Eve, hating the defensiveness in her own voice.

'What I don't get,' he was saying, 'is why you didn't know about any of this? I mean, I can sort of understand that he's always on good form when he stays with me and Lou, because he doesn't see us all the time, so it's exciting when he comes to our house – and a bit special. But he's with you for most of the week, so I would have thought you'd see a wider range of behaviour?'

'What are you suggesting – that he's not as happy with me?'

'I'm not saying that. But you'll see him, warts and all, whereas we see a different side of him. And, of course, Keira's there and he just adores her, so that keeps him cheerful. They spend a lot of time together playing and just hanging out, watching TV.'

Mention of Ben's pretty, blonde daughter reminded Eve about what Daniel had said on Sunday. She had been trying not to think about it, which wasn't easy because it seemed to be the only thing Daniel wanted to talk about. She'd snapped at him last night, when he'd been chatting – yet again – about his new brother.

'I want him to be called Jack!' he'd said. 'Lou likes Jack as well but Daddy likes Oscar or Joshua. But they say we'll all get to choose his name together when he's born. We'll wait to see what he looks like, and Lou says that when we see his face we'll know if one of our names suits him more than the others.'

'Okay, Daniel, that's enough about the baby!' she'd said, immediately feeling awful when she saw the look on his face. 'Sweetheart, I'm sorry, I don't mean that. I know you're excited. We're all excited! It's such a wonderful thing to be happening. But it's going to be a long time before the baby arrives and I'm sure you'll all have thought of other names by then.'

Daniel had glared at her before turning back to the television and, in the set of his jaw, he had reminded her so much of his father. Now Ben was sitting opposite her at the table, glaring at her in a similar way.

'The thing is, Eve, I'm just surprised you didn't pick up on any of this. You're his mother, you're the one who sees him most of the time. Surely you should have noticed things weren't right?'

'Oh, that's great, blame me–'

'I'm not blaming you. I'm just saying that we don't see as

much of him, so we can't be expected to pick up on signals in the same way.'

It was that bloody *we* again. She hated it. 'Of course you should be able to notice when things aren't right. He's your son too, Ben. I would have thought you'd like to claim you know him just as well as I do.'

'What's that meant to mean? I'd *like to claim…?*'

'You just can't lay all of this on me,' said Eve. 'It's not fair.'

'Oh, grow up,' said Ben. 'Life's not fair.'

'Anyway, he's sometimes quite unsettled when he comes back from yours. It must be really hard for him having to slot into two families. I try to keep things steady and consistent, to counteract whatever happens when he's at yours.'

'What the hell needs counteracting? He has a really good time when he's with us. We give those kids everything they could want and we know he's happy. We make sure he feels part of a secure family unit.'

That stung. She grasped the stem of her wine glass tightly, imagining herself throwing the contents at him and watching wine dribble down the side of his face.

'Oh yes, speaking of which, I hear you're expanding that lovely family unit. Congratulations – another son on the way! Goodness, you and Lou will have your hands full. I hope this isn't going to mean your firstborn gets less of your attention, Ben. In fact, I wonder if that has occurred to him as well? It wouldn't be surprising if Daniel is already worrying about being pushed out over the next few months – scared you'll have less time for him and won't be able to do as much with him. Or he may be worrying you won't even want him around like you do now? You and Lou having another little boy isn't going to help him feel any more secure and confident, is it?'

As the words came out of her mouth, she hated herself for saying them. None of it was even true: she *knew* Daniel's six-year-old brain was thrilled at the prospect of having a brother. He hadn't for one moment begun to wonder if his daddy would love him a little less.

'God, when did you turn into such a mean bitch?' said Ben. 'I know you're trying to put all of this on to me, but it's just pathetic. You're his mother, you're the one who should have noticed something wasn't right, and if you stopped feeling so hard done by for a minute, you'd start to realise that's true. To be honest, it's worrying me that you're the one in sole charge of him for the majority of the time. You're so wrapped up in yourself, you can't even see what's happening under your nose and how unhappy your son must be.'

'That's unfair,' said Eve, her heart thumping so hard her voice quavered. 'I'm not wrapped up in myself. God, I have no time at all to worry about my own life!'

'It's the truth, Eve,' he said. 'I don't think Daniel is a priority for you anymore, and that concerns me.'

He picked up his phone and his wallet and stood up, pulling his coat off the back of the chair.

'I've been thinking a lot about our move to Glasgow, and worrying whether we're doing the right thing. I've been saying to Lou that maybe it's not fair on Daniel to uproot him – and last week I even said to her that what we're planning isn't fair on you! God, it's crazy but I've been fighting your corner, even though this should be about me and Lou – it's our life and our future. Well, I can see now I've been an idiot. You're not a fit mother and you're not doing a great job of looking after our son, so maybe it's a good thing he's going to come and live with us. You don't deserve to have him.'

THIRTY

It started to rain, but she didn't move. The skin on the top of her hands tingled as it got damp, and she could smell the fresh earthiness of the raindrops on the sleeves of her coat.

Her face was already wet, the skin on her cheeks tight from the tears that had streamed down them. Her eyes itched and her nose was so snotty she could hardly breathe, but she didn't have the energy to root in her bag to look for a tissue. Her arms felt like lead and every sinew in her body ached, as if the blood had been drained from her veins. She wasn't sure how long she'd been sitting here, but she couldn't think about going anywhere yet; there was no way she could arrive home looking like this.

After Ben had walked out of the pub, Eve had sat at the table for a few seconds before pulling on her coat and putting her phone into her bag. She did it all calmly, without urgency, aware that the group of girls at the next table were staring across at her, open-mouthed at the way Ben had shouted at her.

She also knew that, after she walked out, they would lean forward, gasping, enjoying the intrigue and the fact that they could now discuss what the hell had been going on with that couple. The entire pub had just listened to Ben tell her she was a bad mother, and every head turned to watch her as she walked out. She left with as much dignity as she could muster, but was aware her face was blazing. Despite the fact that she didn't know any of these people, the humiliation was overwhelming.

It was only when she got out onto the pavement that she began to cry. She walked quickly past a row of houses before turning into a small park and collapsing onto a bench, just inside the railings.

Then she just sat there, for goodness knows how long. Around her, city life carried on as normal: cars drove past the park, music drifted out of windows, front doors slammed, passers-by talked and laughed. She tipped her head back and gazed up into the night sky, watching an aeroplane make a slow arc overhead, the flashing red light on its underbelly marking it out in the darkness.

She was in pieces. Was this all her fault? She ran through every word he'd said, time and time again. It wasn't fair that he was blaming her for all this. She wasn't the only one responsible for Daniel, but she'd always felt proud that she was doing a bloody good job – effectively as a single mother. It would have been nice to have got the occasional thank you, or for Ben to have acknowledged she was doing more than her share, but she'd never asked for that, or expected it. Just as well: he hadn't said anything supportive in the last five years. Instead, he had dipped in and out of fatherhood when it suited him and when it fitted in with his wonderful new life. Now he was telling her what a mess she'd made of bringing up their son.

There was no doubt he'd fight her for custody after this. She bent forwards and put her head in her hands, sobs welling up in her throat again. How had she messed up everything so badly? She remembered what the young solicitor had said: the suggestion that, since she and Ben had such a good ongoing relationship when it came to Daniel, they ought to try to sort out future arrangements amongst themselves.

Hah! What a bloody joke; there was no chance of that now. Ben would take her to court and ask a judge to let him move Daniel to Glasgow so he could become a proper, permanent part of his other family. The judge would look at them both and see Ben: an upright, respectable man with a decent job and steady income, who was married and had a beautiful, contented family. Then he would look at her, and see an exhausted, overwrought single mother, who had been so preoccupied by complications at work and problems relating to the care of her own elderly parent, that she hadn't given enough time and attention to her son.

Maybe this was what she deserved. She'd been so wrapped up in herself that she'd failed to notice that her gorgeous little boy, whom she loved more than anyone in the world, was desperately unhappy at school and had turned into a playground bully.

She cried again, feeling the rain drip down the back of her neck as she bent forward, burying her face in her hands. But after a while it began to feel as if she had hollowed out inside; there were no tears left. She leant back against the bench, so drained she could hardly lift her hands from her lap.

A young couple walked in through the gate, arms flung carelessly around each other's shoulders, heads together, their laughter carrying on the breeze. She couldn't hear their exact words but it sounded as if he was teasing her about something: she was arguing back, but playfully, enjoying the faux quarrel, safe in the knowledge that he loved her deeply enough for there not to be any hidden meaning or criticism in what he was saying. Had she and Ben ever been like that? Eve was sure they had, but it was all such a long time ago, and looking back now she could remember so few of the good times.

Instead, what came to mind were the arguments and exhausted bickering after Daniel was born, the resentment and misunderstandings; the evenings when Ben slammed out of the door and went in search of a mate or a pint. There were many nights when he slept in the spare room – at first, because it meant at least one of them got a decent amount of sleep, but later on because sleeping in different beds had come to feel like the norm.

When she woke to feed Daniel in the night, she would tiptoe out onto the landing afterwards, rocking a full, sleepy baby on her shoulder, and peer in through the crack in the bedroom door at Ben's sleeping form in the spare bed, his back turned to her.

But Ben was right; she hadn't been doing her best by Daniel. There had been so much going on with Flora over the last year, so many concerns and worrying symptoms, so many medical appointments and decisions that needed to be made. Daniel had been dragged along to view care homes after school and left to play on her phone in doctors' surgery waiting rooms or in the back seat of the car while she popped into the chemist to pick up an amended prescription. It hadn't been unusual for her to do what she'd done yesterday: pick up Daniel at the end of a school day and take him back into work with her, because there was something urgent which she hadn't finished. But none of it was fair on him.

The young couple had now reached the other side of the park and were standing by a gate onto the road. They looked like they were going their separate ways and, as Eve watched, the man reached out and pulled the girl towards him, enveloping her in a hug and putting his face down towards hers. Their kiss was long and lingering. She felt like a voyeur, but couldn't drag her eyes away.

Now that she'd stopped crying, the breeze felt cool on her

cheeks. She looked in her bag for a tissue, but couldn't find one, so wiped her eyes with the sleeve of her coat and pushed her hands back through her hair, scraping it away from her face. Her eyes were swollen and puffy and it would be a while until they'd look normal again. She would have to walk around for a bit, maybe find some water to splash onto her skin. Daniel would be asleep when she got home, but there was no way she could let Katie see her in this state. She forced herself to take in a deep lungful of air, then breathe out again slowly. In and out. There was a kind of comfort in the rhythm, a sense of regaining control.

She didn't want to keep thinking about all this, but her head was buzzing with Ben's words, which were cruel and cutting, but also true. There must have been signs that Daniel wasn't happy at school – he wasn't old enough to be able to hide his feelings. Maybe he had tried to talk to her, or had mentioned something – however small – that was actually a cry for help? But she'd missed the warnings.

There was no excuse: it didn't matter that she'd been busy and stressed and worried. She had failed her son.

THIRTY-ONE

The office door was shoved open so roughly it crashed against Eve's desk, jolting everything on it. She gave an involuntary scream and reached out to steady her mug of coffee, some of which had splashed perilously close to her laptop.

'Who's responsible for this?' yelled the man standing in the doorway. He was in his fifties, wearing a suit that suggested he'd come from work and he brandished a piece of paper in his left hand.

'Can I help you?' Caroline had started to get up from her desk on the other side of the room.

'If you're the one who's lost me this house, then yes you bloody well can help me! We've spent money on surveys and solicitors, we were just about to agree a date to exchange – and now I get *this!*'

The man was advancing towards her, holding the paper out in front of him like a weapon, and Caroline looked terrified.

Eve came out from behind her desk. 'I'm really sorry, but we don't know what you're talking about. Is that a letter from someone in this office?'

'Don't pretend you don't know what's been going on,' the

man said. 'You've done the dirty on us. I thought you lot were some of the decent ones. What an idiot I've been. You're all the same: bloody estate agents – no wonder your industry has a reputation for being a bunch of thieves.'

'Are you buying a property through us?' asked Eve. She'd never seen this man before, but that didn't mean he wasn't on their books: someone else in the sales team could have done viewings with him.

'Thirty-seven Newbury Street,' he said. 'The name's Giddings. I've not only been for three viewings there, and had a full-price offer accepted, but I paid for a survey with the company you lot recommended, and then I agreed to use your preferred solicitor – all of which no doubt means plenty of commission for you. I did everything you advised, and now I get this letter, telling me the vendor has backed out of our agreement because he's accepted another offer!'

Eve blanched; now she knew exactly what this was about. Bloody Gav. He'd been laughing about this a few days ago. A couple had wandered in off the street, saying they were cash buyers and were interested in the house in Newbury Street; despite the fact that it was under offer and the vendors had agreed to take it off the market, Gav had offered to show the couple round. It was unethical, and everyone else in the office knew it. Eve hadn't been in when they called to make a higher offer on the house, but Caroline told her Gav had encouraged the vendor to pull out of the original sale and go with the new buyers. This poor man standing in front of them had been gazumped and there was absolutely nothing he could do about it.

'Gav, that's awful,' Eve had said, when she heard what he'd done.

'Oh, get off your high horse, princess,' he said. 'Nothing illegal about it, and you know it. As their agent I was under an obligation to pass on the details of the offer. It was entirely up to them whether or not they decided to accept it. But an extra ten grand isn't to be sniffed at nowadays.'

'But you shouldn't have shown the other people the property!' said Eve.

Gav had waved a hand dismissively. 'It's a dog-eat-dog world out there, Eve. You know it as well as I do.'

She hadn't thought about it again, until now. So, this poor man was the one on the receiving end of Gav's disreputable behaviour. Typically, he wasn't in the office to take the flak.

'I'm really sorry, Mr Giddings,' she said. 'What's happened to you is dreadful.'

Caroline was looking at her nervously, but Eve didn't give a damn about loyalty or defending the agency's reputation. 'My colleague handled this, and I think what he has done is appalling. Gazumping isn't illegal in this country, as I'm sure you know, but it is immoral and it's not something the majority of reputable agents would condone.'

The man was looking at her in surprise, he clearly hadn't been expecting this sort of reaction.

'I'm so sorry you've lost money on this transaction, and that you've wasted weeks of your time going through the process,' she said. 'I know that having found this house you must have set your heart on it, which is probably the hardest thing of all.'

The man was looking deflated now, his arms hanging by his sides, the letter drooping from one hand. 'My wife had fallen in love with the place,' he said. 'She was so happy. She'd already been planning where all the furniture was going to go, and she's ordered a new wardrobe for the bedroom. She was so excited about it.'

Eve nodded. 'I bet she was. I can only imagine how upset you both are.' She leant over her desk and scribbled something on a piece of paper. 'Here,' she said, handing it to him. 'This is the personal mobile number for my colleague, Gavin Williams, who encouraged those other buyers. Please don't tell him how you got hold of his number, but feel free to call him, Mr Giddings, as many times as you want – any time of the day or night – and make his life as miserable as you possibly can.'

The man looked at the piece of paper. 'Well, it won't change anything, but it might make me feel better,' he said. 'Thanks for being sympathetic, I was expecting you all to close ranks.'

After he'd gone, Eve sat back down in her chair. Caroline was grinning at her from across the room. 'That,' she said, 'was genius. Let's hope Gav's in the office when those calls come through.'

As Eve turned back to her laptop and started rereading the email she'd been typing, she realised her hands were trembling. She hated confrontation of any kind, but that poor man had every right to come in and yell at them. Even by Gav's questionable standards, his actions had been unfair and heartless. The awful thing was that everyone in the office was guilty by association, however much they hated what Gav had done. Hopefully this man and his wife would find another property to fall in love with, but it was highly unlikely they'd be using this agency for their search.

The confrontation dragged her mind back to the drink with Ben, last night. Her head had been pounding all morning – not from an excess of alcohol this time, but from the hours of distraught crying she'd done as she sat on the bench in the park – and she felt wrung out, her limbs throbbing as if she'd been running for hours. She'd spent most of the morning replaying their conversation over and over in her head, remembering the look on Ben's face: his disgust at her and his throwaway comment that life was unfair. He was right. Poor gazumped Mr Giddings had provided another example of that.

She was desperate to speak to someone about their row. The

things Ben had said had been so hurtful – even if there was some truth in them – that she wanted to talk about them to someone who would sympathise and put their arm round her, tell her she wasn't a completely dreadful human being.

Until recently, the person she would have confided in was Flora. She'd always been able to use her mother as a sounding board, whether she needed advice about work, or had problems with Daniel – she even used to discuss her love life with her, although recently there hadn't been much call for that. Over the years Flora had provided a shoulder to cry on and a box of tissues when Eve had been going through all sorts of emotional crises. But now her mother was no longer there for her. Or rather, she was there, but only physically; Eve wasn't able to open up to her about any of the things that were causing her sleepless nights because Flora wouldn't understand.

The front door crashed opened again and Gav came striding into the office, shrugging off his coat as he walked past Eve's desk, showering her with droplets of rain. 'Hello girls and guys!' he yelled. He'd been the only male who worked in the office for years, but his habitual greeting never changed. 'How are we all today? Selling, selling, selling, I hope!'

As he flung his coat onto a hook on the side wall, Eve swept her palm across her desk, wiping away the moisture that had already blurred the signature on a contract she'd been about to file.

'Right!' shouted Gav, rubbing his hands together. 'I want a couple more sales from you lovely people before the end of the week. Our figures are pretty good for this month, looks like we're going to beat the Bath office, hands down. Losers!'

As he walked towards his office, the sound of Whitney Houston singing *I will always love you* filled the office. Eve hated Gav's ringtone, but right at this moment she was delighted to hear it. She and Caroline caught each other's eye, as he pulled his mobile from his back pocket.

'What's that?' he yelled. 'Giddings?'

Eve kept her eyes on the screen in front of her, pretending she wasn't listening. *Give him hell, Mr Giddings,* she thought. *Both barrels.*

THIRTY-TWO

The young woman sitting in the chair next to Eve's, kept sniffing. She had a sleeping toddler sprawled on her lap and was flicking through a magazine, not pausing long enough to actually read any of the articles: flick, sniff, flick, sniff. Eve's hands itched to reach across and rip the magazine out of her fingers and throw it across the room.

'Sam Hughes?'

A boy got up from a chair in the row in front and followed the nurse out of the waiting room.

Sniff.

Eve sighed deeply and shifted away slightly, crossing her legs so that she was facing the other way.

Sniff.

'Oooh, look at this! Custard tarts with raspberries.' Flora was sitting on her other side, her head buried in a copy of *BBC Good Food*. 'I haven't had a custard tart in years! Do you like custard tarts, Eve?'

'Not really, Mum,' said Eve.

Sniff.

She ought to say something. She was too British when it

came to stuff like this, afraid to make a scene. She should just come straight out with it and ask the woman to go and blow her bloody nose. Or, better still, pull some tissues from her own bag and hand them over, her actions speaking so much louder than any words. Unfortunately, she had no tissues; she'd used the last one earlier this morning to wipe the remains of Daniel's breakfast off his school jumper when she dropped him at the gates, scrubbing so hard she'd left a patch of white fuzz across the burgundy wool.

'I don't know why they use figs in cakes,' Flora was saying. 'I don't like figs, I never have done. Those little pippy bits get stuck in your teeth.'

Eve kept her eyes on her book. She'd been reading the same sentence over and over for the last few minutes, unable to concentrate, but unwilling to put the book down in case it encouraged Flora to chat even more. She was being mean, but felt so tired this afternoon.

'Now that's a useful little thing,' Flora said, holding the magazine closer to her face. 'A kitchen tap that gives out boiling water so you don't need to boil a kettle. Eve, have you ever seen anything like it? How clever.'

'Yes, Mum, most new properties have them.' She must stop snapping, it wasn't fair. She forced herself to look up and smile. 'You're right, I'm sure they must be very useful.'

Flora was studying the magazine intently again, so Eve allowed her eyes to drop back down to her book. This place always made her feel uncomfortable. It wasn't just the smell of it – disinfectant blended with floor polish and a base note of vomit – it was the awkwardness of being in a room full of people who might have cancer, depression, asthma or just a tickly cough, but who all needed help and support.

Ironically, this was the sort of place where Flora's slightly odd behaviour shouldn't matter; these people were strangers, why should she care if they were listening to their conversation and passing judgement on the quirkiness of a little old lady? But, to Eve's shame, it did matter. She hated knowing that people were staring as Flora chatted away to herself. She sensed some of them shifting uncomfortably in their seats as her mother's thin, wobbly voice rang out across the waiting room.

'La, la, la, laaaa...'

'Mum,' she whispered. 'Don't sing here.'

'All is calm, all is bright...'

'Mum, please?'

Flora turned, her brow furrowed. 'What's the matter?'

'Please don't sing in here.'

'Why not?'

'There are other people trying to concentrate on what they're doing. It's a bit antisocial.'

Flora snorted. 'So what? I am practising my carols! La, la, laaaaa – virgin mother and child...'

The door opened at the far end of the room and one of the doctors stuck his head around it. 'Mrs Glover?'

'That's us. Come on, Mum.' Eve bundled her book into her bag and took Flora's arm to help her up from the seat.

'Here,' said Flora, turning to the overweight man sitting next to her and pushing the magazine into his hands. 'You'd better have this. It's all about food – you obviously like a bit of that.'

They hadn't seen this GP before, which wasn't surprising. The surgery was oversubscribed and Eve knew that two of the regular doctors had left recently, their places taken by locums. It was hard enough to get through to a human being on the main phone number, let alone ask to be seen by a specific doctor. But having waited ten days for this appointment, she really didn't care who they saw.

'What can I do for you today?' asked the man. He was

possibly half Eve's age with untamed curly brown hair and a fresh face showing no signs that he'd experienced much of life.

'It's a six-monthly check-up,' said Eve, irritated at the need to explain. 'To assess whether my mother is still on the right medication?'

He swung round and started reading the notes on his computer, tapping his finger on the desk. 'Ah, yes. I see. Excellent. Right then, Mrs Glover, can you tell me what medication you're currently taking?'

Flora stared at him, confused.

'Do you remember any of the names?'

'Oh no, dear, not at all,' she said. 'They're all in Latin.'

He grinned at her. 'You're right, that was a silly thing to ask. How about the way it's making you feel. Would you say your anxiety levels are generally better now than they were a few months ago?'

Flora shrugged.

He looked questioningly at Eve.

'Well, there have been a lot of changes over the last six months,' she said. 'My mother is now living in a care home and the move wasn't easy. It took her a while to get used to being somewhere new, and to settle there.'

He nodded. 'That's not surprising. How about your motivation, Mrs Glover? Do you have plenty of energy?'

'Well, dear, I don't really know about that.' Flora turned to Eve and rolled her eyes. 'Why is this boy asking all these questions? We ought to be getting back because it's nearly time for the tea trolley. I don't want to be out too long.'

Eve put a reassuring hand on her arm. 'It will be fine, I'll get you back in time, don't worry.' She turned back to the young GP. 'I think there are increasing memory problems. I was wondering if it might be possible to repeat some of the tests my mother had earlier in the year? The previous doctor we saw suggested he might alter the medication if the current dose didn't seem to be as effective.'

The young man nodded and started scribbling something on a pad on the desk in front of him. 'We can certainly do that. I'll need to book your mother in for a longer consultation, though I'm afraid I can't do that today.'

'I want to go home now, Eve,' whispered Flora, grasping her sleeve with her fingers.

'But why can't you do any of the tests now?' asked Eve. 'Just a couple of the quick ones? It seems crazy not to, since we're here.'

The doctor shook his head and turned back to the screen. 'This is only a single appointment: six minutes.'

'Eve, I need to go to the toilet!' said Flora. 'I need to go now.'

'Okay, Mum. Listen – doctor – when I called to make this appointment, I specifically said it was to have these tests done. The woman said she'd book us a double slot to give us enough time?'

'Eve!' wailed Flora. 'I don't like this place.'

The young doctor was tapping something into his screen. 'Make another appointment outside at the desk,' he said, not turning back towards them. 'We'll run through it all properly next time.'

Eve grabbed her bag, slamming it against the side of the desk as she stood up. What a waste of time. She could stand her ground and refuse to leave? This fresh-faced young doctor had no idea what a struggle it had been to get Flora along to this appointment today: her mother had been worried when Eve told her she would need to leave the home, nervous about even getting into Eve's car for the first time in weeks. Not only that, but it wasn't exactly easy for Eve to get time off from work. This whole visit had been planned and scheduled and they were here now, so why couldn't they just get on with it?

'Let's go home, Eve.' Flora was crying, her hands shaking in her lap. 'I don't like this place.'

Eve glared at the doctor, but his back was still turned. She helped her mother out of the chair and they went towards the door.

'I don't want to miss the tea trolley,' Flora was saying. 'They might have Hobnobs today.'

'Don't worry, Mum, we're going back.' Eve linked her arm through her mother's as they walked out through the waiting room. The woman with the sleeping toddler was still sitting there, flicking rapidly through the pages of yet another magazine. She sniffed loudly as they walked past her chair.

'For goodness' sake!' said Flora, turning to stare and dragging Eve to a halt. 'Young lady! Stop sniffing, get a tissue and blow your bloody nose!'

THIRTY-THREE

'Daddy says the new baby will sleep with him and Lou at first, but then when he gets a bit bigger, he'll have his own room. But I'd like it if he could sleep in my room, with me. I don't mind if he shares all my toys, even though he might break some of them because he'll be very little and won't understand how to play nicely. Keira sometimes breaks things of mine, but she doesn't mean to – last weekend she drew on the wall of the kitchen with a green pen and Lou had to send her up to her room because–'

'Daniel, for God's sake, shut up!'

That had come out too abruptly. It shouldn't have come out at all; the words should have stayed in her head. He looked confused, then his face crumpled and she knew he was about to cry.

'Sweetheart, I'm so sorry. I didn't mean to shout, I'm just tired...'

But the little boy had turned and was running out of the room. She heard him sob as he bounded up the stairs, then the thump of his door closing echoed through the house.

What the hell was wrong with her? Eve sat on the sofa, staring out through the window onto the street, feeling sick. Nothing could excuse the way she'd just snapped at her son, but she knew why she was so short-tempered: it was Saturday and Ben was coming over as usual to pick up Daniel in a couple of hours. She always hated Saturday mornings for precisely that reason, but today was particularly bad. This would be the first time they'd seen each other, or communicated, since he walked out of the pub.

But that wasn't Daniel's fault. Why had she yelled at him? The trouble was, like most little boys, he had no off switch, and she'd had just about all she could take of his chatter about the precious new baby. But it was only natural he was going to talk about it all the time; he was excited. Ben was right, she'd turned into a mean bitch.

She got up from the sofa and flicked the remote to turn off the garish cartoon Daniel had been watching on CBBC. As she walked upstairs, she could hear him sobbing, and she stopped on the landing outside his room, her hand on the banister, her heart thundering. This was all too awful.

She knocked on the door gently, then pushed it open and peered through. He was lying face down on the bed, his head buried in his arms.

'Daniel,' she said softly, as she walked over to him and sat down. 'Daniel, I'm so sorry I shouted at you. It was horrible of me. Please forgive me?'

He was still crying, but more softly now. She knew he was listening: waiting for her to carry on. She reached out and stroked his hair, the warmth of his little body radiating through her hand.

'I'm not being very nice at the moment, am I?' she said.

He lay still for a few seconds, then rolled over and looked up at her.

'It's okay, you can agree with me.' She smiled. 'I know I've been grumpy and snappy, and that's not fair on you.'

He sniffed and slowly stretched out his hand towards her, starting to fiddle with the button on the front of her cardigan.

'I've had a lot of things on my mind recently – things that have been worrying me – and that's made me upset and I've behaved badly,' she said. 'But there's no reason for me to take it out on you.'

He looked up at her, his eyes still glistening with tears. 'That's all right, Mummy. I know you've been sad.'

The surprise must have shown on her face.

'You've been sad because of Granny,' he said. 'About her having to go into the horrible old people's place. But when we go and see her now, she's always happy and she's got her new friend, the lady with the funny teeth, so maybe you don't need to be so sad about it anymore?'

Eve pulled him towards her in a hug, inhaling deeply to get a full fix of the sweet smell of his skin against hers, the shampoo in his hair, the washing powder on his clothes. She loved everything about this child; adored him so much that the love was a physical ache inside her.

She suddenly realised this was the first time they'd really spoken about what was happening with Flora. She hadn't given him credit for being perceptive enough to know – or care – what was going on. She had presumed the regular visits to Three Elms were just an inconvenience in his six-year-old world, an hour or so of enforced boredom before he could get home and switch on the TV or play with his Lego or his Nerf gun.

'Granny has been taking up a lot of my time recently, but that's already changing and things are getting easier,' she said. 'You're right, she's happier now, so I don't need to speak to her so often or go over to see her all the time. But I still need to be there for her, because she's my Mummy and I love her. The most important thing though, is that I'm your Mummy too and I need to be here for you.'

He lay back on the bed and nodded. 'You are,' he said. 'Most of the time.'

They looked at each other and grinned, and she put out her hand and swept his unruly fringe out of his eyes. He was overdue a haircut; she'd have to sort that out one day after school next week. Unless Ben could do it this afternoon? At the thought of asking Ben for anything, her heart flipped again.

'The way things have been here, at home...' she began, not sure this was the right time for this conversation, but deciding to risk it anyway. 'Has that had any effect on you at school? I mean, I know you haven't been happy there sometimes, and you've been getting into trouble. Is that because I've been so busy and you felt I was ignoring you?'

He shook his head, concentrating on the button on her cardigan again. 'Not really. It's not about you.'

'So, what's going on with this other boy, then; Liam?'

Daniel's eyes shot up to meet hers. He looked startled.

'Mrs Russell said the two of you don't get on, and you've been hitting Liam and fighting with him. I know it's hard when you don't like someone, but it's really important you try to be nice to everyone in your class.'

Daniel whispered something that she couldn't hear.

'Sorry, tell me that again?'

'I said, he's not nice to me. I don't know why, but he hates me. He hated me last year as well, but he hates me more now. He says stuff to me.'

'What sort of stuff?' asked Eve.

'He says I've got big ears and big feet, and that I do smelly farts. And when I don't wear the right uniform to school, he laughs at me and tells everyone I'm a loser.'

'Oh, that's horrible.' God, this was her fault: a couple of days ago she had yet again sent Daniel into school wearing a non-regulation sweatshirt, because she'd put a load of washing into the machine late at night and forgotten to get it out again, so his school jumper was still wet in the morning. He hadn't seemed to mind when she packed him off to school and she'd had no idea that the clothes she dressed him in were being used to make him feel bad. She needed to pull her finger out. There was already another full laundry basket of dirty clothes downstairs right now; as soon as she finished speaking to Daniel she would go and throw it all into the machine.

'I'm going to do something about this,' she said. 'I'm going to make sure that you have a proper uniform to wear every day. But you have *not* got big ears, or big feet, and so what if your farts smell? Everyone does smelly farts.'

He looked up at her again and started to smile.

'The thing is though, sweetheart, just because someone is being nasty to you, it doesn't mean you can hit them or kick them. You're going to have to learn to ignore whatever Liam says and walk away.'

'I do,' said Daniel. 'But he follows me. He pinches my legs under the desk and he kicks my feet when we're in the queue at lunchtime. The other day he bent one of my fingers back when we were washing the brushes from art. It really hurt.'

'Why doesn't Mrs Russell tell him off?'

The boy shrugged. 'She never sees when he does it; he waits until she's looking the other way. She only sees me doing things back to him.'

Eve sighed. It sounded as if Liam whatever-his-name-was had got school and Mrs Russell sussed. Unlike Daniel. 'I know it's hard, but you have to stop hurting him in return, when he hurts you. The main thing is to stay away from him, so he doesn't have the chance to do anything to you. You also need to learn a thing or two from him about staying under the radar – if you really can't stop yourself from giving him a kick, make sure you do it when Mrs Russell isn't looking! Not that I'm suggesting you should *ever* kick someone. Obviously. But if your foot should happen to slip when you're near him...'

She winked at Daniel, then got up and grabbed him by the hands, swinging him off the bed so he was standing up beside her. 'But right now, we're going to go down and have some milk and a biscuit, so you're not hungry when Daddy picks you up. Is that a good idea?'

Daniel nodded, his tears now dry and his eyes shining. As they went back down the stairs, he hopped from one leg to the other, still clutching her hand. 'Will you be okay when I've gone to Daddy's?'

'Of course I will, how do you mean?'

'Will you be lonely?'

She suddenly realised that he wasn't talking about this afternoon, once she'd waved Ben's Audi off down the street. He was thinking about Glasgow.

She sat down on the bottom step and gently pulled him round to face her. 'I'll be fine, you don't need to worry about me. But what about you – will you be okay at Daddy's?'

He nodded, staring down at his fingers as he twisted them around each other.

'Are you looking forward to it?' she asked, not really wanting to hear his answer.

He nodded again. 'But I don't want you to be lonely. You'll be here all by yourself and I won't be back when the weekend finishes. What will you do without me?'

She made herself smile, although in all honesty she had no idea what she would do. But this wasn't good; the fact that he was so concerned about her that he couldn't be excited about his own future. 'You mustn't worry about me; you should be looking forward to having a new bedroom and going to a new school in

Glasgow. It's all going to be really exciting! Whatever happens, we will make it work, and if you move away with Daddy – when you move away – I'll be fine here on my own. I'll keep your room clean and tidy, and you can come back whenever you want to see your friends, I'm sure you'll want to come back so you can play with Robbie in the holidays, won't you? I'll come up to see you as well – maybe some weekends I can come up on the train after work. I'll miss you, but I'll be happy knowing you're having a good time.'

'What if I get lonely without you?' he asked, in a small voice.

She pulled him into a hug, so he couldn't see that her face was crumpling as she tried not to cry. 'Well, in that case, Daddy and Lou will look after you for me,' she said, squeezing her eyes shut. 'You're bound to get lonely sometimes and feel miserable because you're away from me. But you'll have them all to take care of you and cheer you up again. Daddy and Lou both love you very much and they will be there for you all the time. Every single minute of the day and night. If you're feeling sad or if you're missing me, then you can ask for a special hug from Daddy... or from Lou.'

THIRTY-FOUR

The teacher from St Barnabas was standing in the middle of the room, wearing a Christmas jumper; it had a huge reindeer's head on the front, with a black bobble nose, googly eyes, velvet antlers and what appeared to be a red flashing collar. It was one of the most tasteless things Eve had ever seen.

'Wow!' said Daniel. 'Look at that – it's brilliant. I want one!'

They were late, as always, and there was barely even standing room at the back of the lounge. Eve squeezed herself in, apologising as she knocked into elbows and trod on toes, then pushed Daniel forward through the crowd ahead of her, so he could see. From her spot by the wall, she could just make out the top of a white head, which might or might not be Flora.

Today, the sofas and armchairs had been turned so that the residents sitting on them were facing into the room, with some of the children from St Barnabas perched amongst them, others standing at the back or fidgeting cross-legged on the floor at the front. Their parents had clearly come out en masse to support today's concert, along with the residents' relatives, and there were so many people in the room that the windows had steamed up. Crammed together like sardines, people were jostling against each other as they tried to shrug off their coats in the warm, wintery fug.

The singing wasn't bad. They sailed through *O Little Town of Bethlehem* and *Away in a Manger*, then one of the children did a warbling solo at the start of *Silent Night*. As she finished, an older voice took over: slightly quavery on the top notes, but strong and steady. Daniel pushed his way back through the people standing between them to grab Eve's hand excitedly, whispering: 'That's Granny singing!' before ploughing back to his spot at the front again.

Eve was amazed. Her mother could sing, but she'd never heard her perform like this. When Eve was a child and the two of them were driving somewhere in the car, they used to sing along to whatever was on the radio. They usually listened to Radio 2 – sometimes Radio 1 if Eve could persuade Flora to put up with what she called the 'stupid DJ chatter' – and when a song came on that they both loved, Eve would spin the volume dial, and they'd sing out at the tops of their voices. They had been word-perfect to *Love Shack* and, to this day, hearing that song took Eve back to the complete happiness her ten-year-old self had felt on those car journeys.

But that was a lifetime ago. As an adult she'd only heard Flora's voice on a handful of occasions: mostly when she was standing beside her at weddings or funerals. Or when her mother was singing loudly in an otherwise silent doctor's waiting room.

There were several more carols, each one applauded enthusiastically by the onlookers, then the teacher thanked everyone for coming. 'It has been an honour to be involved in this,' he said. 'Being able to bring old and young together in this way has been so special. And we've all learnt such a lot from it – and from each other. We're hoping the children will continue to come to Three Elms at least once a month to meet up with their new friends here.'

It took a while for Eve to work her way through the groups of people standing chatting and, when she got to Flora's side, she realised her mother was also wearing a Christmas jumper: bright blue with a snowman knitted onto the front. It was several sizes too large for her and hung in baggy folds down past her thighs.

'Daniel, this is my friend, Olivia,' Flora was saying. 'She and I have been spending quite a lot of time together over the last few weeks.' The two children eyed each other cautiously. 'And her parents are here too,' said Flora, turning to Eve. 'Hello darling, did you enjoy it?'

'That was fantastic,' said Eve, smiling at the young couple standing beside her. 'Olivia was great, they all seem to have had a wonderful time taking part in this.'

The children were being called over to the door by their teacher, and the girl turned to Flora and threw herself at her, squeezing her arms so tightly around her neck that Flora shrieked with laughter. 'Sweetheart, you'll strangle me!'

'Coming into Three Elms has been so good for her,' said Olivia's mother, as the girl ran off. 'She isn't settled at school and we worry she's a bit lonely. She doesn't have a grandmother of her own anymore, so it's lovely the two of you have struck up this friendship.'

'I've enjoyed it too,' said Flora. 'I don't have a granddaughter, so we're perfectly matched.'

'Well, you've got me!' said Daniel.

'Yes, of course I have,' said Flora, pulling him into a hug. 'And you are my very best boy.'

He nodded, looking serious. 'It's okay, Granny, I don't mind sharing you,' he said. 'Olivia can have a bit of you as well.

Especially when I go to Glasgow – then she can have you all of the time, if she wants.'

Flora looked confused, and Eve quickly changed the subject, saying goodbye to Olivia's parents and suggesting to Flora that they move out of the crowded lounge.

'That was great, you've got a lovely voice,' she said, one hand through her mother's arm, the other clutching Daniel. 'But you didn't tell me you were doing a solo. Did you have to audition for that?'

Flora turned to look at her. 'What do you mean?'

'Well, did that schoolteacher choose you, or did you just volunteer for it?'

Flora was shaking her head. 'I don't know what you're going on about, Eve,' she said. 'I can't sing for toffee. Why would I want to sing a solo in front of a room full of strangers?'

There were a handful of people in the library, but it was quiet and less stuffy than the lounge. As they walked in, Eve saw Barbara sunk into one of the deep armchairs; she was reading a book, and lowered it as she saw them coming. She was also wearing a Christmas jumper: it was identical to Flora's, but several sizes smaller, so the head of the snowman was stretched tightly across her chest and the sleeves ended halfway up her forearms. Eve had no idea how she'd managed to squeeze herself into it, but getting it off again was going to be a challenge.

'Ah, there you are,' said Barbara. 'Is that wretched carol thing over at last? I could hardly concentrate on my book with all that racket.'

Flora lowered herself into a chair beside her. 'It was actually very lovely,' she said. 'And all the better for not having you there, yowling alongside us.'

When the two women were sitting side by side, it was very obvious that each would be better off wearing the other's jumper. Eve wondered if she ought to say something, but it would only complicate matters. Besides, she didn't want to be the one who had to try and extract Barbara from the massively stretched snowman.

'The children were a delight,' said Flora. 'Real little angels.'

Barbara sniffed and picked up her book again. Eve noticed she had managed to get hold of a Jilly Cooper. 'I am far too busy for that sort of nonsense,' she said. 'I've got to a very exciting bit where Rupert is having a lot of casual sex.'

'Goodness!' said Flora. 'Lucky Rupert.'

'What's casual sex?' asked Daniel. 'Can I get some?'

When they got home, Eve unlocked the front door and sent Daniel inside, then went next door and rang the bell. Jake answered, holding a wooden spoon and wearing an apron with a picture on the front of a woman's body in a bikini.

'Hello stranger!' He grinned. 'Nice to see you. Do you fancy coming in for spag bol?'

She laughed. 'Nice offer, but I need to get Daniel sorted. Thank you though. I just wondered if Katie was free to babysit tomorrow night?'

Jake shrugged. 'No idea, my delightful daughter doesn't generally tell me her plans in advance. She's due back soon though, I'll ask her to pop round if you like?'

'That would be great.' Eve couldn't help noticing that he had a lump of bolognaise sauce in his fringe, and she reached up to wipe it away.

'Oh, thanks,' he said. 'I'm not the neatest chef. I wouldn't eat that bit if I were you, it probably needs cooking for longer. So, are you going anywhere nice, tomorrow night?'

Eve nodded. 'I am, actually. I'm going out for a drink, to that rather nice wine bar down on the corner.'

He nodded. 'I know it. The rather nice wine bar has got a rather nice Chablis on offer at the moment. You ought to try it.'

'Thanks,' said Eve. 'That sounds good. Do you drink a lot of Chablis?'

Jake grinned. 'Not on my salary,' he said. 'But every now and then a special occasion demands it.'

'Good,' said Eve. 'Because this is a special occasion.' He looked confused. 'You'll need to drink some Chablis tomorrow night,' she continued. 'Because you're coming out with me, to that rather nice wine bar on the corner.'

THIRTY-FIVE

Daniel needed to be a Wise Man for the school nativity play. And he needed to be one urgently.

'A letter was sent home in the book bags several weeks ago,' said Mrs Russell with a sigh, her arms crossed, her glare no more friendly than the last time Eve had seen her. 'All the other children have already brought their costumes into school, Miss Glover. The dress rehearsal is tomorrow afternoon and the nativity performance itself is on Thursday. Presumably you have heard about that and have ordered your ticket?'

'Of course,' said Eve, who hadn't ordered anything.

'Please ensure Daniel brings in his costume first thing in the morning, and, as usual, everything needs to be labelled.'

'No problem,' said Eve, smiling so much her cheeks hurt.

She grabbed Daniel's hand and started walking away towards the car. 'Which other boys are Wise Men?' she hissed at him. 'I need to speak to their mothers to find out what you're supposed to be wearing.'

'Jonathan's one of them,' said Daniel. 'His mummy hired him a costume from the theatre; he's got a big shiny pot as well, with frankly sense in it.'

'Oh, great.' There was no way she had time to get to a costume hire shop. This would have to be a cobbled-together, homemade effort. 'What about the other Wise Man? Quick, Daniel, who is it?'

'Toby. But he's not here today.'

'Damn and bugger,' said Eve. 'Okay, we'll have to wing this. Let's go home and look up some pictures online.'

'Mummy, you shouldn't swear,' said Daniel. 'Especially when you're talking about our nativity play. God wouldn't like it.'

Jake and Katie were due at 7pm, but by the time the doorbell rang, Eve had only just served up Daniel's tea.

'We've had a crisis,' she explained, letting them in. 'Daniel has to be a Wise Man in the school nativity and I forgot – or rather, I didn't forget, I just didn't get the letter. So, I've made him a costume, but I'm not really sure it works. Daniel, stand up and show them.'

The boy put down his knife and fork and scraped his chair back from the table.

Katie and Jake stared at him.

'What do you think?' asked Eve. 'It's one of my old shirts, and the cord is from a curtain. I'm quite pleased with the crown though – apart from the wonky bits at the back. What do you think?'

'Seriously?' asked Katie. 'It's awful. It won't do at all.'

Eve put her hands up to her head and groaned. 'But I haven't got time to sort out anything else – he has to take it into school in the morning.'

Katie put her hands on Daniel's shoulders and turned him around to get a better look. 'Don't worry,' she said. 'Leave it with me.'

By the time Eve and Jake got down to the wine bar, there was only one free table, beside the door to the gents' toilets.

'Sit here and I'll get the drinks in,' said Jake. 'Wine? Prosecco? Gin?'

'Yes please,' she said. 'All of those.'

He came back with a bottle of white wine and two large glasses. 'I thought you ought to stick to this,' he said. 'It's that Chablis we were talking about. Gin might make you maudlin and you'll get pissed too quickly on fizz. Cheers!'

Talking to this man was so easy. They started with Eve's appalling attempts at costume-making, and went on to discuss their children, their work, their irritating colleagues and all the repair jobs that neither of them had got around to tackling in their respective homes.

'I'm sorry I was useless with the mower,' said Jake. 'I'm much better with an electric screwdriver if you have any DIY that needs doing? I can put up shelves or take down shelves. I can paint shelves. I can do anything with shelves really.'

Eve went to buy another bottle of wine; when she came back Jake had loosened his tie and undone the top button of his shirt. She wished he'd taken the tie off: it had cartoon Dalmatians on it. He refilled their glasses and held out his to clink against hers.

'Cheers again,' he said. 'Your very good health. I hope you don't mind me asking, but how are things, with Ben?'

Her face flared as she remembered the afternoon a few weeks ago when she had gone round to thank Jake for the flowers, and ended up bawling on his sofa while he provided her with tissues and an increasingly damp shoulder.

'Fine,' she answered automatically, before realising there was no need to put on any kind of brave face. 'Actually, not fine at all. Things are a bit shit. Ben and Lou are still planning on moving to Glasgow, and we fell out the other night, over Daniel. He told me I was a bad mother and didn't deserve to have custody of him, so I'm now waiting to find out whether he's going to challenge me through the courts.'

'That's dreadful,' said Jake. 'How can he accuse you of being a bad mother? You do a great job with that little boy.'

'Not great enough,' said Eve, looking down as she twisted the stem of the wine glass between her finger and thumb. 'Ben said I've been distracted recently and I haven't noticed Daniel's not happy at school. And that's true. There's so much going on at the moment; I feel I'm pulled in so many directions and I'm not dealing with anything properly. Take the nativity. I bet none of the other mothers have completely missed all the letters about providing costumes. I just can't seem to get myself organised and keep all the balls in the air.'

'So, what has Ben done to help?' asked Jake.

'How do you mean?'

'Does he know what's going on in Daniel's life at school? Does he empty his bag every night to check for letters? Does he speak to the teacher? Does he fill in his reading record? Does he make his packed lunch in the morning? Does he iron his uniform?'

Eve smiled. 'I don't do that last one either,' she said. 'I've got the most wrinkled child in the road, in case you hadn't noticed.'

'You know what I mean,' said Jake. 'He's blaming you for not coping well, but I bet he doesn't do any of those things himself.'

There was a question Eve suddenly wanted to ask. It was possibly something that should wait until she knew Jake a little better, but she was fuelled by Chablis, and also felt he wouldn't mind if she asked it now. 'Have you always been on your own with Katie? I've never heard you talk about her mother.'

'You won't have done,' he said. 'We separated when Katie was five and Michelle moved to France. She had mental health issues and having a young child caused her lots of emotional problems. She promised she would stay in touch with Katie, but she didn't. We haven't heard from her now in about ten years.'

Eve's mouth fell open: how could a mother just walk out on her own child? She was distraught at the prospect of Ben taking Daniel to live hundreds of miles away; the thought of never having any more contact with him was unbearable.

'For a while I worried Katie had turned into a vile teenager because she didn't have a mother around during such an important stage in her life,' said Jake. 'But actually, we're surrounded by some wonderful women – friends and family – who have been involved in her upbringing and been great role models. I've decided Katie is a vile teenager because of a combination of hormones and social media. It has much less to do with my single dad parenting skills – or lack of them.'

Eve smiled. 'It can't have been easy, bringing her up on your own.'

'Not always, but it's been a lot of fun too,' said Jake. 'Things have got even more interesting now that boys are on the scene. I have to play it cool and pretend not to care whether she tells me about her love life or not. If I do that, I know she'll tell me everything. She split up with her latest boyfriend last week, and she told me about it in great detail – most of it was stuff I'd rather not have heard.'

Jake drained his glass and stood it beside hers on the table. 'It's really important to me to be a decent father. My own dad was a bit of a bastard, to tell the truth. He had a nasty temper and a cruel tongue. He was never violent or anything like that, but he wasn't loving and he didn't have any time for whatever my sister and I were doing. He didn't care how we did at school or whether or not we got good grades. When I applied to study sociology at university, he said it was a namby-pamby subject and not the sort of thing a son of his should be studying. Bizarrely, the fact that I was the first person in our family to go to university didn't seem to matter. He was just pissed off that I wasn't doing something manly like physics or engineering.'

'Given the family history, it sounds as if Katie has been lucky you've turned out to be such a great dad,' said Eve.

'Ah, but you don't know I have,' said Jake. 'You don't know me very well at all, Eve.'

'No,' she said, leaning forward over her empty glass, and running her finger down a Dalmatian's tail. 'But I think I'd quite like to get to know you better.'

'Hussy,' he said, and winked at her.

THIRTY-SIX

With just seven days left until Christmas, Eve was beginning to panic about her lack of planning. She had ordered a few stocking fillers online for Daniel, but had no idea what to buy him in the way of a proper present, although he'd given her some suggestions.

'I would like an iPhone 15,' he'd announced. 'Everyone in my class is getting one of those at Christmas.'

'What, everyone?'

'Yes.' He nodded. 'Although some of the girls are getting Disney princess stuff as well.'

'The thing is, sweetheart,' said Eve. 'I haven't got an iPhone 15 myself, and I don't think I'm likely to get one until they're so outdated they'll be available on eBay for about fifty quid. I'm afraid I can't afford to buy you something like that.'

'I don't want one from you, Mummy!' said Daniel, rolling his eyes. 'I know you can't pay for it. But it doesn't matter because I'm going to ask for one from Father Christmas; he can put it in my stocking.'

Eve had been thinking about buying him some walkie-talkies, imagining the fun he and Robbie would have with them:

one outside in the garden hiding in the shed, the other crawling behind the sofa in the sitting room, their tinny voices being relayed the twenty metres between them as they spoke in a code they'd made up themselves. Hopefully the excitement of that would help Daniel forget Father Christmas hadn't delivered the goods.

Now she was elbowing her way around the shops, along with hundreds of others who had also thought that particular Wednesday afternoon, a week before Christmas, would be a good time to go out and scramble for last-minute presents. Bags with sharp edges scraped her shins and strangers trod on her toes as they pushed each other aside to grab items from shelves. When it began to drizzle, she went into a café, ordered a hot chocolate and collapsed into a seat.

She'd been thinking about her conversation with Jake last night: how sad it was that he'd had such a bad relationship with his father. Her own childhood had been so secure and she'd constantly been made to feel special; she couldn't imagine having a parent who didn't care what you did, let alone one who shouted and swore and made home an awkward place to be. You would need a lot of confidence and self-belief to deal with it: Jake clearly had that, she wondered if his sister was the same.

What if she managed to trace Alan Baker, but discovered he was a similar sort of man: selfish, arrogant, caring nothing for other people's feelings? That wasn't a comforting prospect, but perhaps it was the most likely outcome if he was also the sort of man who had ignored a young woman's attempts to contact him and tell him she was pregnant.

A huge mug of hot chocolate, topped with cream, marshmallows and chocolate sprinkles, was delivered to her table by a stick-thin teenage boy who looked like he could do with drinking it himself.

'Thanks.' She smiled up at him. 'I shouldn't really be having this, but I've told myself I deserve it!'

The boy stared at her blankly: he was far too young to understand the concept of middle-aged guilt.

It was ironic, Eve thought, as she sipped the drink and licked away a chocolate moustache, that Jake had a real father who did a bad job and was a prize bastard, while she had grown up thinking she had a kind, loving father who adored her, but who turned out to be a figment of her mother's imagination.

A couple at the table next to hers were bickering, snapping at each other, then lapsing into long silences, both bristling at whatever had been left unsaid. Their two teenage children slumped sullenly in their chairs, swiping at mobile phones. The woman angrily stirred a spoon around in her tea, while her husband fiddled with sachets of sugar, folding them in half, then in half again, discarding each one and picking up another when the paper tore and the sugar began to spill onto the table.

'It is *not* my fault,' the woman hissed. 'You said you'd do it, but as usual, you left it all to me.'

'Oh nag, nag, bloody nag,' said the man. 'You're like a broken record.'

The teenagers didn't raise their eyes from their phones; they were clearly used to this kind of exchange. Eve turned her face away. How awful for them. At least Daniel would never have to witness his parents slagging each other off in public.

Did Ben and Lou bicker at all? It seemed unlikely – they'd only been together for a few years and Daniel never mentioned anything like that when he came back from his weekends at their house. But you never knew what went on behind closed doors and even Ben's new relationship couldn't be constant sweetness and light.

Part of Eve – a mean part – hoped they did get on each other's nerves every now and then. Maybe Lou got fed up with hearing Ben go on and on about how busy and stressed he was at work. Or perhaps he resented the fact that he had to look after Keira most Saturdays while she was in the shop. It would mean they were only human, rather than near perfect.

'The problem is you never listen,' the woman at the next table was saying. 'I tell you things and you nod and say you'll do them, to get me off your back. But then nothing happens!'

Eve ran her spoon around the bottom of the mug to scrape up the last of the chocolate. This was the best bit, the congealed mass that hadn't been dissolved by the boiling milk.

The thing about looking for Alan was that it would be heart-breaking if he turned out to be a less than perfect human being. But she needed to accept that the chances of him being anything else were slim. If he had hung around and done the right thing by Flora, they might have ended up being unhappily married: irritated by everything the other said and did, staying together for the sake of their daughter, resenting every minute of it. Her mother saw the relationship as perfect – because it had never had a chance to go wrong.

Eve finished her hot chocolate and started to gather the various plastic bags around her feet. It would probably help her move on from all this if she got rid of those letters; apart from a pinpointed location on Google Maps, they were the only tangible connection she had to her father. She should toss the contents of the shoebox onto a bonfire or hold a match to the envelopes and watch them burn, one by one. Would that feel too final, though? Too brutal? Maybe she ought to hang onto them for a while – then at least it would feel as if she still had a small piece of her father. There wasn't anything physical or concrete in that shoebox, and the irony was that Alan Baker himself hadn't volunteered any of the information in there. But those letters would always remind her how Flora had felt about this man and how she had tried to involve him in their lives.

Her phone rang, Ben's name lighting up the display. Her stomach lurched: they still hadn't spoken. When he'd picked up and dropped off Daniel, last weekend, Lou and Keira had been in the car, so it had been easier to give a friendly little wave, and a 'See you soon!' than to start a serious conversation. Maybe that was why he'd brought them along? It meant neither of them had to say anything about the move to Glasgow or the hurtful comments they'd hurled at each other.

'Hi!' she said. 'This is a surprise.' She regretted it immediately: she sounded unnecessarily upbeat – verging on sarcastic. He probably hadn't been thinking about any of this as much as she had. Eve knew she was a very insignificant part of Ben's life now, and one he was possibly irritated at having to take into consideration. Whereas his plans for the future were dominating her life. It was up to her to clear some air.

'Listen, Ben, I'm glad you called. I just wanted to apologise for being so out of order, when we met for a drink the other night. I didn't mean it when I said that Daniel is unsettled when he comes back from yours, he isn't. I was just lashing out, feeling a bit insecure I guess.' There was silence on the other end of the phone. 'I'm also sorry I made that horrible remark about your new baby and how Daniel wouldn't get as much of your attention. That was such a bitchy thing to say, and I'm embarrassed about it. I know it's not true.'

There was a pause. Then he cleared his throat. 'I'm sorry too. All that stuff about you not being a good mother. I'm not sure why I said it. You're a great mother, Eve – you've always done such an amazing job with Daniel.'

The silence stretched between them again, but this time it didn't feel so deafening. Should she say anything else about that night? Maybe this was enough; they'd broken the ice.

'So, how are you all?' she continued. 'Daniel's really looking forward to this weekend – he says you're going to take him to see Santa's grotto in Winter Wonderland.'

She'd been planning to take him there herself, but having seen how excited he was about the trip with his dad, she'd decided against it. It would be magical for him to go on Saturday afternoon, with darkness falling and the place sparkling with fairy lights, and it would be more fun if he was there with Keira – his half-sister's excitement bubbling up to match his own. Deep inside, there was a part of her that was disappointed to be missing out on seeing the delight on his face, but she had to stop being self-indulgent. There would be other Christmases.

'Yes, that's the plan,' Ben was saying. 'But I was calling to let you know I'll be a bit late picking him up on Saturday. Lou's not feeling great at the moment so I need to run a few errands for her, first thing.'

'Oh dear, poor Lou,' said Eve. To her surprise, she realised she meant it.

'Would midday be okay?' asked Ben.

'Yes, fine.'

'Great, see you then.'

'Ben?' she said, sensing he was bringing the call to an end. 'I just wanted to let you know that Daniel and I have been talking about a lot of things recently – the problems at school, and you moving to Glasgow...' She paused, but he didn't say anything. 'He's been telling me about the other boy he's been fighting with, Liam, and it does sound as if he's the one who's causing all the trouble, not Daniel. I know we thought that would be the case, but it really set my mind at rest to hear his side of the story. I think it would be a good thing if we both reassured him about school and the fact that we're going to back him up about what's been going on. Maybe we can arrange to have a proper meeting with Mrs Russell after Christmas?' Still silence. Eve knew what Ben was thinking. 'I'm not saying things are going to improve instantly,' she added. 'Or that he's suddenly going to start loving school and not want to move away. This has nothing to do with you going to Glasgow. I just wanted to update you.'

'Okay...' She heard the hesitation in his voice.

'I realise the move is going to happen, and I understand why you want to take Daniel with you.' There was a slight wobble in her voice; she hoped he couldn't hear it. 'And I just wanted to say that, whatever happens, we will make it work. But Daniel is the most important person in all this, not me or you, and we have to remember that. So, we need to talk it through properly – you, me and Lou – and really think about how to make sure it all goes smoothly. I'm not going to stand in your way, Ben, but I need to know that our son is happy.'

She had closed her eyes while she was talking, resting her head against the wall beside her; when she opened them again, she found herself staring at the family who were sitting at the next table; the woman's cheeks were flushed and her mouth screwed up with anger as she glared at her husband.

'Well... that's great. Sounds good to me,' said Ben, his voice softer than it had been before. 'Thanks Eve. I appreciate it. See you Saturday.'

As Eve gathered together her bags and got up, the woman threw herself back in her chair and crossed her arms, shaking her head.

'What do you expect me to do about it?' her husband was saying.

'Nothing!' She sighed. 'Absolutely nothing. Which is what you've done for the last twenty years.'

Her teenage son looked up from his phone and caught Eve's eye. She grinned at him, without thinking, and he smiled back, rolling his eyes and grimacing. She hoped the life he was living on social media was a hundred times better than the one he was living in reality with his squabbling parents.

THIRTY-SEVEN

Even Mrs Russell was impressed, although Eve sensed she didn't want to be. 'Daniel, you look magnificent,' she said, smiling down at him. 'That crown is a work of art. Where did you get the jewels for it, Miss Glover? And that ermine trim is very effective.'

Eve smiled and accepted the praise, knowing she didn't deserve it. By the time she and Jake stumbled in from the wine bar on Tuesday night, Katie had been putting the finishing touches to the costume.

'Don't worry, Daniel has been in bed for hours,' she said. 'But after you left, we went next door to hunt through my old dressing-up box. We got this amazing purple cape and a big gold chain to go around his neck, and I've made a new crown. No offence, Eve, but Daniel and I both thought your crown was a bit crap.'

Eve wasn't offended at all; she was relieved – and rather impressed. Katie had clearly done enough dressing up in her time to be able to cobble together an outfit which was not only sophisticated and appropriate for a six-year-old Wise Man, but also had sufficient homemade touches to impress the other parents.

This afternoon the school hall was full of them, with small children balanced on laps and buggies blocking the aisles. Eve was surprised staff weren't running up and down with clipboards handing out health and safety notices. She took Flora's hand, squeezing it and smiling as her mother turned to look at her. She hadn't been sure it was a good idea to bring Flora along to this afternoon's performance, and it had taken some time to cajole her into her coat and get her out of the front door of Three Elms.

'Where are we going this time?' Flora had asked for the fifth time as Eve got her into the passenger seat of the car and pulled the seatbelt across. 'I'm not sure this is something we should be doing, Eve.'

But now they were sitting in the second row of chairs in the school hall, Flora had cheered up. 'I must say, this is a real treat,' she kept saying. 'I haven't been to the theatre in years!'

As the nativity started, they watched flocks of sheep circle the stage, followed by gatherings of angels, most of them Reception children whose parents oohed and aahed as their offspring did a higgledy-piggledy dance, clutching toppling halos and tripping over untied laces on ballet shoes.

Eventually, once Mary and Joseph were safely installed in a makeshift stable with a Tiny Tears doll swaddled in a crocheted blanket, Daniel walked onto the stage, resplendent in his cape and crown.

'That's Daniel!' exclaimed Flora loudly, grabbing Eve's hand and not noticing the heads turning in her direction. 'I didn't realise he was an actor now. Isn't that something!'

Eve squeezed her hand. She was right, it really was something. Her little boy stood up tall on the stage, bellowing out his lines and grinning down at them, waving excitedly when he'd finished speaking. His costume was impressive, his acting less so, but she couldn't have been more proud.

'Is he going to sing?' asked Flora.

'No, Mum, I really hope not.'

Eve looked at the rapt expression on her mother's face; Flora had been as happy as this after the carol concert the other week, but it was good to see her out and about, rather than stuck inside Three Elms. She just hoped that these trips and a taste of the outside world wouldn't make Flora unhappy when she had to go back, in a couple of hours' time. She seemed settled at the home now, but each time she went to visit, Eve was still plagued by uncertainty: worried her mother would turn back into the miserable, confused old lady who had threatened to kill herself all those weeks ago. It was going to take a long time for the memories of those early days to fade.

'Where's this theatre again?' Flora asked loudly, as the Angel Gabriel stomped in from stage left and began to speak to Mary and Joseph. 'Why hasn't Daniel got any more words? He's very good, isn't he?'

Her voice rang out in the darkened hall, cutting across the quavering voice of the angel-in-chief. A man in the row behind them leant forward and tapped Flora on the shoulder: 'Shhhh!'

Eve turned around. 'Shhhh yourself!' she hissed back. The man crossed his arms in front of his chest and glared at her, and Eve glared back until he eventually shook his head and turned his attention to what was happening on the stage. She put an arm around Flora's shoulders and hugged her close. This afternoon she was not going to be made to feel ashamed of her mother.

Up on stage the children burst into a loud rendition of *While shepherds watched their flocks.* Flora clapped her hands and started singing along.

Her dementia was more advanced than it had been just a

few weeks ago, when she moved into Three Elms but, ironically, she seemed calmer and happier. Or maybe the whole thing felt easier because Eve herself was less stressed about what was happening? It had occurred to her, only recently, that she'd spent much of the last year waging war against something she didn't stand a chance of beating. That ongoing fight, together with the fact that she constantly felt she was failing, had been demoralising, as well as exhausting. Accepting Flora's dementia and acknowledging she didn't need to keep battling against it anymore, was like having a weight lifted from her shoulders.

They'd been handed a programme when they arrived earlier and, reading through the names of the cast, Eve noticed Daniel was one of the few children in his year to have been given a speaking part. She beamed back up at him, not quite sure why he'd been singled out, but proud anyway. She scanned the long lists of children who were grouped together in crowd scenes, as villagers and a host of relatively minor angels. The name Liam Boxall caught her eye: one of a dozen sheep. She looked across at them, penned to one side of the stage under the watchful eye of the teacher who was sitting at the piano. She had no idea what he looked like, but it wouldn't have been possible to pick him out from the crowd anyway, amongst the mass of fluffy white bobble hats and hairbands festooned with cotton wool.

The PTA had laid on some wine for proud parents after the performance, and Eve and Flora filed into one of the downstairs classrooms to accept a glass of lukewarm Chardonnay. It flashed through Eve's mind that she shouldn't be allowing her mother to have wine at this time in the afternoon – what if she carried on drinking when she was back at Three Elms later?

But it was too late.

'Yes please, I'll have some of that,' said Flora, stepping forward and holding out her hand. A mum Eve vaguely recognised was standing at a trestle table, behind rows of prepoured glasses of wine. She picked up one and handed it to Flora, smiling so widely that Eve could see the gums above her front teeth.

'Wasn't the show fantastic?' she said. 'I think we should all be very proud. My daughter has been so excited about this afternoon. She's been practising her lines and singing away at home.'

'Oh, mine too,' said Flora. 'All the time.'

The woman looked confused, and Eve put her arm on her mother's elbow and moved her away from the table, grabbing a glass for herself as she did so.

'Are you sure you want that?' she asked, looking at the wine.

'Of course I do,' said Flora. 'Why wouldn't I?'

Eve wished she hadn't said anything. Why indeed? What right did she have to stop her mother from enjoying one of the few pleasures she had left in life. Anyway, it was only a small glass of cheap Chardonnay. She put out her glass and clinked it against Flora's. 'Cheers,' she said. 'Happy Christmas, Mum.'

'Ooh, is it Christmas already?' said Flora. 'Lovely – I like Christmas.' She took a sip of her wine. 'This is nice,' she said, before tipping up her glass and draining it. 'Yes, very nice indeed.'

She stepped past Eve and moved back to the table, holding out the empty glass to the smiley mum standing behind it. 'Can I have some more of this, please?'

THIRTY-EIGHT

For once Daniel wasn't ready when Ben arrived on Saturday. 'I can't find my trainers!' he yelled from upstairs, as the doorbell rang.

'They're under your bed,' she called back. 'Brush your teeth while you're up there, please.'

When she opened the front door, Ben had his back to her, hands in pockets; she could hear him jingling his loose change.

'Sorry,' she said. 'He's not quite ready. He'll be down in a minute.'

Ben swung round, bouncing slightly on the balls of his feet, hands still in his pockets. He was wearing his designer sunglasses again, even though it was nearly Christmas.

'The sun's pretty blinding out there today, isn't it?' said Eve, smiling to show she wasn't really having a go at him.

Ben reached up to pull off the glasses. 'Better?'

'Much,' she said. 'You've got nice eyes. You ought to be showing them off.' She had always loved his eyes: they were a rich brown, the colour of the conkers Daniel scrabbled to collect each autumn. Ben looked taken aback, and she realised that was probably the first compliment she'd paid him in years.

'Do you want to come in? He's just brushing his teeth.'

'No, don't worry. I'll go and wait in the car. Don't want to disturb you.'

'Ben, you're not disturbing me. Come in for a bit. Please?' She stood back in the hall, opening the door wide. This was probably the last thing he wanted to do: he had lived with her in this house for several years and, even after all this time, it must still feel familiar – while at the same time, terribly strange. Stepping past the front door which they'd painted letterbox red, standing on the wooden floorboards they'd painstakingly sanded and polished together, looking up the stairs at the carpet they'd taken such a long time to choose. It must feel very odd.

In some ways it was just as odd for her to have him in front of her in the hallway. He never came in when he collected Daniel and, over the years, she had forgotten what it was like to see him here, standing awkwardly beside the coat hooks where he used to hang his jackets, absently tapping his toe against the frame of the sitting-room door, where once he used to kick off his shoes and leave them lying in the doorway.

'I bet Keira's excited about this afternoon,' said Eve.

He leant back against the wall, nodding. 'We're going back to pick her up now, then I'll buy them some lunch before we go to Winter Wonderland,' he said. 'I have a feeling the place will be heaving.'

She laughed. 'It will be hell,' she said. 'I don't envy you, to be honest.'

He smiled back at her, then looked away again quickly. 'Nice picture,' he said, noticing a print on the wall at the bottom of the stairs.

'Yes, Mum bought it for me,' she said. 'It was done by a local artist. We went to see his exhibition.' *Years ago,* she nearly added. Before Daniel even started school. That watercolour print was so familiar in its spot on the wall now, she was almost surprised to be reminded it hadn't been there when Ben lived in this house.

They stood in silence for a few seconds, not meeting each other's eye, listening to the bumps and crashes as their son moved about in the bathroom upstairs. The cold tap was running so hard, Eve could picture the water splashing over the edge of the basin as he brushed his teeth, drenching his T-shirt, splattering onto the tiled floor and leaving puddles she would later slip on.

'How *is* your mum?' asked Ben.

'Oh, well... she's okay. She has good days and bad days, but she's settling in much better at the home now. It was tricky for a while.'

He nodded. 'That's good news. Say hello to her for me, will you?'

Eve tried not to show her surprise. She couldn't remember him ever saying anything like that before. She didn't like to tell him that Flora might not even remember the unofficial son-in-law who hadn't played a part in her life for the last five years.

'The new job's not really going to plan,' said Ben, suddenly.

She stared at him, confused.

'They won't be sending so many people up to Glasgow. Seems like they'd overestimated the size of the team they'll need there, so the whole thing has been scaled back a bit.'

'Oh, I'm sorry,' she said. 'But it will still be a challenge, I mean you'll still be in charge of setting up the new office. Maybe it will be less stressful if you've got a smaller team to oversee?'

Ben shook his head. 'No, everything has changed. They made a decision on it yesterday. They think it would be more constructive for me to stay down in Bristol, manage some ongoing projects here.'

Eve's brain was hearing what he was saying, but running to catch up. Did this mean he wasn't moving away at all? No

Glasgow. No promotion. No massive salary hike. No new shop for Lou. But most important of all: Daniel wouldn't be going anywhere either. She knew she ought to say something, but couldn't speak.

'Of course, they'll probably give me some increased responsibility down here as well,' Ben was saying. 'There's talk of putting in new systems and restructuring the way we allocate work between different departments, so I'm hoping they'll be using me to oversee some of that.'

His voice was upbeat, but she knew him well enough to see that this was hurting: the way he was holding his chin slightly too high, the fact that he wasn't meeting her eye as he talked. Disappointment was written all over him. This forty-year-old man, whom she had once loved so dearly, looked like a little boy who'd been sent away by Father Christmas and told he would be getting sod-all in his stocking this year.

'Oh Ben, I'm sorry,' she said.

He'd been staring up the stairs, as if waiting for Daniel to appear at the top of them, but now turned to look at her, possibly doubting she meant it.

'Seriously,' she said. 'I really am sorry. I know how much you and Lou were looking forward to this.'

'We were,' he said. 'I guess it felt like a way we could both make a new start together. There are lots of memories here in Bristol, not all of them good.'

She nodded, feeling the stab of hurt.

'Oh shit, that came out wrong!' he said. 'I just meant that a move would have been good for both of us. Lou was ready to walk away from the shop, she wanted a new challenge, and with the baby and everything...' He trailed off.

'I know what you mean,' she said. 'A new start would have been good for both of you.'

'We put the house on the market a few weeks ago, when all

this happened,' he said. 'I had to call the agent this morning to tell them we're not selling. They weren't happy about it at all, said they had a potential buyer who was going to put in an offer in the next couple of days.'

Eve grinned. 'I bet they did – that's what we always say. As a profession we're skilled at being economical with the truth.'

He laughed. 'I should have put the house on with your lot, shouldn't I? We did think about it, but to be honest we decided that would be a bit weird. Sorry.'

'Don't be,' she said. 'It would have been very weird.'

Daniel came thundering down the stairs, his backpack dragging behind him, banging against each step. A crash came from inside it, sounding suspiciously like something breaking.

'Daddy!' yelled Daniel, launching himself into Ben's arms.

'Hello Danny boy, how are you doing?'

'Do they have food at Winter Wonderland? Can we get chocolate doughnuts, like we did at Lunar City the other time?'

'Do you know, I'm pretty sure they sell chocolate doughnuts,' said Ben, putting the boy back down on the floor. 'But if not, we'll find something else to eat.'

'But I don't want anything else – I want chocolate doughnuts! Lou likes them too!'

'Lou's a bit tired at the moment, so it's just going to be you, me and Keira this afternoon.'

'But I want chocolate doughnuts!' yelled Daniel, colour rising in his cheeks.

'We'll talk about it in the car,' said Ben. 'Come on, let's go.'

'Sorry to hear Lou's not feeling great,' said Eve, as their son ran down the path. 'How many weeks is she now?'

'Nearly fourteen,' said Ben. 'She's had awful morning sickness and she's wiped out all the time. Some days she doesn't even go into the shop until lunchtime. It's strange, I don't remember her being this bad with Keira.'

Eve wondered if he remembered anything about those nine long months when she'd been pregnant with Daniel. It was unlikely. She had also felt shattered for most of the time: dragging herself out of bed in the morning was such an effort, and by the end of the day she could hardly lift her feet to carry herself back up the stairs to bed. She had once fallen asleep at her desk at work, lowering her head onto her arms and giving in as the gentle swell of sleep overtook her, despite the ringing phones and background chatter. She found out later that Gav had been throwing paper aeroplanes at her from the other end of the office but, even when one landed on her head, she hadn't stirred.

'She's bloody grumpy too,' Ben said. 'I can't seem to do anything right.' He grinned at Eve; a smile that was part conspiratorial.

'I was the same, wasn't I?' She laughed. 'Do you remember that time you came back from the takeaway with poppadoms instead of naan?'

'God, yes!' he snorted. 'You got so pissed off, I thought you were going to throw them at me, and you refused to eat any of the curry – all that fuss over a bloody naan!'

'Daddy!' shouted Daniel. 'Come on, I want to go and see Keira!'

He had left his backpack lying on the floor and, as she picked it up, Eve peered inside to check what had broken. It looked as if the only casualties were broken leads in a few pencils, which had fallen out of their metal tin as it crashed open. As she tucked the tin back into the bag, she saw a piece of paper down the side, partly hidden underneath a T-shirt and an empty chocolate wrapper. Pulling it out, she saw it was a letter from Mrs Russell, headed *Nativity*. The words *Wise Man* were typed in big bold letters, followed by a list of suggestions for what Daniel could wear for the role.

THIRTY-NINE

With three days to go until Christmas, it seemed as if everyone in possession of a driving licence was out on the roads. But Eve filled a travel flask with coffee, loaded up a podcast and set off in a positive frame of mind, trying to ignore the little voice inside her head that was telling her it was insane to be making any sort of trip today, let alone a one-hundred-and-sixty-five-mile journey to the south coast.

Five hours later, after she'd been held up by an accident on the M4, moved at a snail's pace through the car park masquerading as the M25 and got lost in a diversion on the outskirts of Brighton, Google Maps informed her that she'd reached her destination.

It had been dark for the last two hours and, as she pulled into a space on the opposite side of the road to 17 Lewes Close, the house was only partly illuminated by the artificial glow from a nearby street lamp. She peered through the passenger window; it was a sizeable red-brick property, with a neat front garden and white wooden gate. The curtains were closed in the downstairs bay window, but there was a light on behind them.

Eve took a couple of deep breaths, her hands shaking on the

steering wheel. Now she was actually here, the whole thing seemed crazy. She'd made a last-minute, impulsive decision to drive to this unknown address and knock on the door, but hadn't thought any further than that. In the back of her mind there had been an expectation – almost a hope – that no one would be home. In that case she would be able to turn around and go back to Bristol, knowing she'd tried to find out more about her father, but failed – through no fault of her own – which would mean she could draw a line under the whole business.

Except, it looked as if someone *was* at home. Which meant she had to get out of the car, walk across the road and knock on that front door. Eve took another deep breath and wondered what she'd say; how on earth she would explain all this to a stranger?

It was no good, she couldn't do it. She started the engine again, putting the car into gear and releasing the handbrake. There was no way she could go through with this. 'Stupid bloody idea,' she muttered. 'What a waste of a day.'

Suddenly, her phone began to ring and the screen lit up with Ben's photo.

'Ben? Is everything okay? Is something wrong with Daniel?'

'Mummy, it's *me!*' Daniel's voice sounded squeaky and strangely high; Eve wasn't used to speaking to him on the phone, he never usually called her while he was with his dad for the weekend.

'Hello, gorgeous boy! Are you all right?'

'Yes, it's *brilliant!* We've been to Winter Wonderland and we had chocolate doughnuts and Daddy and I did ice skating and he fell over on his bottom – it was so funny! Then Keira went on a baby train with a whistle and I went with her because she's too small to go on her own, and we saw Father Christmas and I asked him for an iPhone 15 and Keira asked him for sweets, but Daddy said sweets were okay but Father Christmas might not be able to fit too many expensive things on his sleigh because he has to go all over the world and *lots* of children want phones and the elves won't be able to carry them all back from the Apple store...'

Eve smiled as she listened to his chatter, picturing him clinging tightly to Ben's phone, so many miles away, stumbling over his words in his excitement to tell her about his day.

'...and Daddy said I could call to tell you what we've been doing because he said you'd like to hear about it, but I've got to go now because we've stopped to get pizza for Lou because she's feeling sick and Daddy says pizza will cheer her up, and Keira is asleep in the car next to me so we'll need to wake her up when we get home, and we're nearly there now. So, I've got to go, Mummy! Bye, see you tomorrow.'

As the phone screen went dark, Eve sat back in the driver's seat and reached forward to turn off the car engine again. In the silence, she watched spots of rain fill the windscreen in front of her, her head still full of her little boy's voice. He'd said they were nearly home, so Ben's house was home. Such a casual reference, thrown into the conversation without a thought. It hurt like hell, but she shouldn't be surprised – of course that was his home too, and they were his family. It was yet another reminder – as if she needed one – that she was just one small part of Daniel's life, even though he was almost all of hers.

She turned towards the house again, which had a plaque with 17 attached to the white gate. There was no way she could go back to Bristol without knocking on this door. It didn't matter what she found, even if she found nothing at all. That in itself would be closure, and – much as she hated the term – closure was probably the reason she had driven all this way.

Eve undid her seatbelt, opened the car door and got out, her legs stiff after hours of driving. She took a deep breath as she pushed open the gate and walked up the path to the front door.

There was no bell, so she lifted the heavy brass knocker and brought it back down against the wood. In the darkness of the empty street, the echoing rap was shockingly loud.

A light came on in the glass panel above the door and there was the sound of a lock clicking. Eve took a step back, her heart beating so furiously, it felt like someone was tapping on her ribcage with a drumstick.

'Hello?' A women stood in the doorway, the hall light behind her making it hard to see any of her features. 'Can I help you?'

'Yes, I hope so,' Eve said. 'I'm sorry to bother you, and this will probably sound mad, but I was looking for someone who used to live in this house, years ago.'

The woman put her head on one side. 'There's only me and my husband.'

'It was probably before you lived here,' Eve said. 'Back in the late 1970s. I found some letters that were sent to this address, and I just wanted to come and see if I could work out why.'

'Oh, well I may be able to help,' said the woman. 'My family has owned this house since 1965. Who were the letters to?'

'A man called Alan Baker.' Eve had thought about bringing one of the envelopes with her, but in her rush to leave the house she'd left it lying on the kitchen table. 'The first letter was sent to him here, in September 1979, then several others were sent over the next four years.'

The woman's face had changed. She looked surprised, then frowned in confusion. 'That's strange,' she said. 'He didn't actually live here.'

Eve stared at her. 'Do you mean, you know him?'

'Well, of course! He was my uncle. My mum's younger brother. But I don't know why anyone would write to him here. This was my parents' house and he used to come and visit, but I don't remember him ever staying here, or having any post sent to us. There was no reason for him to do that, he didn't live far away.'

Eve's pulse was racing so hard, she could hardly breathe. 'Where did he live?'

'In Hastings, with Aunt Judith and my cousin Sally. They had a house near Halton Park. My sister and I were a few years older than Sally, but we spent lots of time there – and they came to see us as well, obviously.'

There was too much here for Eve to process. Could they really be talking about the same man? 'Is this Alan Derek Baker?' she asked, aware her voice was catching in her throat, making her sound unlike herself.

The woman's brow furrowed. 'I think so,' she said. 'Yes, I'm pretty sure that was his middle name. He was just Uncle Alan to me!' She laughed.

Eve hadn't been expecting to find any answers today, but suddenly it seemed as if she'd not only tracked down Alan Baker, but in a few short seconds had also found out more about him than she'd ever expected; the most important fact being that he was married. With a child.

'It's funny you should be asking about him today, of all days,' the woman continued. 'It's Sally's birthday and I emailed her this morning. She isn't local now, she lives in Lowestoft, but we keep in touch. It's her fiftieth and she's having a big party up there. Ian and I were invited but we decided not to go, it's a long journey anyway, but with all the traffic at this time of year it would have taken hours to get there, then we would have needed to book a hotel for the night...'

Eve was nodding and smiling, as if this chatter was all just that: chatter. Whereas these earth-shattering nuggets were sending her brain into a tailspin. She was dazed, confused, trying to get to grips with these snippets of information as they came at her from so many directions, like sparks flying off an angle grinder. Sally was this woman's cousin. Sally was Alan Baker's daughter. She was fifty years old, which meant she'd been five when Eve was born. So, Alan Derek Baker had been married, with a family of his own, when he met Flora and created another one.

'Lowestoft is lovely, and in normal circumstances we'd quite fancy a weekend up there,' the woman was saying. 'But I think it's odd to have such a big party right before Christmas. I mean, we've all got so much on. If it was me, I would have waited and had a belated celebration in the new year.'

Eve nodded, not listening. 'You said before, that Alan *was* your uncle,' she said. 'Isn't he still alive?'

'Oh no, he died about ten years ago. Pancreatic cancer. Aunty Judith is alive though. She still lives in Hastings, though not in their old house. She's in a retirement village on the way to St Leonards – been there for a few years now. I go and see her every few weeks. I'm sure she'd be interested to hear about your visit. What did you say your name was?'

'I didn't. It's Eve.'

'Nice to meet you, I'm Alison. Do you want to come in and have a cup of tea? Ian's around somewhere. So, what were these letters you were telling me about? The ones to Uncle Alan. Do you know who wrote them? I really can't understand why he would have given our address to anyone, but I guess he must have had some arrangement with my mother and she would have passed letters on to him. Maybe he'd asked her if he could use our address for some business thing he was setting up. He was a bit of a wheeler-dealer. When I was younger, I remember my dad going off to work in an office every day in a boring suit and tie, but Uncle Alan was much more exciting. My sister and I used to think he must be a spy because he went away for weeks on end and brought Sally back all these amazing presents – dolls and jewellery.'

Alison moved back and opened the door wide, beckoning Eve into the house. 'Come in and I'll put the kettle on. My mum died three years ago, so we can't ask her what this was all about. But I'm sure Aunty Judith will be able to shed some light on it all. She's still got all her marbles!'

Eve suddenly found her voice. 'I can't stay, but thank you so much for seeing me. It's been lovely to meet you. Sorry to take up your time.'

'But, why don't you come in and–'

'No! I really can't stay. I've got a long drive ahead of me.' She was backing away down the path, fumbling in her pocket for the car keys, so many thoughts crowding through her head she could hardly think straight. She turned and ran back to the car, starting the engine and pulling away as she reached behind her to grab the seatbelt.

She glanced sideways as she accelerated down Lewes Close and saw Alison silhouetted in the doorway. Alison, who would never know that the strange woman who'd knocked on her front door one Saturday evening just before Christmas, and then rushed away again with no explanation, was her cousin.

FORTY

E ve was crying before she got to the end of the street. By the time the car had crawled through the traffic to where the A23 became a dual carriageway and headed north away from the town, the collar of her shirt was damp with tears that had dripped down from her jaw, tears that felt like they'd never stop.

Alan Derek Baker – the father she'd thought until recently was Alan Derek Glover – had had another family. He had been married when he met and became involved with Flora. Eve had begun to wonder if that might be the case, but it was still a shock to have it confirmed. Not only that, but this man already had a young daughter of his own. Was that why he didn't want another child with Flora? Did he even know he was about to father a second daughter?

It sounded as if his sister – Alison's mother – had known some of his secrets. She might have been the one to scrawl *Return to sender* on the envelopes. Maybe he'd told her there'd been an affair. Or maybe – Eve's breath caught in her throat – there had been more than one. Flora Glover might have been just the latest in a long line of women to fall in love with Alan Baker during his frequent 'business' trips away from home. If he had a wife and child, he clearly couldn't give out his real address, but why give his sister's? If he was that much of a philandering liar, why not make something up so that if a woman came looking for him, she'd find no trace?

But Flora hadn't gone looking for him. Maybe if she had, the whole thing would have turned out very differently. Then Eve wouldn't have been told endless tales about the handsome, kind, doting father who was tragically taken from her when she was just eighteen months old. Instead, she would have had a father who didn't face up to his responsibilities and Flora – knowing she'd been strung along by a man who never told her he was married – might not have worked so hard to maintain an illusion and give her daughter countless happy memories of a man who didn't exist.

By the time she got back onto the M25, the traffic had died down and the rain had stopped, along with Eve's tears. She was left feeling empty, as if every ounce of emotion had been forcibly drained from her body.

Clinging to the steering wheel, she struggled to concentrate as the streams of headlights raced by on the other side of the central reservation. The miles ticked past and she turned off the M25 on to the M4, heading west. When the sign flashed up for Reading Services, she knew she had to take a break. But once she'd pulled into a parking space, she couldn't muster the energy to get out of the car and walk towards the brightly lit double doors of the service station.

Her mobile started to ring, and she frowned when she saw Flora's name come up. 'Mum? Are you okay?'

'Eve! There you are!' Flora sounded cross, but that was a relief. Cross was generally easier to deal with than miserable. 'I haven't bought any Christmas presents!'

'Oh, Mum, that doesn't matter. You don't need to worry about getting presents.'

'Yes, I do. But I think I've left it too late. Nathan has just told me it's nearly Christmas now?'

'He's right, we've got a couple more days and then it will be Christmas Eve. But don't worry about presents – Daniel and I weren't expecting you to get us anything, you haven't had a chance to go shopping!'

'I don't mean for you,' Flora snapped. 'I need to get a present for Barbara, because I've just found out she has bought me something called Cards Against Humidity. So, I need to get her something in return.'

Eve stifled a laugh. 'Humanity, Mum. I think it's called Cards Against Humanity.'

'Well, whatever it's called, she has bloody well gone and bought it for me, which is very embarrassing because I don't have anything to give her. And the thing about presents is that you have to give them back to people, otherwise they get offended.'

'I'm sure we can sort out something,' Eve said. 'I'm not at home at the moment, I've been...' It suddenly occurred to her that she could tell her mother where she'd been. She could mention Brighton and see if there was any reaction. Or Lewes Close. *I've been looking for my father,* she imagined saying. *But I've found out that he was a prize shit and that he lied to you – probably from the moment you met him. He had a wife and a daughter and a whole life that didn't involve you, and he had no intention of giving any of that up for you.* But she was never going to say those words.

'I've been out for the day.' She squeezed her eyes shut. 'But I'm heading home now and I'll pop in and see you tomorrow and we can think of something for you to give to Barbara for Christmas.'

'Good, that's good.' Flora sounded calmer. 'Maybe we can buy her some gin? Or a book with more casual sex in it? She liked that other one.'

Eve laughed. 'I'll have a think and we'll talk about it tomorrow. Night, Mum.'

'Night, night, darling. Sleep tight, don't let the bloody bastard bedbugs bite.'

FORTY-ONE

It felt strange to be telling someone about it all. For so long, Alan Derek Baker had only existed inside her head, trapped there like a fly battering itself against a closed window. Talking about this man suddenly made him real.

'How long were they together?' asked Jake.

'I don't know. In the letters, Mum talked about the summer they'd spent with each other, so it might only have been a few months. But she'd obviously really fallen for him.'

Just a couple of weeks ago, Eve had been considering telling Ben what she'd found out about her father. Desperate to hear someone else's view on the whole thing, and unable to get any sense out of Flora, it had come into her mind suddenly – on her way to meet Ben at the pub for their discussion about Daniel – that he might have an interesting take on it all. He wasn't a part of their lives anymore, and had no emotional baggage to set to one side before considering the options. But he had known Flora for several years while he and Eve were still together, so that small connection might give him some sort of insight into what had happened.

But that night in the pub had got off to a bad start – and an even worse finish – and she'd never got the chance to mention the letters or her confusion about whether or not to try and find her lost father. She was glad now; things seemed better between her and Ben, but he was still too wrapped up in his own life to really care what was happening in hers.

She had no idea what had made her tell Jake. She'd slept in late after her long day trip to Brighton, and had woken to find a text waiting from him:

> Fancy helping me wrap some Christmas presents? I'll bring Sellotape if you provide the coffee x

She'd texted back to say that she was a superior wrapper of gifts and would be delighted to offer her services, and he arrived half an hour later, carrying a plastic bag full of presents, two long tubes of garish cartoon Christmas paper, a pair of pinking shears and a roll of Sellotape.

After she'd boiled the kettle, they sat at the kitchen table and – to her own amazement – the words just came out. Once she started talking, she couldn't stop, it was as if someone had turned on a tap and everything that had been bottled up inside her for the last few weeks came pouring out. After all the emotion and exhaustion of the previous day, it was such a relief.

'So,' he said, remarkably unfazed by the revelation that Eve's past held a messy secret, 'the big unknown is whether or not Alan was aware your mother was pregnant?'

'Yes. Which means that, either he was a nice guy who didn't realise what a mess he'd left behind. Or he was a bastard, who knew but ran away from the problem. Although he wasn't a nice guy at all, because he was having an affair and leading on my Mum.' She pulled out another length of paper and slid it underneath a make-up mirror Jake had bought for Katie.

'But when it comes down to it,' said Jake, breaking off a piece of Sellotape and passing it across, 'does it really matter?'

'Of course it matters!' she said. 'If he had guessed that Mum might be pregnant, then he deliberately ignored her letters and left her to cope with everything on her own. If that was the case, he was a prize shit.'

'Yes, but does it matter *now*?' persisted Jake. 'In some ways, whatever he did forty-five years ago, is irrelevant. The man isn't alive anymore, so you'll never be able to find out the truth. And it doesn't matter to your mother, because you say her memory is failing.'

'Well, it must have mattered to her back then, that she'd been abandoned,' said Eve. 'She would have been devastated.'

'Of course,' he said. 'But you were more important than all of that. From what you've said, she always intended to go through with the pregnancy and have you – however hard that turned out to be.'

He was right; she hadn't thought about it like that. She remembered how ecstatic she'd felt when she discovered she was pregnant with Daniel. Even when Ben didn't seem as enthusiastic as she'd hoped, when he didn't seem to share her excitement, she had deliberately ignored the warning signs. She had wanted the baby and would have gone ahead with the pregnancy, come what may. She hadn't really thought about it before but, even if Ben had been so furious at the news that he'd walked out, she wouldn't have considered any other option. She would never have given up that baby.

They sat without speaking for a while, as Eve used the last section of Jake's paper to wrap a jumper she'd bought for Daniel, folding the edges neatly and taking care to make it perfect, even though she knew her son would rip through the paper in frenzied seconds, not caring how well it was wrapped. The only sound was the zipping of the tape as Jake tore off strips to pass across to her. Eve looked up at him and smiled. This oddball neighbour of hers had a way about him that put her totally at ease; it felt as if she'd known him for years and could talk to him about anything.

'The thing is,' she said eventually. 'However hard I try to tell myself it's all in the past and it doesn't matter anymore, it does. It matters to me.'

'Yes, but it's not about missing the father you never had,' he said. 'All of this only matters because you're angry that everything you believed in, isn't what actually happened.'

'Well, is that surprising?' Eve could hear the defensiveness in her voice. 'It means my whole life has been a lie.'

Jake pulled at the end of the Sellotape too quickly and it ripped unevenly down the middle. 'Bugger.' He dug his thumbnail into the roll. 'I hate this stuff.'

'Give it here,' she said, reaching across. 'That is the hardest bit, though,' she continued, finding the end of the tape and pulling it out. 'Feeling that everything I grew up believing, has been a lie.'

'But you're wrong, Eve,' he said. 'It hasn't. You had a happy childhood, with a mother who adored you and did a really good job of bringing you up on her own. You grew up feeling safe and secure and having been taught some decent values. You learnt to be resilient and independent. Okay, she was creative with the truth when it came to your father. But, so what? She only told you all those things about him for the best possible reason – to make you feel loved and wanted. She was protecting you.'

'I know that,' said Eve.

'There's something else,' said Jake. 'By presuming your real father wasn't the wonderful man your mother always made him out to be, you're undermining that whole relationship. You're suggesting she was a poor judge of character. Maybe you need to give her the benefit of the doubt? That summer they spent

SARAH EDGHILL

together might have been the most wonderful time of her life. Deep down, she may have suspected he was married – especially when he didn't reply to the letters. But she needed to maintain the illusion, for her own sake, as well as yours.'

Eve sat back in her chair and watched as he stood up and went to fill the kettle again. He was right, this wasn't about her: it was about her mother. Even if she'd only known him for a few weeks, Flora had spent long enough in the company of Alan Derek Baker to fall in love with him, so maybe that was all that mattered? And while she'd done an amazing job of bringing up Eve as a single parent, she hadn't really been alone. She'd had that pretend husband beside her, who had been such a big part of their lives and followed Eve through childhood, instilling in her security and self-confidence and the belief that she was adored. Something she now suspected her real father might not have done.

'I've been thinking about the address,' Jake said. 'About why he'd give her a real one – even though it wasn't his own. You thought he might have had lots of affairs and she was just the latest in a long line of lovers. But if that was the case, I think he would have given her a made-up address.'

Eve sat back and watched as he pulled the jar of coffee out of the cupboard and heaped teaspoons into their mugs.

'I think that suggests she was special to him too,' Jake continued. 'Maybe he was subconsciously hoping she'd come looking for him and make some waves. Maybe he was looking for a way out of his own marriage.'

'I don't think that's likely,' Eve said. 'He was having his cake and eating it.'

'Perhaps. But he did trust her enough to give her an address through which she could track him down, if she really wanted to. And he may never have known that his sister returned all the letters.'

With the presents wrapped, they went into the sitting room and Eve arranged Daniel's parcels under the tree. It was only a small one – she'd been horrified at the price of trees in the local garden centre – but the lights draped around it were twinkling prettily, and even Daniel's haphazard efforts at decoration didn't look too bad in the shadowy darkness.

She tried to balance a small present – a packet of felt tip pens – across one of the tree's branches. But despite the thickness of the needles, it slipped through a gap and landed on the floor. She and Jake both leant forward to pick it up at the same time, and her forehead touched his cheek. Suddenly their faces were so close that she could smell something citrussy: moisturiser or maybe shampoo. It was a vaguely familiar smell and she was trying to place it when he leant towards her and she felt his lips gently touch hers.

As he pulled back again, she inhaled sharply, realising there was a tingling in the pit of her stomach, spreading up towards her chest, down her thighs. She stared straight ahead into his eyes. Even in this light she could see how blue they were: pale cornflower blue with dark rings around the irises.

'Sorry, should I have done that?' whispered Jake.

'Probably not,' she whispered back. 'But I'd quite like you to do it again.'

He leant forward and kissed her once more, this time he didn't pull away. It was a gentle kiss, a careful one, and she allowed herself to fall into it as she closed her eyes. When she felt his lips move away again, she opened her eyes and saw him smiling at her.

'Miss Glover,' he said, as he put out his hand and ran the back of his fingers down her cheek. 'I think this is going to be fun.'

FORTY-TWO

'Good grief!' said Jake, stopping in front of the Christmas tree in the reception area. 'Look at the size of that thing – it's as big as the one in Trafalgar Square. What the hell is that on the top?'

'It's a fairy,' said Eve. 'Knitted by one of the residents. Just keep walking, Jake. Pretend it's the sort of thing you see every day.'

As they approached the open doors of the lounge, Mrs Donaldson stumbled out, wearing a pink paper hat and holding the end of the cracker it had probably come from.

'Merry Christmas!' she trilled. 'Welcome one and all! There's a glass of sherry waiting for you just in there, and the kitchen staff have produced some wonderful canapés.'

'Excellent,' said Jake, rubbing his hands together. 'I thought something smelt good. And to think you didn't want me to come!'

Eve had tried very hard to persuade him to stay at home. She wanted to spend time with Flora on Christmas Day, but had been dreading the forced bonhomie of Three Elms, anticipating there would be elevator-style Christmas music playing in the background, packets of shop-bought mince pies sitting on the coffee tables, and a dried-out, institutional Christmas lunch to be tackled. This hadn't felt like the right time to introduce her mother to Jake, or to introduce him to the musty, claustrophobic corridors of the care home and the eccentricities of its residents.

But he had insisted. 'I can't stay in the house while Katie's cooking,' he'd said. 'She's a really messy cook. Unbelievable.'

'I'm creative!' Katie had called from the other room.

'She burns holes in pans and throws food at the walls,' said Jake. 'I'll need to get out of the place for a couple of hours to preserve my sanity.'

So, while Katie stayed at home to create a Christmas lunch for them, Jake and Eve had driven to Three Elms, their arms full of gifts for Flora.

'Happy Christmas, Mum!' said Eve, leaning down to hug her mother. 'How are you?'

'Oh, I'm tip-top, thank you darling,' said Flora. 'Tippedy-top. Yes indeed. I am having a rather marvellous day.' She lifted up a glass from the coffee table beside her chair. 'Cheers! Down the hatch we go.'

Eve felt a tap on her shoulder, and turned to see Nathan standing behind her. 'Merry Christmas!' he said, beaming.

'You too, Nathan,' she said. 'How many sherries has she had?'

'Oh, three or four.' He laughed at the expression on her face. 'Don't worry, I'm keeping an eye on her. Anyway, she doesn't notice when I water down the sherry, so she's not going to get nearly as drunk as she hopes she is.'

'Who is this?' asked Flora, pointing her glass up at Jake.

'Mum, this is my neighbour – and good friend – Jake. His daughter Katie is cooking us lunch today, so Jake and I thought we'd come to see you first.'

SARAH EDGHILL

Flora was peering at Jake's chest, her head tilted to one side. 'What,' she asked, 'is that?'

Jake knelt down beside her chair and proudly puffed out his chest. 'It's my best Christmas jumper,' he said. 'So here we've got Father Christmas, on a unicorn, carrying a Christmas stocking. Do you like it?'

Flora looked up at him and smiled. 'I like it very much, young man. It is extremely tasteful. Do you like mine?' She sat back and tugged at the bottom of her own jumper, pulling it forwards to show Jake the snowman. Eve wished she'd had the nerve to suggest she and Barbara swap: the outsized pale blue jumper was now baggier than ever on her mother, nearly reaching her knees.

'Mrs Glover, that is exquisite,' said Jake. 'What an amazing snowman.' There was no trace of irony in his voice; Eve knew he really meant it.

Flora beamed. 'I think you and I are going to get on like a house on fire, Eve's good neighbour friend,' she said, raising her empty glass. 'Get me another one of these will you, and one for yourself while you're at it.'

Eve had bought Flora a new cushion for her bed, some lavender hand cream and a pretty mother-of-pearl photo frame. All her gifts were carefully wrapped, alongside Daniel's present, a Chocolate Orange, which he had wrapped himself – so badly it looked as if it had exploded inside the paper.

'Daniel got you this,' she said, passing it over. 'I'm sorry he's not here today, he would have loved seeing you at Christmas.' Her voice caught slightly and she took a deep breath, feeling Jake's hand on the small of her back. It was fine. She was fine. 'He's at Ben's today. They asked if he could spend Christmas with them this year, and he was very excited about it.'

And I cried, she wanted to add. *I smiled and said, 'Yes, that would be great. What a lucky boy you are, you'll have a fabulous*

*day with Daddy and Lou.' Then I went upstairs and lay down on
my bed and wept.*

It was only fair that Ben got to spend Christmas with their
son, she'd had him all to herself every year so far. But she'd been
dreading the prospect, and had felt physically sick as she waved
him off yesterday afternoon, listening to his excited chatter as
Ben strapped him into the back seat of the car.

But strangely, now that Christmas Day was here, the whole
thing wasn't as bad as she'd been anticipating. She had woken
ridiculously early and made herself a cup of tea to take back to
bed, sitting watching dawn seep through the curtains,
wondering whether her boy was already awake – certain he
must be. Last year, he had got up at 4.15am and run into her
bedroom screaming with excitement, clutching his bulging red
stocking to his chest. 'Mummy, he was here! Father Christmas
came and I didn't even wake up!'

Nothing she said could persuade him to go back to bed, so
she lay dozing as he rifled through the contents of the stocking,
littering the duvet with bits of plastic wrapping and cardboard,
shrieking with delight at each new discovery. She had been
exhausted for the rest of the day and had snapped at him several
times as she tried to cook lunch.

But this year she would have given anything to have been
woken up in the middle of the night by her overexcited child.
She had sipped her tea and listened to the radio, imagining the
chaos that was engulfing Ben's house. What would they put in
his stocking? Would they lay it carefully on the end of his bed,
like she did, or leave it downstairs by the fireplace? What
presents would they buy him? Would they all rush downstairs
and open everything at once, before it was even light, or did they
eke out the presents, like she did, with a couple after breakfast,
then a couple more before lunch.

When it was finally light enough to get up, she had made

herself a piece of toast, and eaten it standing up, looking out into the garden. Had Daniel eaten anything vaguely sensible for breakfast, or just stuffed himself with chocolate from his stocking? She always let him do that on Christmas Day. Where was the harm? It was only once a year.

Later – still too early to call anyone – the house had felt horribly quiet, so she went onto Spotify to find some Christmas songs. As Wizzard yelled that they wished it could be Christmas every day, she sat flicking through photographs on her phone, looking at memories of Christmas past: pictures of Daniel opening presents, playing with new toys, working his way through a heaped plate of Christmas dinner.

Eventually, a text from Jake had helped her snap out of the self-indulgence.

> Happy Christmas lovely neighbour person! I'll
> be round at 11am so we can go and do the
> Royal visit. Katie is already peeling sprouts.
> Send help… x

And now here he was, standing next to her in the lounge at Three Elms, proudly showing Flora his appalling Christmas jumper and pushing a glass of watered-down sherry into Eve's hands.

'Cheers, and a bloody happy Christmas,' he whispered, leaning forward to kiss her briefly on the lips.

'Oh goodness me!' said Flora. 'I saw that. Who is this young man, Eve – do you know him?'

Eve grinned at him and then stood up on her toes to kiss him back. He smelt of toothpaste and washing powder, with a touch of sherry around the edges. This wasn't as thrilling as their first proper kiss, but it was the first public show of affection and it made her feel about fourteen years old.

'Yes, Mum,' she said. 'I do know this young man. But I'm intending to get to know him even better.'

Christmas lunch was being served in the dining room at midday, and some relatives used it as an excuse to leave, keen to rush away to the cosier familiarity of their own festivities. But Jake and Eve walked along the hallway on either side of Flora, and found her a place at a round table, its centre decorated with sprigs of red-berried holly, with crackers and snowflake-patterned napkins laid out at each place setting.

'I can't believe you're working today as well, Nathan,' said Eve, as the young man passed round plates of steaming turkey, roast potatoes and vegetables. 'Didn't you want to take time off to be with your family?'

'They're all here,' he said, smiling. 'My sister works in the kitchens, and that's my mum – over there.'

Eve looked at the woman carrying plates on the other side of the room. She had seen her at Three Elms before, but wouldn't have noticed a resemblance.

'We're having our own Christmas at home, tonight,' said Nathan, as he went back towards the kitchen. 'It means we get to do it twice!'

Jake had helped Flora pull her cracker and was patiently waiting for her to decipher the joke.

'Who has a... no, who holds... no, hides in a bakery at Christmas?' she read, holding the scrap of paper close to her face. 'A mince pie! No, that's not right. It says a mince spy!' She looked up at Jake. 'What on earth does that mean? How silly.'

The lunch took a long time; there was much chewing and gumming of food. Barbara was sitting at a different table, and Eve went over to wish her a happy Christmas.

'Well, it would be, if I could get through this turkey,' she said, sawing at the meat with her knife. 'Tough as old boots.'

The man sitting next to her, who – judging by the amount

of food on the tablecloth – had also been struggling with his meal, suddenly put his fingers into his mouth and pulled out his false teeth, setting them carefully on his side plate. He turned to Barbara and winked. 'Thass better.'

'Wish I could do that,' said Barbara.

Eventually the staff began to clear away the empty plates. Eve was conscious that she kept looking at her watch, but couldn't stop herself.

'Don't worry, we won't be eating for ages,' said Jake, grinning. 'If Katie says she's aiming for 3pm, it will be at least an hour later.'

But she wasn't worrying about their own schedule: she was wondering what Daniel was doing. What time had Lou planned their meal? Would the children be watching Christmas cartoons while the grown-ups worked in the kitchen? Maybe Lou's family would be there, even Ben's parents. Theirs would be a noisy, happy family house, crammed with people who wanted to be together to eat, drink and celebrate. Her own house was so quiet and empty. Thank God she didn't have to be there.

'You're looking maudlin,' Jake whispered in her ear. 'Have another glass of watered-down sherry. We just need to get through the Christmas pudding, then we're out of here.'

As he spoke, Mrs Donaldson appeared in the doorway, holding aloft a plate on which sat what looked like a blackened cannonball, blue flames licking the sides and curling around the sprig of holly in the top. 'Who's going to get the lucky twenty pence!' she called out, as she lowered the plate onto the nearest table. 'It's in here somewhere.'

Flora looked at Eve and frowned. 'It should be a sixpence!' she said. 'That's what you put in there, not twenty pence!'

'I know, Mum. You're right. But that's the twenty-first century for you. Traditions get reworked I'm afraid.'

She was kneeling beside Flora's chair, her hand covering her mother's, feeling the warmth from her skin. Flora smiled at her as she spooned up the food. 'This is delicious!' she said. 'I do love Christmas pudding.'

Looking around the dining room, Eve realised she now recognised most of the other residents, and knew many of them by name. It was surprising how quickly this warm little community had become the new normal for both her and Flora. They had come a long way since they'd wheeled her battered old suitcase down the corridor for the first time.

After just a few months of coming here, she could hardly remember how it felt to visit Flora in her previous life: driving into the communal parking area outside her old flat, waiting for the noisy lift to descend to the ground floor, taking her out to the shops every week for groceries.

Flora always used to come over for an early supper on Sundays, once Daniel had been dropped home by Ben, and the three of them would then slump onto the sofa and watch *Countryfile* before Eve drove Flora back home. It had always been a late bedtime on Sunday for Daniel, but it was only once a week. Those days felt like a lifetime ago.

'Do you know, Eve,' her mother was saying now, 'I remember one Christmas, when you were very little, when you nearly choked on the sixpence I'd put in the Christmas pudding.'

'Really?'

'I'd mashed up a portion with a fork and put it on the table of your highchair, and you were stuffing it into your mouth, using your hands!' Flora laughed and shook her head. 'Oh Eve, you were such a funny child. Then your father tried to feed you with the spoon and you kept pushing his hand away, telling him you could do it yourself.'

At some stage, this will stop hurting, thought Eve, as she watched her mother's face light up. *I will stop caring that what she's telling me isn't true.*

'You were such a feisty little thing!' Flora was saying. 'You grabbed the spoon from his hand and started banging it on the side of your chair. Food flew everywhere and your father and I laughed so much.'

Not yet though. At the moment, there was still a part of her that wanted to put her hands over her ears and tell Flora to stop talking with such animation about a moment in their lives that never happened. She felt Jake's hand resting on her shoulder, squeezing it gently.

'Come on, Flora,' said Jake. 'Eat that up or I'll have to help you out with it.'

'I don't want any more,' said Flora. 'I hate Christmas pudding.'

The noise level increased around the tables, as the residents finished their food and carers delivered cups of tea and coffee.

'We're going to head off soon, Mum,' said Eve. 'We're going back to Jake's for our lunch. Nathan says you'll be playing some games this afternoon?'

Flora nodded, but she was looking vague again, her brow furrowing as she stared around her, seeming unsure about what they were all doing there. Just twelve months ago, she had sat in Eve's kitchen, playing Daniel's favourite game, Simon Says, as the remains of their turkey congealed on their plates.

'Simon says put your hands on your head!' Daniel had shouted, and Eve and Flora threw up their hands.

'Simon says pull your pants down!'

'Well, I'm not doing that one,' Flora had huffed, folding her arms across her chest. 'My pants are far too big, Daniel. It would take all day to get them back up again!'

Even just a year ago, her mother had been so much more her old self.

Barbara appeared at Eve's elbow. 'Right, we're going back into the lounge,' she announced. She was holding a short, elderly man by the hand, pulling him along beside her. He looked confused.

'This,' she said, 'is Terry. He's in here for respite. His daughter has gone to the Bahamas for Christmas. All right for some. I've told him he can sit with us for Scrabble, Flora, because he says he's very good at Scrabble.'

'What a lovely idea,' said Flora, pushing her chair back from the table and getting up. 'We're very good at it too, aren't we?' She took the old man's other elbow and the three of them moved towards the hallway.

'Mum, we'll be off then,' said Eve, to her retreating back.

Flora waved a hand at her, then turned her attention back to Terry. 'I used to play with my husband, many years ago,' Eve heard her mother saying. 'He came up with all these clever words. But I was better at using the triple word scores.'

As the three of them disappeared into the lounge, Jake put his arm around Eve's waist. 'Well done, you,' he said. 'Job done. Wasn't so bad, was it?'

Eve smiled. 'It was actually rather lovely. Thanks for coming with me. Now, let's get out of here and see how much damage Katie has managed to inflict on that turkey.'

ALSO BY SARAH EDGHILL

A Thousand Tiny Disappointments

~ A gripping novel about grief and friendship

———

His Other Woman

~ A compelling and suspenseful women's fiction novel

———

The Bad Wife

~ A totally absorbing psychological suspense

———

Memory Road

~ A charming and uplifting novel about family and relationships

———

The Pool

~ A gripping novel about family and secrets

ACKNOWLEDGEMENTS

A book never appears in the world without having gone through many edits and rewrites and – occasionally – major plot changes along the way, and authors are never on their own during this process. Not only do we have ongoing encouragement from friends and family, but the writing community is an extremely supportive one, and other authors often give insightful advice that can change the whole course of a novel. With *The Good Daughter,* I was lucky enough to get this input from two fantastic writers, Ericka Waller and Alison May. They both give so much help to fellow authors that they've probably forgotten they were involved with a version of this book several years ago, but I'm grateful to them for reading early drafts and giving invaluable feedback.

Friends also play a huge part and I'm so lucky to be surrounded by some of best in the world. Not only do they generously buy my books, but they come back time and time again to get more copies to give as presents to friends of their own – which is the most wonderful compliment. A heartfelt thank you in particular to Gaynor, Helen, Liza, Amanda and Val, and a special mention to the Brown Cows – hope you enjoy this one, ladies!

Finally, no amount of thanks can ever be enough for the most important people in my life – Mat, Sam, Maddy and Jessie. You are my inspiration and make me the happiest woman on the planet. Love you to the moon and back.

If you'd like to find out more about me and my writing, please visit www.sarahedghill.com *or follow my Amazon Author page by clicking on any of my novels.*

A NOTE FROM THE PUBLISHER

Thank you for reading this book. If you enjoyed it please do consider leaving a review on Amazon to help others find it too.

We hate typos. All of our books have been rigorously edited and proofread, but sometimes mistakes do slip through. If you have spotted a typo, please do let us know and we can get it amended within hours.

info@bloodhoundbooks.com

Printed in Great Britain
by Amazon

49536564R10159